Praise for
PRETTY IN PUNXSUTAWNEY

"Like the vintage movies sprinkled throughout the story, *Pretty in Punxsutawney* is destined to be an instant classic. In mashup style, this young adult rom-com cleverly overlays the age-old desires to fit in and be popular with a brilliantly funny and magical problem. It will appeal to readers of all ages . . . even if they've never heard of John Hughes or Bill Murray!"

PATTY BLOUNT, author of *Some Boys*

"Now playing: *Pretty in Punxsutawney* by Laurie Boyle Crompton. Pop a bowl of buttery popcorn and curl up for the perfect romantic comedy. I fell in love with Andie as she's caught in an endless loop, reliving a horrific first day at her new high school over and over again. Fun, adorable, and so identifiable, I found myself cheering Andie on. Bring out the red carpet for *Pretty in Punxsutawney*. It will have you swooning and laughing all the way to the credits!"

CHRISTINA FARLEY, author of the Gilded series and *The Princess and the Page*

"*Pretty in Punxsutawney* is a delightful read, full of whimsy, wisdom, and classic movie trivia. Starry-eyed Andie is a likable heroine whose personal growth throughout the novel is realistic and relatable. Cinephile or not, YA readers will relish their trip to Punxsutawney!"

LAURA NOWLIN, *New York Times* bestselling author of *If He Had Been with Me*

"For many 1980s-era teens, the iconic movie *Pretty in Pink* captured the possibility of finding true love, be it through fashion, music, or a star-crossed romance that felt destined from the start. In her new book, *Pretty in Punxsutawney*, author Laurie Boyle Crompton has resurrected that same sense of possibility; from the apropos dedication to Molly Ringwald to the satisfying final scene, Boyle Crompton maintains a nostalgic link to a true movie classic by creating a cast of characters readers can truly rally behind and by proving that 'happily ever afters' can appear on the page in ways that are both wonderfully familiar and entirely unexpected."

KELLY FIORE-STULTZ, author of *Taste Test*, *Just Like the Movies*, and *Thicker than Water*

"From the first meet-cute to the last truth bomb, it's impossible not to fall for Andie and her fumbling quest for true love. In a country more divided than ever, this gem of a book is an important reminder that appearances can be deceiving, our hopes and dreams are universal, and despite all our differences, sometimes we need to break down the walls between us."

STEWART LEWIS, author of *Stealing Candy*

"Laurie Boyle Crompton's clever story proves that 'getting things right' doesn't always look like you think it does. I loved it!"

AMY FINNEGAN, author of *Not in the Script*

pretty
IN
PUNXSUTAWNEY

LAURIE BOYLE CROMPTON

BLINK®

BLINK°

Pretty in Punxsutawney
Copyright © 2019 by Laurie Boyle Crompton

Requests for information should be addressed to:
Blink, *3900 Sparks Dr. SE, Grand Rapids, Michigan 49546*

ISBN 978-0-310-76216-4 (hardcover)

ISBN 978-0-310-76221-8 (ebook)

This is a work of fiction. Names, characters, places, and incidents are products of the author's imagination or are used fictitiously and are not to be construed as real. Any resemblance to actual events, locales, organizations, or persons, living or dead, is entirely coincidental.

Cover design: Brand Navigation
Interior design: Denise Froehlich

Printed in the United States of America

19 20 21 22 22 / LSC / 10 9 8 7 6 5 4 3 2 1

* * *

To Molly Ringwald
for proving that as long as we believe in
ourselves, nothing can break us
(not even riding in a loathsome, smelly school bus).
Thank you for making us feel less alone.

* * *

chapter 1

The ground races toward me so fast that my muscles tense instinctively. With a nauseating dip downward, everything goes dark for a beat before an explosion rattles the walls.

Good old Dolby digital cinema surround sound.

The hero striding toward us onscreen is so cool, he doesn't even give a backward glance toward the burning ball of fire growing behind him.

"Yes!" Colton punches the air in triumph and aims his 3D glasses in my direction.

I grin at him just as the theater door swings open and light spills over his handsome smile. "Shoot." He grabs the glasses off his face and shoves a final handful of Raisinets into his mouth.

The theater manager, Tom—aka, the bane of our existence—makes his way toward us. "Break's over, Colt."

Colton's grin bounces back as he quickly chews. "No problem, boss-man." He brushes his hand along my arm as he stands. "You want to stay, Andie?"

I glance at the screen. One of the best scenes is coming up, but I've already watched this movie with him twice, and I find that CGI explosions lose their appeal around the third viewing. Besides, action movies are only my sixth-favorite type of movie. They come after romantic dramas, rom coms, regular coms, suspense, and parodies, but just before horror and foreign films—unless, of course, the foreign film is an epic romance, in which case, *swoon*. Speaking of swooning, I can still feel the trail of warmth Colton's fingers left on my arm.

Following him out of the theater, I squint at the brightness of the lobby and stagger slightly as if I've just woken up. Post-movie disorientation: one of my favorite feelings.

It's amazing to think that when we moved to Punxsutawney just two months ago, I was sure my life was over. Summer break had barely begun, but I was already anxious about starting at a new school. Now the first day of senior year is tomorrow, and I can't wait. Colton is giving me a ride, and he's promised to show me around and act as my student guide. I'm fairly confident he'll be acting as my first boyfriend very soon as well. If my wishes have any power to come true, the two of us are *definitely* happening.

He gives me a micro-wink as we both move behind the lobby's glass snack counter. I twist my auburn hair into a knot and secure it with a cheap plastic pen from the pile beside the register before I start handing out 3D glasses to a family of five.

"Whoops, let's try that again," I say to a sticky-looking little girl who grabs hers by the lenses. I give her a clean pair and hold the smeared ones up to the light. Somehow, she managed to deposit about one hundred teeny-tiny fingerprints during the split second she held them.

Tom is standing at the far end of the counter, spraying cleaner into a rag. He aims the bottle my way as if to ask if I need it, but I just shake my head and use the edge of my T-shirt to wipe the glasses. Tom shrugs as he starts wiping the counter. He's a bit older than us, but takes his job so seriously that I'll always think of him as "boss-man."

"Hey, Colt," Tom calls, "make sure your *girlfriend's* clear she's fine helping out, but you're responsible for the register."

Even though Tom already knows Colton and I are not together, we tell him in stereo that I'm *not his girlfriend*. Of course, saying it out loud makes my insides go all slasher-flick angry. I've had a thing for Colton ever since our adorable meet-cute.

In case you don't know, a meet-cute is the point in a romantic movie where the two lead characters meet each other for the very first time. I'm not sure where the name comes from, but I assume it has something to do with how quirky and adorable these meet-cutes always are. Colton and I had ours the first week my parents and I moved here, when I came to the theater alone so I could drown my sorrows in a nice light romantic comedy called *Sundae Sunday*.

I was looking forward to the movie, whose trailer promised the comforting formula of girl-meets-boy, girl-loses-boy, girl-and-boy-realize-they-are-each-other's-everythings-and-finally-get-to-the-point-of-the-whole-film: *true love's kiss*.

When I walked into the cinema, Tom greeted me from behind the snack counter with a genuine smile. "What would you like to see today?" he asked with such enthusiasm that his love for his job was immediately clear.

He struck me as borderline cute, so I tried not to look like a friendless freak as I told him, "One for *Sundae Sunday*."

"You must be new around here," he said as he rang up my ticket.

"We just moved into town." I reached into my shoulder bag to get my wallet, and the plastic bag I was holding slipped from my hand. The bag dropped to the red carpet and the carton of malted milk balls inside rattled loudly. *Very* loudly.

Tom peered over the counter to see what was happening down by my feet. "Care to explain that rattling sound?" His friendly voice had turned crisp.

"Oh, that's just my Whoppers." I picked up the bag, pulled out the large tan carton, and grinned at him as I gave it a hearty shake.

"No outside food." He looked offended, as if he was some aspiring Willy Wonka who'd made the theater candy by hand and I'd insulted him by bringing my own personal stash.

"Sorry, I didn't know if you sold them or not, and I can't watch a movie without my malted milk balls." I scanned the snack menu. "Either way, it's cool because I'm buying popcorn."

"Why would buying popcorn make it cool for you to sneak food into the movie theater?"

"I wasn't *sneaking* it." I raised the flimsy bag and waved it in his face. The milk balls rattled noisily. "This bag is totally see-through."

He put his hands on his hips. "I'm going to need to confiscate those chocolates."

"Listen"—I squinted at his nametag—"*Tom*. This is my favorite movie treat . . ."

"Do you have any idea how much a theater like this depends on refreshment profits? Do you even care if we keep our doors open? There is *no outside food* allowed. I'm sorry. No exceptions."

I gestured to the row of candy under glass. "You don't even

carry Whoppers, so it's not like you're missing out on a sale. My old theater didn't carry them either, so they just let me bring my own."

"You are welcome to leave your malted milk balls with me. And may I interest you in one of *our* tasty chocolate confections to enjoy with your popcorn?"

Tom and I stared each other down for a few beats. He steepled his fingers like a Bond villain, and I noticed he was trying to hide a grin. Like he'd been hoping to have a Whopper standoff against someone all morning.

Finally, I snapped, "Fine." I pulled out my carton and peeled open the spout on one side. Shaking out a large handful of the chocolaty balls, I defiantly shoved them into my mouth and started chewing in his face with a loud *crunch, crunch, crunch.*

I found his wide-eyed reaction satisfying enough to push a *second* handful into my already bulging cheeks.

Which was exactly when the best-looking boy I'd ever seen in real life swooped in behind him. It was Colton.

Everything in the theater lobby shifted to slow motion when I saw him for the first time. I could practically feel my pupils dilate. My hearing sharpened. I began to salivate. Literally. As in, the milk balls in my mouth were dissolving into thick chocolate drool.

Colton—who I immediately dubbed "Drop-dead handsome-face" before I knew his name—gave an easy grin and asked us what was happening. Tom threw a hand over his mouth, covering his shocked laugh, and all I could do was stand there, breathing through my nose and trying not to choke on my chocolaty spit.

Tom filled him in on the contraband candy situation, empha-sizing how much outside snacks were hurting the theater. "She's new to town." Tom gestured to my face. "I had no idea she'd take it this hard."

Colton leaned over and handed me a napkin, presumably to wipe the trail of brown drool off my chin. I tried to smile at him, but my cheeks were already stretched as wide as they could go.

"What did you do, frisk her?" Colton asked, looking at me curiously.

"No, the carton of Mighty Malts dropped and made a huge racket," Tom said. "I couldn't just ignore them."

I tried to correct him with a muffled, "Whoppers," which only served to send a fresh stream of chocolate drool down my chin.

Colton handed me a new napkin and winked at me. "Perhaps you're willing to buy an extra-large tub of popcorn for your snacking pleasure? You can keep your candy and we'll call things even."

I nodded and tried again. "They're Whoppers." More drool. I swiped the napkin Colton had given me across my chin.

"Missed a spot there," Colton said, and then—get this—he took the napkin from my hand and gently guided it along my chin. Meanwhile, his other hand swiped two Whoppers and popped them right into his beautiful mouth. "Mmmmm, choco-laty." His voice was so deep and his eye contact so intense, I had to take the napkin from his hand before I impulsively tried to lick his fingers.

Even if my mouth hadn't been packed with dissolved malt and chocolate, I would've been speechless.

Tom looked back and forth between us before finally giving

a laugh of disbelief. With a shake of his head, he plucked an extra-large popcorn tub off the stack of empties, placed it on the counter, and said, "She's all yours, horse man."

"That's *Colt*." He leaned in closer to me. "Name's Colton."

I glanced down and saw he wasn't wearing a nametag like Tom's. I smiled. "Hi, Colton." This fountain of handsomeness hadn't only made me swoon with his gaze; he'd also rescued me from having to spite-eat an entire carton of Whoppers right in the lobby of my new town's only theater.

I remained mute as Colton prepared my enormous bucket of popcorn, but I noticed he slathered on extra butter and gave me another quick wink just before he took my money.

As I made my way toward the theater doors in my sugar-rush-enhanced state of happiness, I turned back to admire my rescuer one last time and . . . walked directly into a giant, life-sized cutout of an armored superhero.

I screamed as my trough of popcorn went flying in all directions. I found myself flat on my back with the cardboard cutout lying on top of me. Colton rushed out from behind the counter and kneeled at my side. "Sorry, I told the boss we need to get rid of this thing. Victory Man has been trying to grab pretty girls all month."

As I lay there, my heart palpitating over his use of the word *pretty*, Colton lifted the cardboard cutout and pretended to slap Victory Man's masked face. I laughed as I accepted his hand of assistance, and then the two of us stood looking at each other awkwardly. Too late, I thought of the quip, "Victory Man needs to learn that some girls prefer to be their own hero," but the moment had passed.

If only I'd delivered that perfectly timed line during our meet-cute, I'd probably be Colton's girlfriend by now. Instead, my reaction was to drop to the floor on my hands and knees and maniacally start scooping the scattered popcorn back into the bucket.

"Don't worry about that," Colton said.

Tom must've been watching us, because he suddenly appeared with a broom and dustpan. "Here, this should help."

Colton took the broom and pretended to swat his boss in the butt. "Such a *gentleman*," he said. "Come on, I'll get you fresh popcorn. Er, or I should say fresh-*ish* popcorn."

I melodramatically batted my eyelashes, and gave a girlie "My hero" that *thankfully* made him laugh.

Before following him back over to the counter, I gathered up the last lingering kernels. Tom was busy straightening Victory Man's bent arm as I walked by, and I had to resist the urge to dump the salvaged popcorn over his head on my way to the garbage can.

Once I'd been given a brand-new popcorn bucket bigger than my head, Colton insisted on escorting me all the way to one of the red velvet fold-down seats. And from *Sundae Sunday* on, I was utterly his.

Our meet-cute had it all: quirky humiliation, a pratfall, and even adorable chocolate drool. At least, I've convinced myself my brown drool was somehow adorable. I pretend it's my genuine obsession with movies that's kept me coming back all summer, but I'm pretty sure it's obvious I'm only here during Colton's shifts.

He leans on the counter now and asks if I'm ready for

tomorrow. I grin and nod as I scan my brain for a pithy comment about the first day of school. Before I can come up with anything, he turns to watch a couple walking through the theater's glass doors.

I can read their pinched expressions from across the room. *Uh-oh.* Desperation Date Night. Trying to fix a broken relationship with a trip to the local Cineplex.

The guy slides his hand over the woman's shoulder, and she shoots him a look as if he just wiped toxic slime on her. His hand drops back to his side. Couples like this are even worse than those first-date pairings where the awkwardness is so palpable, they should have to buy it a separate ticket. But at least first dates are *supposed* to be uncomfortable. Timeworn couples like these two are walking marques, warning of the misery that awaits if we choose the wrong partner.

This is why I will never settle for anything less than epic love. Magical, all-consuming, life-changing love. It's what I've been saving my first kiss for. I went out with exactly one boy from my microscopic old town, and I certainly wasn't about to waste my first kiss on someone who thought the movie *Stand by Me* was "just okay." I mean, honestly. My first kiss is going to count.

Colton politely sells the couple their tickets, but avoids making eye contact. Once they're out of earshot, he rubs his arms. "I think I need a sweater after that chill."

"I don't know why people even bother when things get that obviously bad."

"What's the point in staying together when there's zero passion?" he says, and my whole face feels like a warm, slow-motion explosion.

Gazing at his solid jaw, I sense that this could be it. My chance to actually move our love story a step forward. I'm filled with what must be hysterical post-action-flick boldness and give Colton a hip check, saying, "You know, I love passion fruit."

Colton looks at me as if I've sneezed directly into the popcorn warmer. Not the reaction I was hoping for. I straighten, and the two of us stare at each other.

I try to think of something else to say. *Anything* that will erase my weird produce affection confession. But as the silence grows between us, I curse my ability to always think up the perfect pithy remark *after* it's too late.

"So . . . are you, um, wearing new school clothes tomorrow?" I ask.

"I do plan on being fully clothed." He cracks a smile, and I relax. "But I haven't really thought about what I'm wearing."

"My mom is always buying me outrageous outfits from the thrift store that I would *never* wear," I say. "This one time, she came home with a whole pile of jeans from, like, the nineteen eighties. One pair had such a high waist, the fly was about three feet long . . ." I continue babbling about crotch zippers and weird vintage clothes as if I have an acute form of Social Tourette's. Colton just nods as he helps the next customers.

I don't even realize Tom is listening in until he interjects, "You should go with a wild new look for your first day of school, Andie."

"Gee, thanks?" I widen my eyes at Colton and he laughs.

"I mean, wearing a unique thrift-store outfit will really trademark you as an independent thinker." He points down to his black-and-white wing-tipped old-man shoes and shakes a toe at me. "Gives a vastly more interesting first impression."

"Andie doesn't need some outfit to make her interesting," Colton says, and I grin maniacally.

"Just saying." Tom shrugs. "Punx High is filled with boring drones who dress alike. It's nice when someone isn't afraid to sprinkle the place with a little originality."

"You and your crew provide more than enough originality, Tom. More like you hose down the whole school with your bizarreness."

"Wait a second," I say to Tom. "You're still in high school?"

He and Colton laugh hard at this while I look back and forth between them. "Don't let the pole up his butt fool you," Colton says. "Tom's a senior like us."

I know he doesn't look *old* old, but I definitely figured Tom was in college. Maybe a college from the 1950s, since he's wearing tight plaid pants with his wingtips. "You don't really act like a high school student."

"Thank you, I'll take that as a compliment." Tom strokes his face as if he has a long beard. "I'm wise beyond my years."

"And what sort of outfit will you be sporting for the first day, O ancient one?" Colton asks him.

"Still deciding," Tom says before straightening up like he just remembered he has a pole up his butt. I get that he loves this theater and all, but the guy is way too serious. As if reading my mind, he announces to Colton, "Fun's over. Time to clean out the popcorn maker."

He turns away and Colton whispers to me, "Fun's just starting."

I laugh, and he pulls out a large plastic bag and two empty paper cups. He dramatically holds up one of the cups as if it is a holy chalice and hands it to me. We fold back the glass doors of the popcorn maker and get busy scooping out the warm kernels left at the bottom of the machine.

Holding the bag open between us, we take turns with our cups, and I can't stop staring at the way the neon POPCORN sign lights up Colton's face each time he leans forward. Like, *hello handsome . . . hello handsome . . . hello handsome . . .*

The two of us laugh and discuss our favorite parts of the action movie we were just watching, while the strong aroma of warm butter wafts around us. It smells an awful lot like falling in love.

It isn't until Tom finishes sweeping the floor and comes over to inspect the popcorn maker that I finally think of something to say that will tie in my bizarre proclamation of love for passion fruit from a half hour ago.

"You should see the way juice runs down my face when I eat passion fruit." I laugh and gesture to my chin as if it's covered in juice right now.

Colton is wiping his hands on a napkin, and he and Tom both stop and look at me like I've just projectile vomited into the freshly cleaned popcorn maker.

"Um, I mean . . . remember that chocolate drool I had the first time we ever met?" I'm pointing energetically to my chin. "The Whoppers?"

"Oh, yeah," the two of them say together.

"It was just . . . very drooly." I am doing a horrible job redeeming the passion fruit comment. I seriously wish I'd let it go.

Tom says, "I've busted plenty of people sneaking in snacks, but *no one* ever started wolfing down their contraband food before. I couldn't believe you shoved that first handful of malted milk balls into your mouth. And then you doubled down and just kept on going?" He laughs. "I think you would've eaten that whole carton."

"And you'd have just stood there watching her, huh?" Colton shakes his head. "Chivalry is truly dead."

"Come on, that would've been *epic*," Tom says. "I didn't even get a chance to snag a video clip of her before you butted in."

Colton tells me, "You did look fairly hilarious with your cheeks all stretched out like a chipmunk." He slaps Tom on the back, laughing. It's the friendliest I've ever seen them.

I don't know how this conversation turned on me so quickly.

The next shift of theater workers is arriving in their red vests and nametags. Tom moves to the register and pops the money drawer open. I need to flip this back around fast.

"Well . . ." I lean in closer to Colton. "It was still a pretty sweet meet-cute, don't you think?"

Colton looks at me with a furrowed brow, and my grin dies on my face. Meanwhile, Tom is counting bills, but nods with distracted amusement.

"What's a meet-cute?" Colton asks.

I blink, surprised. *How does he work in a movie theater and not know what a meet-cute is?*

"How did you get this job again?" Tom asks, stopping his counting.

"My mom knows the owner." Colton shrugs.

Tom closes his eyes and gives a groan before going back to counting. "*Of course* she does." He glances over to me. "You believe this one? Not even a movie buff."

How am I blowing things so epically that now Tom thinks he and I are bonding? I launch into a quick explanation of a meet-cute as Colton gets to work wiping down the soda machine nozzles. Since he and Tom only seem to be half listening, I get nervous and start babbling about how I became obsessed with movies. Which would be fine if I were describing some cool story, like having my mind blown the first time I saw *Star Wars* or something. But instead, I'm describing how I inherited my love of cinema from my mother.

Over the years, Mom has taken me to every Pixar and Potter film on opening night, and the first moment anything good is released on DVD, we spend hours together exploring the special features. I've listened to more directors' commentaries than most film students, and I was picking out act breaks when other kids my age were still searching for Waldo.

Mom even has this locked glass cabinet filled with all her favorite movies from the eighties and nineties that she's been watching with me at key moments in my life. For instance, the first time I stayed home sick as a teen was an excuse for her to break out *Ferris Bueller's Day Off*. Then, when I was having trouble with chemistry, we watched *Weird Science* together, and I'm still awful at chemistry, but it was fun to see what they thought future computers might be capable of back in the 1980s.

Of all Mom's movies, the ones by John Hughes are the holiest vestiges of her own adolescence. As the two of us watch these movies, sitting side by side, we don't speak at all, because, well, talking during movies is an obnoxious habit. But we always discuss the films after, which has resulted in some amazing revelations about life and each other.

And now here I am babbling to my crush about how movies make me feel more connected and understood and close to my *mother.*

"She's been saving up her favorites," I'm saying. "And tonight, my mom and I are supposed to watch *Pretty in Pink*. Since we moved here, she's talked about waiting for the last day of summer vacation to share it with me."

Tom raises his head from the garbage bag he's just tied up. "Did she name you Andie after the main character in that movie?"

I blush and nod, looking down at my hands. "Because of my red hair. Both of my parents love the movie, and according to my mom, watching it will change my life." I laugh. "Of course, she *has* made this claim about other movies before."

Tom grins, and I realize Colton is looking back and forth between the two of us as if we're both speaking a foreign language. I want to crawl inside the garbage pail and roll away into a sticky, buttery oblivion.

"Well, I'd better go catch that movie. With my mom." I pull the car keys from my purse and jingle them in the air.

"Give my regards to Duckie," Tom says with a smile.

"Um, yeah," Colton says. "I'll see you first thing tomorrow for school."

"You have my address, right?" I hate that my voice sounds so desperate. "I mean, if you're still planning to give me a ride and tour of the school."

"Righto. You're over on Cherry Street. Seven a.m." I can't tell from his expression if he regrets making the offer to drive me. But before he can back out, I wave good-bye and run from the theater.

As I turn the key in the ignition of my mom's vintage Mercedes, I wish I could rewind the last half hour of the night and act like less of a weirdo. Hopefully I can turn things around with Colton tomorrow, because I can sense our epic rom-com could be heading for a fade-out much too soon.

And I've been counting on my magical first kiss being with him.

chapter 2

By the time I pull into our driveway, triggering the motion-detection lights, I'm already on my third replay of every single word I said to Colton tonight. And most of it is not good.

At least 60 percent of my comments were downright cringeworthy, not to mention that embarrassing bit at the end with me oversharing about my mom. She may be cool as mothers go, but I'm pretty sure my acting all dorky about it to Colton isn't going to make him swoon.

Mom flings open our chartreuse front door and steps onto the front porch with a big-toothed smile and a wave. "You won't believe what I scored at the thrift store today!"

I give an inward groan as I climb out of the car and walk across our driveway. Mom's wearing a minidress composed of purple and white panels of material that desperately cling to each other around her hips. When it comes to thrift store bargain shopping, "perfect fit" is not her top priority.

"Great dress," I say. "Let me guess . . . half-off ticket?"

"Oh, no, the dress isn't the big score," she says. "Although six bucks was a really sweet deal." Her bright red bob swings as she spins around, exposing the puckered zipper in the back. "And it only needs a few stitches to be flawless."

I sigh and give her a kiss on the cheek. Mom might not technically qualify as a clothing hoarder, but she's incapable of passing up bargains. Even bizarro ones. About one-third of the boxes we moved from our old house were filled with Mom's questionable thrift store fashion "scores."

I step into the living room and stop with a gasp. A giant pink couch has taken over the whole room. It is the longest couch I have ever seen in my life, and the cushions look like they're about to explode out of the tight leather. The radiant monstrosity is partially blocking the pathway to the stairs. And did I mention this thing is a *giant pink leather couch*?

When I stop being speechless, I ask, "Has Dad seen it yet?"

Mom pats my back reassuringly. "He'll *love* it."

"So, you haven't even sent him a photo of it yet?"

"You know I hate that camera phone thingy," Mom says. "He'll just have to be surprised."

"Oh, yes, he will. Be surprised." I widen my eyes. "Did you stop to ask yourself if we really needed a *pink* leather sofa?"

"The woman at the thrift store labeled it pink on the delivery slip too." Mom runs her hand along the couch's low back. "But that's silly. Anyone can see this couch is red. It's just a little faded, so it's a light shade of red."

I laugh. "Light red is another way of saying *pink*." I drop my butt onto the center cushion and bounce a bit. "Wow, is it comfortable though."

"Lie on it!" Mom shoves my shoulders, forcing me down.

I fold my hands across my chest and snuggle in deeper. "Maybe Dad can use it for his patients."

She pulls up an ottoman and sits primly, pretending to hold a pencil against her upturned palm. "Okay, Andie. Tell me, how do you *feel* about starting at a brand-new school tomorrow?"

We both laugh and I sit up. My dad is a psychologist who was fine with being mostly an author, until his advances got so small he had to go back to being mostly a psychologist again. That's why he, and by extension *we*, had to move to a town with more patients for him to treat. Punxsutawney isn't exactly a bustling metropolis, but it's bigger than the teeny-tiny two-store "town" I grew up in.

The closest business in our old town was a semi-truck dealership three miles away, and we bought our groceries from a small general store on the first floor of my best friend, Rhonda's, two-story home. With a sigh, I think of the sleepovers we used to have there. My favorite was the time we snuck down to grab ingredients to make midnight cookies. We ate so much dough, there were only three large (very-stuck-to-the-pan) cookies in the end. It was awesome.

Rhonda is the only person I've met who loves talking about movies almost as much as I do. We fit perfectly as best friends, which is pretty amazing, since it's not like the town had a huge best friend lake to go swimming in or anything.

My old high school only had 172 students total, and that was junior and senior high combined, so to me, Punxsutawney is practically urban.

To be honest, I'm nervous about diving into the new high school waters tomorrow. Colton is the only friend I've made since moving here, and I haven't even spoken to anyone my age besides him and Tom.

Mom furrows her brow. "*Are* you feeling ready for tomorrow?" My parents have been over-anticipating how damaged I'll be due to a big upheaval during such a "vital stage in my development." (Dad's words, not mine.) I've tried reassuring them as best I can, but Mom has been counting down the days to tomorrow as if I'm about to start preschool.

I say, "I'll be fine, I'm sure." I don't add how much I'll miss having Rhonda by my side. Or how nervous I am about winning Colton's heart.

"What are you planning to wear?" she asks.

"Jeans and a T-shirt?" I shrug, but Mom launches into a monologue about how crucial my first day outfit is.

"This isn't just about you entering your senior year, Andie. *Nobody* here knows you. You will be judged solely on what you wear that first day."

"Thanks a bunch," I say. "Dad always tells me I should just be myself."

"Of course you should be yourself." Mom pats my hand. "Just be yourself, wearing something *fabulous*."

She rises and moves to a bin in the corner, where she roots around for a few moments, selectively gathering an armload of dresses as if she's picking an oversized bouquet of bright, patterned flowers. With a flourish, she spreads them out one by one down the length of our new pink couch.

I let her have her fun, since I have to admit she does have some crazy-cool taste in clothing. That is, with an emphasis on the *crazy*.

Within minutes, the living room is covered in fitted pinup-style dresses and silk-screened prints, black crinoline skirts, wild designs, colorful stripes, peek-a-boo cutouts, and lots and *lots* of ribbon. It's like the couch has become a vintage fashion cornucopia.

Mom turns up the stereo to act as a soundtrack for our montage of trying on outfits together. My mother wouldn't be my mother without massive amounts of quirk. As usual, just like the cheesy special effects vortex they used in the movie *Weird Science*, her enthusiasm sucks me right in.

Between outfit changes, Mom keeps insisting I try on a sleeveless pink dress covered with white polka dots. The bright pink color clashes with my hair, so I resist, but she eventually wears me down. Once it's zippered, I must admit the cinched waist does create the illusion I have a great figure, and I can't seem to help spinning around in it. The poufy skirt just insists on being twirled.

When Dad walks in the door, he looks back and forth at the two of us wearing zany dresses with our hair all static-y, and he starts laughing.

Mom sings him the line from her favorite Cyndi Lauper song, "Girls Just Wanna Have Fun," and blows him a kiss.

Dad pretends to catch her kiss as he moves into the room, but stops at the new couch blocking his way.

"This place wasn't Barbie's Dream House enough for you two already? Did we really need to start collecting pink furniture?" He's referring to the periwinkle-painted exterior of our new house, but he sounds more amused than angry.

"It's red." Mom pouts as she drops onto the couch, tugging

at the tight, yellow pencil skirt she landed in after our fashion experimentation. "The leather's just a little faded."

Dad and I look at each other and in unison call out, "*Pink!*"

He says, "I know you're excited that this thrift store sells furniture, sweetheart, but we can honestly afford to order something online and have it delivered. Anything you'd like."

"What's the fun of that?" Mom says. "Shopping is about the thrill of the *hunt*."

"Maybe the next time you're out on safari, you can target a sofa that's a more neutral color," Dad teases as he pulls her to her feet. Holding her hand, he spins her quickly, and they slide into an embrace. I look away until they disengage and Dad heads for the kitchen.

It's nice that my parents still love each other and all, but I could do with a little less PDA in my own living room. Especially since I'm so anxious about trying to make my very first kiss happen with Colton.

Mom drops back into the pink leather abyss and asks me what time the bus comes in the morning. It's as if she's been reading my thoughts. I shyly confess that Colton is picking me up early in the morning and will be taking me on a tour of the school. Mom has pieced together the fact that I like him, since apparently I "light up" every time I say his name, but this is the first time I openly confess how deep my crush goes.

"I'm really excited and nervous," I admit, playing with the pink hem of my dress.

"Oh, honey." Mom's pencil skirt threatens to rip as she jumps up and toddles over to the glass DVD cabinet. With a flourish, she pulls the key from the chain around her neck and bends down to open the door. Her fingers roll along the titles and delicately pluck one from the shelf. From her crouched position, she announces with a serious tone, "It's time."

Spinning around and holding up the pink DVD case like it's baby Simba from *The Lion King*, she announces, "You are about to get … *Pretty in Pink*."

The tulle on the pink polka-dot dress I'm wearing makes a crinkling sound as I cross my arms. If a dress could laugh, it almost seems like that's what it's doing. A chill runs up the zippered spine of the stiff pink material and tickles the hairs on the back of my neck. Which is strange, since the *Pretty in Pink* movie choice isn't even a surprise to me.

"This movie." Mom taps the cover. "Oh, Andie, *this movie*! This is the movie your father and I fell in love to. As soon as we saw your red hair, we knew your name. Andie, this movie is about to change your life."

And there it is. Each time Mom's opened her magical glass movie case and presented me with one of her movies from the 1980s, she has labeled it life-changing. While most of them have been largely entertaining, my world has yet to flip on its axis the way she keeps warning.

Still, this film does sound really special. Could it offer some insight into my destiny? More importantly, my *romantic* destiny? I realize lots of people look to things like horoscopes and fortunetellers for guidance and direction, but movies have always held all the wisdom I need.

With a crunch of pink crinoline, I drop onto our new leather sofa. Mom starts the movie and slides in beside me, and we are both instantly, utterly absorbed in *Pretty in Pink*.

I must admit Molly Ringwald does put together some "volcanic ensembles," as her best friend Duckie calls them. And while Duckie is hopelessly dorky and strange, he's also hilarious and kind of adorable. Not to mention Blane (the character, not the appliance) who is every bit as blue-eyed and dreamy as Colton.

The zany owner of the record store where Andie works is named Iona, and she acts as a sort of mentor-ish-type-person to Andie. Iona reminds me so much of my mom that I have to pause the movie and ask her, "Did John Hughes know you back then or something?"

Mom points to the screen, where Iona is standing frozen, midsentence, with her bright red lips twisted. "Well, I did have a tight rubber dress like hers, but my hair was never spiked that aggressively."

"But you did spike your hair?"

"Not *aggressively*." She gives my arm a playful shove. "I'll have you know, everyone dressed like that back in the eighties."

I look at her. "Sure, if by *everyone*, you mean mostly you and Cyndi Lauper."

She poses dramatically. "Me, Cyndi, *and* Iona as played by Annie Potts in *Pretty in Pink*."

We both laugh, and I hit play on the remote, enjoying every second of this cinematic time capsule.

Halfway through the movie Mom yawns and stretches, announcing she's heading to bed early. This is a plot twist, since we're both night owls and she usually stays through till the ending credits with me. It is fairly late, but I'm completely engrossed in the film. Without taking my eyes off the television screen, I accept her light kiss goodnight on my cheek and relax beneath the fuzzy blanket that she tucks under my chin.

"Don't stay up too late," Mom warns from the stairs. "You want to be fresh for your first day."

I keep my attention on the movie, but snap my hand into a formal salute. "Good job mothering there, lady." She chuckles as she heads up to bed.

Onscreen, my *Pretty in Pink* namesake is agonizing over whether or not to go to her prom. Of course, Iona responds in the most eccentric way possible; by changing into a tight pink formal dress, donning a beehive hairdo, and forcing Andie to slow dance with her as she reminisces about her own prom. It's basically what my mom would probably do if the subject of prom came up.

I realize the dress I'm still wearing is very similar to the one Iona gives to Andie, and I feel my face pull into a smile. I wonder if Colton and I will go to the Punxsutawney High School prom together.

As I imagine the flowers he'll bring me, and the tux he'll wear, I feel my eye blinks getting slower and lasting longer. The movie continues humming on in the background, and the next thing I know I'm in a beautiful ballroom wearing a pale prom dress and slow dancing with Colton.

It's a dream I wish would never end.

chapter 3

When I drag my eyes open, the living room has been cast in a rosy sheen. I peel my face off the leather arm of the sofa and rub my cheek. I'm still wearing the pink polka-dot dress from last night. It's early morning, and I've spent the night underneath the fuzzy blanket here on the giant pink couch. A glance toward the windows tells me it's going to be an overcast day.

A fragment of music is playing over and over, and I see the main menu for the *Pretty in Pink* DVD looping on the television screen in front of me. Overnight, the music's cheesy drumbeats have ingrained themselves fully into the folds of my brain. Reaching for the remote, I click *mute* and wonder why they didn't use a better song from the soundtrack for the menu theme. The portion of the film I saw before drifting off had some fairly stellar music.

I haven't fallen asleep to a movie since I was a kid, and now I'm dying to find out what happened between Andie, my favorite character, Duckie, and my newest movie-crush, Blane. It's also the first time I've slept in this living room, and I wonder if I should go upstairs to bed and try to get another hour of sleep or if I should just put the movie back on.

Then I remember: *Colton is picking me up for school today!* An involuntary grin presses my cheeks up so high, I can see them.

I hear happy whistling sounds floating from above. The whistling gets louder as it gets closer, and I look up to see Dad coming down the stairs. "Good morning, sweetheart. You up for pancakes?"

"Isn't it a little early for pancakes?"

He shrugs and resumes whistling as he heads for the kitchen. I call out after him, "Okay, maybe just one pancake. Or, like, four, tops." There's something irresistible about pancakes that have been whistled over. Like the joy of the tune works its way into the batter and makes them taste better.

Mom bustles in and spreads her arms wide. "Happy first day at your new school, Andie!"

I pull the blanket up to my chin and mumble, "Thanks, Mom. Wake me when the pancakes are ready."

Mom yanks the fuzzy material off me, but I close my eyes and feign being asleep. "The pink dress was my favorite!" she says excitedly. "Is this the outfit you decided on for today?"

"Nope. This is the outfit I slept in." I keep my eyes closed. "Going to school in jeans and a T-shirt."

"Jeans and a T-shirt?" I can hear her pout without looking. "Are you sure?"

I shrug. "I guess."

"You *guess*?" Mom's voice has just enough of a screechy edge to get me to open my eyes.

"It's just the first day of school, Mom. I've never dressed up for it before."

"Back at home, you never had a handsome young man escorting you. This is basically a first date."

"Mom. I assure you, this is *not* a date."

Ignoring me, she pulls a white dress off the top of the pile from last night's try-on montage. "What did you think of this one? It's positively angelic."

"The zipper sticks a little—and, also, I'd rather not show up for my first day at a new school dressed as a teenaged bride."

Mom gives the dress a closer look and shrugs before tossing it behind the couch. "Don't worry, we'll find you something."

As she holds up dress after dress, I continue rejecting them. She insists the dress I'm wearing looks amazing, but I explain what she should already know; this dress is just not me. It may be impeccably made and voguish, and okay, yes, very flattering *on* me, but this vintage pink polka-dot dress is decidedly *not* me. With a sigh, Mom asks me what I thought of the movie last night.

"It was really cool up to the point where I fell asleep."

She freezes and stares at me as if I've just pulled out a lit cigarette. "You fell *asleep*? To *Pretty in Pink*?"

At my sheepish nod, she mutters under her breath and rushes to turn on the television. "I knew I never should've gone to bed early." Scrolling through the scene selection screen, she asks me, "Did you see this? Did you see this?" over and over, until I finally grab the remote from her and hit play.

As the movie's soundtrack thumps around us, Mom sets up snack trays in front of the TV for us so we can eat our delicious whistle-cooked pancakes as we watch. I genuinely love the rest of the movie, but I can't help noticing something seems off about the ending.

To start, there is this tremendous build-up as we watch

Andie working to assemble her custom-designed pink prom dress. Based on Andie's funky vintage style throughout the movie, this dress promises to be the most epic wearable creation of all time. Anticipation grows as we wait to see her looking ever so pretty in pink, and then we finally get to the big reveal and . . . the thing is a hot mess.

Onscreen, Andie holds her head high as she enters the prom in a shapeless pink sack. I realize Andie made this prom outfit all by herself, and she was combining two very different styles, but the dress Iona gave her looked sort of cool on its own. This thing looks like it was sewn together by an ape. And not one of those clever *Planet of the Apes* sort of apes either. I'm saying an *actual* ape could've designed this dress.

I smooth the skirt on the pink polka-dotted number I'm still wearing and think maybe my dress is not quite as eye-bleedingly awful as I thought.

The other issue I have with the movie is that the ending feels a bit tacked on. Like, I saw things heading in a very different direction. I'm happy for Andie (spoiler alert) winning Blane, and there is no denying the movie-magic moment of them kissing while silhouetted by his car's headlights, but I say to Mom, "Something feels a little *off* about the ending." I turn to see she's wiping sappy tears from her eyes and add, "Uh, never mind."

"I'm telling you, Andie, that movie really holds up." Mom blows her nose. "It's every bit as romantic as it was that first night when I saw it with your father."

"I don't know." I stand and begin clearing our sticky pancake dishes. "I thought Blane was super cute and all, and he and Andie definitely had some chemistry, but by the end I was kind of rooting for Duckie to get the girl. He's the one who truly loved her and understood her."

Mom tilts her head at me. "Duckie is a funny character and, okay, I admit that dance he performs in the record store is pure genius. But trust me, sweetie, Andie and Blane are the ones who belong together."

"But didn't it seem odd to you that they didn't have much to talk about any time they weren't kissing?"

She laughs and waves her hand as if dismissing the air that holds my very valid question. "You'll understand once you've shared a kiss with your one true love," she says. She takes my face in her hands and looks me in the eye. "My wish is that your first real kiss will be with your true love."

We smile at each other for a beat, and I make my own small wish for the same thing.

There's a knock at the door, and I glance at the digital clock on the front of the DVD player. "No, no, no!" I panic-whisper. "That must be *Colton*!" My heart starts thumping in time with the drums on the *Pretty in Pink* movie menu that's playing once again.

I look down at my dress. "I can't wear this!" Despite Molly Ringwald's ability to pull off the color, pink is a wide-awake nightmare for most redheads. Particularly hot pink. And especially on already-goofy-enough-without-calling-even-more-attention-to-myself me.

I give my armpit a quick sniff. "Oh God! I should've showered! What was I thinking?" I curse *Pretty in Pink* for distracting me for so long.

"Everything's going to be okay," Mom commands. "This

dress looks amazing on you, and it is fate that you are wearing it today. You *are* pretty in pink. Just go upstairs and rub a dryer sheet over the material. I'll let your date in, and you can make your grand entrance down the stairs when you're ready."

"I don't need a grand entrance," I say as I sprint up the steps. "And this *isn't* a date."

"Whatever you say." When I glance back, Mom gives me a super cheesy double-thumbs-up signal and calls to the door, "Be right there!"

I rush to the bathroom, where I get to work on a quick sink shower, careful not to drip on the material of my dress. This dress that is apparently my *fate*.

I hear Mom introduce herself to Colton as "Andie's mom" and offer him a seat. "Annn-diiiie," she calls casually. "Your ride is here."

"Be there in a sec!" I'm beyond grateful she didn't say my "date" is here.

"Who's this?" Dad's voice rises from the living room.

"Andie's date," Mom announces. She must hear my horrified squeal because she quickly corrects, "I mean, Colton is showing our daughter around her new high school this morning."

I drag on a pair of fishnets too fast, and all of my toes burst through the stockings. On both sides. Sliding black ballet flats over the holes, I scrape my hair into a classic "didn't wash my hair" high ponytail and take a few swipes at my lashes with a nearby mascara wand.

Pausing for a beat, I consider myself in the mirror over the sink. My face looks flushed but not bad, except that I'm already regretting this whole pretty-in-pink dress. I should've just ignored Mom's romantic notions and thrown on a pair of comfortable jeans with a basic T-shirt. *No time to change now*; I need to get Colton away from my parents.

I'm startled by an impatient knock on the bathroom door. My dad calls, "You okay in there, Andie?"

"I'll be right out." As we pass each other in the hallway, I give him a quick, "Thanks for the pancakes, Pops," before rushing down the steps.

My heart starts drumming as soon as Colton comes into view. He's sitting on the pink leather sofa with his head down, elbows resting on his knees as he types something into his phone. He's completely absorbed and I slow down, panic rising. I know I wasn't really going for a big, grand entrance, but now that it's set up to happen, I think it *would* be a nice way to mark this beginning of our future together.

I look to Mom, who gives a knowing smile. "Oh, Andie, that dress is a little too low-cut for school, don't you think?"

Colton's attention darts up from his phone, and thankfully he catches the final few steps of my gliding descent. His reaction to my dress is to laugh and say, "What're you *wearing*?" I just stare at him with my knees buckled until he adds, "I mean, it's fine, Andie. You look nice. Lots of people dress up for the first day of school."

I take in his worn jeans and tight T-shirt, showing off his muscles, and wonder if I was drunk on pancake syrup when I let Mom talk me into this dress. She insists on taking a photo of Colton and me together before letting us go, which isn't helping our current mother/daughter dynamic one bit.

I glare at her through the camera lens, but she still takes five more rapid-fire shots before saying, "Okay, you two go on and have a great day."

I step across the threshold with Colton, ready to greet my very first day in my brand-new life. As we make our way down the walk toward the curb where Colton's car is parked, I imagine my pink polka-dot dress is giggling with every swish of its skirt. The idea fills me with a ping of unexpected hope.

chapter 4

When we arrive at school, I decide I'll be staying in Colton's boxy blue Honda Element for the rest of the day to avoid letting anyone see me in this dress. *Why was my brain too busy to be bothered with thinking this morning?* Amidst the ocean of normally dressed teenagers, I'm clearly the only one who mindlessly decided to select my first day of school outfit from a random pile of my mom's thrift store scores.

Obviously, my dress's swishing skirt has been laughing *at* me.

Colton is walking away before he realizes I haven't left the car. Coming back, he opens my door and offers me his hand. With a tight smile, I allow him to lead me toward the school. Embarrassment washes over my body as the river of staring students flows around me like I'm a rock. A weird, redheaded rock in polka-dotted pink. I smooth my skirt and feel another spike in my normally mild level of resentment toward my mother.

The oversized doors to the school are held open by a pretty blonde girl. "Hi, Colton," she says in a milkshake voice, thick with flirtation. His casual nod as we move inside is deeply satisfying, and I lift my chin as high as I can.

Another pretty girl—this one with black hair—walks by cooing, "Missed you, Colt," and he thankfully seems oblivious to how genuinely attractive she is.

I do remember a few wide-eyed females stalking him at the movie theater over the summer, but none of them stuck around and helped him out behind the counter the way I did. In fact, I was the only one who visited him during his shifts on a consistent-slash-obsessive basis.

Moving through the school, I stay glued to his side while he introduces me as "the new girl" to various athletic-looking guys who eye my dress with confusion. None of them are nearly as good-looking as Colton.

When we reach the cafeteria, he grabs my shoulders dramatically. "The only food you can trust in this place is the pizza."

He asks me what time I have lunch, and I dig in my bag for my class schedule. It turns out the two of us have the same lunch, and my hope surges as he points to a table in the corner. "I'll meet you right over there. Don't worry if I'm a little late—I need to talk to my coach before lunch."

"I take it that's the *cool kids'* table?" I bump him playfully with my hip.

He grins at me. "You know it."

"My old school was too small to have cliques. We mostly all got along."

"Yeah, it's kind of the same here. Although, I guess we do each have our own crowd."

Looking around, I can't help but think this is a drastic understatement. People appear to be segregated into clumps, based on mode of dress as well as facial expressions. Surly frowns? Over here with this group. Shyly looking at the ground? Step right this way.

Aside from the modern clothes and diverse races, the way the groups are gathered feels a little like we're in an eighties teen movie. I wonder, will the athletes end up acting like bullies and are the shy, awkward outcasts hiding their soft hearts behind snarky comments? And just how bad have everybody's parents messed them up already?

Of course, back in the eighties, there weren't selfie-takers to trip over every few feet, not to mention people bouncing off each other as they all stare at their smart phones. But at least I'm not surrounded by a totally whitewashed group of movie-poster-attractive people.

Still, it feels like this scene could totally be the fade-in for a living, updated version of a John Hughes movie. I'm busy imagining the rocking music that should be playing as the soundtrack right now when I get the sensation I'm being watched.

A girl with an eyebrow ring and wearing all black widens her heavily lined eyes at me, and I nearly recoil in fear. By the time I notice her small smile and realize she's not menacing, just acting friendly, it's too late for me to smile back.

I should probably stop trying to view everything through the lens of archaic teen movies.

Leaving the cafeteria, the hallways have grown suddenly more crowded, and I can't help but notice that Colton is apparently *super* popular. *This must be what it's like to date a celebrity*, I think as he returns hellos with nods, punctuated by a few manly fist bumps and an occasional, "*Hey-oh*." One girl gives me an up and down look that's so deliberate, I can feel it in my knees.

I seriously wish I wasn't dressed like such a freak.

When we reach the gymnasium, three manic blonde girls wearing matching cheerleading outfits flock around him. "Wow, Colton, have you been working out this summer?" the least-blonde one with dark skin purrs.

He grins at her and flexes a muscle. She swoons and my jealousy pops out, solid as his bicep.

"You're new," the blondest-blonde informs me.

The lesser-blonde asks, "Are you coming to squad tryouts after school?"

"The *cheerleading* squad?" I laugh.

At her "Duh," I violently shake my head *no*. I picture myself breaking my neck while attempting a cartwheel. Or trying to clap with any sort of rhythm. My mom once took me to a Zumba exercise dance class, and the frustrated instructor actually grabbed my hands to force me to clap on the beat.

The least-blonde is adjusting her cheer skirt in a way that is clearly designed to draw Colton's eye. Just as he notices her skirt's hem edging up her left thigh, I say, "We'd better finish up our tour." Taking him by the arm, I lead him away from the magnetic pull of the girls. "I want to be on time for homeroom."

I give least-blonde a fake smile over my shoulder and she calls, "See you later, Colt," with a familiarity that makes me wince.

He leads me into the stairwell, and I spot a group of students dressed in head-to-toe black, (or rather neck-tattoo-to-combat-boot black) tucked underneath the stairs. The back wall of their cave is covered in cartoons, some of which deserve an NC-17 rating.

The eyebrow ring girl who I recently flinched away from

gives me a cold look as she pushes past us to join the group. I can't exactly blame her, but now she's pointing a finger in my direction while saying something to the others, and I imagine them all judging me. *Look at you, Andie*—already making friends.

Colton smoothly guides me up the steps and whispers, "Goth Central. Stay for too long and risk losing your soul." He winks and says, "Kidding," and I force myself to wink back.

Once upstairs, we approach double doors that open to a high-ceilinged classroom. "And here we have . . . these people."

I peer inside the room. It's huge, with choir bleachers lining the back wall. A group of students that can best be described as "eclectic" is gathered around a piano in front. They're wearing everything from hats with feathers to stilettos and suspenders, with so many colors and patterns that my mind can't sort it all. Clearly, my mom isn't the only one who knows how to score vintage threads. I feel myself smile.

A kid with straight posture and a slicked-back hairdo from the 1920s moves into view and says, "Nice dress, Andie. Now *that's* what I'm talking about." It actually takes me a minute to realize the guy is Tom.

I cringe as Colton seems to notice my dress all over again. *Great.* This is not at all the way he looked at the cheerleader's skirts. I'm mortified to realize my pink, crinoline-lined, polka-dotted dress and black fishnets go perfectly with the crazy getups gathered around the piano.

I call, "Thanks, um, Tom," and guide Colton away from the doorway before he decides to dump me here. My tongue is paralyzed by dress regret, and an awkward silence catches stride between Colton and me as we walk down the hallway.

I've never been the type to care about what outfit I'm wearing, but today, I get why some people do.

I spot two girls taking a selfie as they stand side by side in front of a locker with their heads tipped toward each other. On impulse, I hold out my phone and pull Colton's head next to mine.

"Say selfie!" I snap a picture of the two of us together.

He asks, "Is it technically a selfie when there's more than one person in it?"

"I don't know," I admit. He looks surprised in the shot, and I must have snapped it just as I got to the f-sound in *selfie*, because I bear a striking resemblance to the local celebrity groundhog, Punxsutawney Phil. I reach up and take a few more multi-person selfies of us together.

Colton's smile is less genuine in these, and I stop before I get as annoying as my mother. Picking the most natural-looking shot, I pause to post it on online, adding the caption, "Rocking my first day at Punxsutawney High!" For some reason, reporting this to my handful of followers from my old school makes me feel like less of a loser.

Of the 172 kids in my old school, there were only fifty-four in what would have been my graduating class. We all grew up together, so everyone was pretty much friends with everyone else. Even though I didn't check in much over the summer, I suddenly miss all fifty-three of my old classmates.

I'm walking with my head down, looking at my phone, when I run smack-dab into someone's chest. The impact is so jarring, I actually reel backward a bit.

Of course, he's another goth, and I immediately want to cry. By now, I've probably turned their whole group against me thanks to my unique social impairment. He bends down to pick up the Sharpie pen that I've knocked out of his hand. By the time he straightens back up, I've mustered a friendly smile, but he only looks even more annoyed by me.

I stare into his green eyes lined with black, willing him to return my smile, until he glances down at my dress and squints as if it's made of direct sunlight. I bow under his look of disgust, and rush to catch up to Colton.

A cluster of kids with backpack-stooped posture moves unevenly toward us, and as we pass, a girl wearing a tight hairband catches my eye. She looks up at me, and I can read her strong IQ in the way she hugs a thick textbook to her chest. Nobody else is carrying books yet. I avoid her gaze before Colton can see that hers is probably the group I belong with, even more than the choir room misfits. My old school may have been a small bubble without cliques, but I was known for being a bit of a brain. I think it helped that zero percent of my fifty-four classmates were hot guys, so there was nothing to distract me from my studies.

I hear a high-pitched, nasally "Hello, Colton" from my right, and look over to see a girl with glossy black hair giving a limp-wristed wave in our direction. She starts striding purposefully toward us, her shoes clicking on the tile floor like a countdown before impact. I grasp for a way to distract Colton.

"So, I guess we should be looking for my homeroom now." I put a hand on his non-flexed bicep, which is still pretty solid.

Colton smiles at my hand, then looks up just in time to catch a dramatic Hollywood "finally reunited" hug from the girl. She's tall, and even up close with no filter, her olive skin looks airbrushed. Over Colton's broad shoulder, her perfectly defined eyes seem mesmerized by my pink polka-dotted torso. I cross my arms in defense. Her rose-red lips stretch into a phony-looking smile, and she asks through her nose, "Who's this?"

Shooting a thumb in my direction, Colton says, "This is the new girl, Andie. She's cool."

His words make me glow from the inside out like a jack-o'-lantern, but Miss Hair Gloss quickly blows out my candle. "I was friends with a redhead once."

I don't know how to respond to this, so I laugh. She gives my dress another puzzled look before turning back to Colton.

And now I notice that he practically has stars in his eyes. It's obvious he and this girl have some serious chemistry and/or romantic history. As the two of them flirt with each other shamelessly, I note that she's wearing the ideal first day of school outfit: perfect-fitting jeans, black kitten heels, and a thin scoop neck top. I want to shred my polka dots to pieces and run away screaming. But I'm not giving up on my first kiss with my one true love without a fight. Also, wearing the worst dress ever is still better than being at school naked.

"We should get moving." I give Hair Gloss a smug grin. "Colton has been so sweet, taking me on a tour of the school before homeroom."

Hair Gloss tilts her head at me. "The bell's going to ring soon. What's your name?"

"Um, Andie?"

She gives an exaggerated sigh. "I mean your *last* name."

"Oh. Knedman?" I wonder if she's planning to put out a hit on me for interrupting her little flirting session. Or it's possible I've watched too many spy movies this summer.

"Fabby, you're with me." She hooks my arm in hers and tells Colton, "Don't worry, I'll take good care of her." Before I can even decide to resist, we're moving down the hallway together. Away from Colton.

"How do you know the Colt?" she asks, her heels clicking confidently as she drops my arm and steers me none-too-gently through the now-crowded hallway.

"Oh, just … from the movie theater," I say.

"That lame job of his?" She shakes her shiny mane. "Such an *inconvenience*."

"Are you two together?" I ask as my heart dives into my ballet flats.

"No. But we're about to be."

I already do not like her. But I don't doubt that she speaks the truth. Colton seemed fully under her spell in a way I've never seen him act before.

Hair Gloss tells me her name is Kaia as she points a shiny maroon fingernail toward a classroom doorway. "Your homeroom's there. If you need any help finding your way around, there's no need to bother Colton anymore. I'm sure you'll find plenty of people happy to talk to you." She points down the hallway. "Oh, look. Here's someone checking out your fashion statement now."

"Hey there, Andie." Tom glances at my dress as he slides past us on his way into the room.

"Go for it," Kaia whispers in my ear. With a slight smile, she turns on one of her kitten heels and heads across the hallway. I'm furious that I let her pull me away from Colton, especially since she isn't even in my stupid homeroom.

I slump into an open desk by the doorway, and Tom leans across the aisle toward me. "That is a *volcanic* ensemble." He raises one eyebrow. "Very Molly Ringwald circa 1986."

I muster up a smile before scrunching lower into my seat. I can't believe I've already completely blown it. If I could have a morning do-over, I'd be getting a can-we-be-more-than-friends hug from Colton right now instead of sitting here having my bizarre wardrobe admired by Tom.

A glance at the big white clock on the wall tells me there is more time left before the first bell than I could possibly know what to do with. I try plastering a smile back on my face, but I'm quite sure I look like a freak on the verge of a panic attack.

"Hey, what did you think of the movie last night?" Tom asks. When I give him a confused look, he adds, "*Pretty in Pink*?"

With a sigh, I let my phony smile drop and lean forward. "I have to be honest. I couldn't help rooting for Duckie half the time."

Tom gives me a full grin. "Yes. The Duckman!" He starts drumming on his desk and humming the song Duckie performs for Andie in the record store. It starts off being kind of funny, but then Tom's hums get progressively louder and he increases his flailing until he's acting completely over the top and the whole class is watching us. He doesn't seem to mind, but I feel like I've gotten more than enough attention for one day.

I slide down in my chair and glare at the looming clock, willing the minute hand to hurry up and move. School hasn't even officially started yet and it already feels like the first day has lasted forever.

● ● ●

The morning stretches and blurs like it's out of focus as I try to find my way around the school's impossible floor plan. It seems to have a hexagonal layout, which is three sides and two angles beyond my spatial grasp. I am late to every class, and grow increasingly stressed as I strive for a chance reunion with Colton that never happens.

Nobody can see past my polka dots, and the only people who speak to me also look like they're dressed in fifties costumes from the seventies movie *Grease*. Or maybe that should be seventies costumes for the fifties movie *Grease*. Either way, by lunchtime I'm ready to be done with this place.

It takes me three wrong turns to find the cafeteria, and when I get there, Kaia is already sitting at the table where I'm supposed to meet Colton, surrounded by a few other girls who look equally airbrushed and intimidating. All of them definitely use the same hair products. I can't handle another showdown with Kaia, especially when I'm pretty sure I'll lose.

I turn and flee, grateful when I spot a blue sign indicating the girls' room. One of the stall doors opens and a tall, athletic-looking girl wearing a sports jersey steps out. Just so I can look like I have something to do, I turn toward the mirror and pull the elastic tie out of my hair. I get busy reworking it into an even higher ponytail as she steps up to the sink beside me.

Once my hair is gathered so high it practically looks like a unicorn horn, I try to reapply the elastic band, and the stupid thing snaps, pinging across the room and nearly hitting the girl. I give a sheepish grin and mumble, "Sorry," but she just dries her hands without breaking eye contact.

"Would've sucked if that hit me," she says, and I don't

know how to react because I can't tell if she's joking or threatening me.

I nod. "Yeah, whew." I pretend to wipe sweat from my brow and realize I'm sweating for real.

She turns and goes, and I start clawing at my hair with the least effective form of hairbrush; namely, hooked-talon finger-combs. I work both hands at once, and before I know it, my hair looks like a giant auburn cloud of cotton candy on top of my head. It is depressing how perfectly it goes with my dress.

At least I've hopefully given Colton enough time to meet with his coach. I stride back into the lunchroom with my confidence hovering somewhere around my cinched waist.

It drops to my knees when I see Colton and Kaia sitting together. The way he tips his face toward hers says he'll probably never notice me again. My stomach groans, and I slink into the lunch line. After rejecting the scoop of dripping brown goo the woman in a hairnet tries to put on my tray, I select the least greasy-looking slice of pizza and make my way over to the registers.

Which is when I realize that in my rush this morning, I *of course* forgot to grab any lunch money. Glancing over, I see Colton and Kaia still glued together, and I feel my stomach cry as I head back to return my pizza to the warmer. Placing my empty tray on top of the stack, I'm startled when Tom sidles up to me. He grabs the slice I've just returned, adding it to his tray that's already carrying a plate of brown goo and tater tots.

"First lunch. My treat," he says simply, and walks over to the register.

"That's okay, I'm not . . ." I try to resist. This is the guy who basically blocked me from Colton all summer long, constantly coming up with busywork anytime the two of us started to connect.

Tom squints at me, comically sliding his lips to one side. "I was watching you. Obviously, you forgot your money today. This is no biggie."

He's wearing what must be his lunchtime fedora, tilted rakishly over one eye. Meanwhile, the other eye is taking in my hair, and after a moment he says, "Nice do."

It's significantly depressing that my hair is more ridiculous than his hat.

I glance once more toward Kaia and Colton, who seem to be starring in their own lunchroom love scene. The rest of us are clearly just subplots and background artists in the cozy couple's feature film.

I numbly follow Tom as he pays for our food and carries the tray from the registers. Our plates clink softly against each other.

I realize he's heading toward the table filled with the eclectic choir room crew as they make extra room for us. *No, no, no . . .* If I sit here, Colton will never think of me as girlfriend material. I know it's pathetic, but I can't give up on true love the very first day.

"Thank you so much. I'll pay you back tomorrow," I say abruptly, and Tom stops walking. I pause a beat before grabbing my pizza off his tray and toppling his plate of brown goo. He catches the sliding plate and I help him rebalance his tray.

"I am so sorry," I say. Half his brown goo has dumped onto the tray. "I'm pretty sure the trays are just as clean as the plates."

He smiles. "That's not actually all that clean."

When he lunged to save his goo, his hat lost its rakish tilt, and it's practically hanging off his ear. Instinctively, my hand that's not holding pizza reaches up and straightens it. "Wait . . ." I tug at the front corner until I've re-created the rakish tilt.

"Thanks." He tips his head and gives me a grin.

"No, thank *you*," I say, holding up the pizza. Then I realize his whole table of friends is watching us.

Looking over, I see Kaia is talking to her friends while Colton scans the lunchroom. I'm sure he's looking for me, wondering where I am.

Tom gestures to the empty space that's been made for us. It's barely enough room for two people. With a glance back toward Colton, I make a choice. Rushing all my words together, I tell him, "I'll-pay-you-back-I-promise-and-sorry-again-about-your-brown-goo-and-if-you-get-sick-from-tray-germs-it's-all-my-fault-and-thank-you-again-and-bye."

Clutching my pizza plate, I turn and zip back toward the girls' room before he has a chance to respond. I probably should've stayed, or at least gone over to confront Kaia on boxing me out, but the lunch period is half over by now and I haven't eaten a thing.

I just need a chance to regroup, and the quiet girls' room seems like the most reasonable place to go.

I will say this: eating greasy cafeteria pizza while crouching on a toilet in a high school bathroom stall would probably be the number one most humiliating experience imaginable if anybody could actually see me doing it. As it is, I feel the confines of the worn metal walls quite comforting.

Chewing slowly, my mind rolls over how neatly Kaia stole

Colton from me. Like the easiest heist ever, she conned me into handing him directly into her manicured clutches.

The doors to the other stalls begin to creak open and slam closed with increased frequency, which I assume means the lunch period is about to end. I watch the shoes coming and going on either side of me and try to picture the owner of each pair. There's probably a sporty girl attached to those plain white sneakers, and most likely a funky punk wearing the glittering high-heeled boots that sashay past the front of my stall. But the shoes' owners are all strangers, and I don't know anybody here. Suddenly, the patheticness of sitting here, alone on a toilet, hits me. Dropping my ballet-slippered feet to the ground, I instantly realize that both of my legs have fallen asleep. Also, my toes have been tangled in the fishnet holes for far too long. Six of the ten are completely numb.

I don't think I can walk, and here's one thing I'm sure of: if I ever hope to have a social life at this school, stumbling awkwardly into the middle of a bathroom filled with chattering girls is *not* an option. Keeping my door locked, I do a few deep knee bends to get blood flowing to my legs and try to kick the feeling back into my toes.

Under the divider, I see a pair of cute black pumps move into position in the stall next to mine. Kaia's kitten heels— I'd recognize them anywhere. Except they're facing the wrong direction. At first, I'm afraid she's about to step up onto the toilet so she can see into my stall, but then I hear the slightest gag. And the *sploosh* of . . . something . . . hitting the water. She gives a small cough, and it takes a moment for me to realize; Kaia is throwing up.

I have a hard time marrying the image of perfect-looking Miss Hair Gloss to the eating-disordered girls from my seventh-grade health video. But the evidence is undeniable. She's just eaten lunch. She's now puking her guts out. Unless she very recently contracted the flu or got instant food poisoning, Kaia must be bulimic.

I'm so shocked, I unlock the door to my stall and haltingly make my way toward the row of sinks.

"Are you drunk, Pinky?" A girl with an eyebrow ring is glaring at my dress. I recognize her as the eyeliner girl whose smile I rejected by accident earlier.

I shake my head *no* to her, trying not to look scared as I twist the closest faucet to cold and splash water on my face. Of course, this makes a mess of my mascara. After being barefaced all summer, I forgot I was wearing any. As I scrub at the stubborn black underneath my eyes, I can feel the stares of the other girls.

Eventually, Kaia moves into place beside me, her eyes slightly red and watery. I wonder who else knows her secret. Pulling a toothbrush and tube of toothpaste from her bag, she proceeds to brush her teeth. Catching my eye in the mirror, she stops and gives me a frothy, "What?"

I turn my attention back to scrubbing my face, wishing I'd stayed hidden in my stall until everyone left. By the time Kaia finishes brushing, reapplies her lipstick, and starts running a completely unnecessary comb through her hair, my face matches my pink dress. But thankfully, my mascara is gone.

I make my escape and hear Kaia give a melodic chuckle as I lunge out the swinging door.

And smack into Colton.

"Whoa, Andie," he says. "Missed you at lunch today." He looks at my hair as if ginger-flavored cotton candy is not really his preference.

Patting him on the chest, I try to mimic Kaia's feminine chuckle and instead bray like an amused donkey. Before I can embarrass myself more, I push off of Colton and make my way down the hall. It isn't until I turn into the doorway of my next class that I realize my ballet flat has a long toilet paper tail attached to the heel. *Because, of course it does.*

Wadding up the white streamer of shame, I shove it into the wastepaper basket at the head of the classroom. This whole day is turning into a slow-moving train wreck. I head for the back of the room, slide into a chair, and lay my big-haired head on the desk. I shift in my seat and swear I hear my stupid dress chuckle out loud at me.

Okay, new strategy: quietly get through the rest of the day without calling any more attention to myself. Which would be *so* much easier without the red bouffant. Not to mention my highly amused, pink polka-dotted dress.

I press my forehead into the smooth surface of my desk. My life is officially over.

● ● ●

When the glorious final bell rings, marking the end of this unending day, I finally track Colton down at his locker. Kaia is already attached to his bicep. "You ready to go?" he asks me with a grin.

Her perfectly symmetrical eyebrows furrow. "But, Colt,

baby," she whines. "You were going to take me to the mall, remember? I have a gift card for Lucy's."

"We can head to the mall right after I drop off Andie," he soothes.

Kaia eyes me. "I'm sure Andie won't mind taking the bus home. It's good for her to learn her way around."

The way Colton has to drag his eyes off of Kaia when he turns to me confirms that my romantic fantasy is ending, and not in a happily-ever-after sense. True love cancelled today due to Typhoon Kaia. Before Colton can say anything, I cut in. "It's really no problem." I feel myself blinking rapidly as I lie. "I love riding the bus."

"Are you positive?" Colton asks. "You're right on our way. I'd be happy to drive you home."

I imagine myself sitting in the back seat of his Honda Element, watching Kaia flirt with him across the center console as she flings her long, glossy hair into my eyes. The healthy-looking blunt ends could probably blind me. "I'm good, really." I say. "Just point me in the right direction."

Colton is such a nice guy that he sees me onto the big yellow school bus, which makes me feel about five years old. At the head of the aisle, I stop and look over the field of green seats sprouting with curious faces. One girl near the back is wearing a straw hat and frilly collar that would go great with my polka dots, but she breaks eye contact. She probably remembers me ditching her choir room crowd along with Tom today at lunch. But that was only because I thought I still had a chance with Colton. I want to tell her, *I'm really not a horrible person.* Though I fleetingly ask myself if ignoring everyone but Colton's crew makes me a horrible person after all. Then, I wonder if worrying that I'm a horrible person automatically makes me not horrible, or if it's evidence I'm most definitely horrible.

The goth girl who's been giving me the eye all day is sitting in the middle of the bus, staring out the window. She starts to turn her head in my direction, and I dive into the seat directly behind the bus driver before she notices me. Keeping my head down, I glare at my stupid pink lap the whole twisting ride home. By the time I climb off the bus at my stop, I've developed motion sickness on top of everything else.

My mother greets me at the door wearing a royal blue miniskirt, asking, "What happened? Where's Colton?" The hope in her eyes makes everything infinitely worse. Instead of making progress toward my first kiss with my one true love, all I got was one giant kiss-*off* today.

"I'm just glad the first day of school is over," I tell Mom, and we move inside so I can spill about my shiny epic romance bursting into a flattened Mylar balloon of tattered silver dreams.

"*Dang*. The two of you looked so adorable together too." Mom holds up her camera with the screen turned in my direction. Displayed is the photo of Colton and me from this morning. He looks a bit surprised, but I look so excited and happy, it's utterly heartbreaking.

"Thanks, Mom. You're making this whole thing *so* much easier." I slump into the pink couch. It seems almost more comfortable than I remember.

With a sigh, she sits down beside me, looking at the picture as if she's the one with the deflated heart.

Since the bus ride home, the greasy pizza I ate inside the

bathroom stall has declared a civil war against my stomach. All I can manage to swallow down for dinner is a sad bowl of Puffs 'o Oats cereal.

Afterward, my dad needs to take his psychology degree out for a spin by trying to figure out why I'm taking Colton's rejection so hard. He digs deep into my psyche and spouts some of his psychobabble wisdom about self-esteem and shame. In the end, he decides my expectations were just too far outside the realm of possibility.

Thanks a bunch, Dad.

Mentally, I burn the beautiful, hopeful pictures of me dancing with Colton at the prom. By the time I change into flowered flannel PJs, I have to admit my father is probably right. No more high expectations for Andie.

I open my phone and count twenty likes for my picture with Colton. A few people have written **#squeee**, and Rhonda gave me an **OMG he's hawt**, which only makes me feel worse. Then some semi-acquaintance who is clearly just jealous of Colton's hotness had to insert the obvious: **Redheads should never wear pink.**

I quickly close the app.

This sad evening can only end in one way. With me sitting on the couch watching a movie, eating ice cream with my mom. She insists I need to re-watch *Pretty in Pink* so I can see just how wrong I am about Duckie being a better match for Andie, but there is no way I can face that final prom scene and Andie's pink sack dress without crying.

Finally, Mom backs down and puts on *The Breakfast Club*, which has a group of teens from different cliques connecting with each other over Saturday detention. She says, "I wanted us to watch this one together before school started, but you were so busy with the movie theater."

"That will no longer be a problem," I say. "Seeing Colton will be too painful."

Patting my hand, she says, "Don't worry. Things seem terrible now, but you never know. They could turn around in an instant."

"Sure, Mom. Maybe Colton just had amnesia for a day, and tomorrow he'll remember I'm his true love."

"That's the spirit." She grins, and I turn away before rolling my eyes. No point in her having hurt feelings on top of my own.

She and I sit side by side, watching and laughing and tearing up and basically losing ourselves in the comforting oversimplification of a high school caste system.

When the movie's over, I immediately restart it from the beginning. "Sorry, Mom, I'm not ready to discuss this one," I explain, but I'm really hoping for some inspiration on how to handle this new world of complex cliques I've entered. Tomorrow I won't have Colton, so I'll be navigating all on my own.

Mom shrugs. "You can't really *know* a movie until you've seen it multiple times."

I couldn't agree more.

Just at the point in the film when Allison is emptying her Pixy Stix onto her sandwich, Mom kisses me on the forehead and heads up to bed. As I lie back on the couch, watching the movie and trying not to cry, my mind won't stop drumming with regret over so many parts of today.

As I haltingly drift off to sleep, I can't help wishing that real life had a restart button. Or at the very least a chapter rewind.

chapter 5

I wake up with my cheek once again sealed to the armrest of the pink leather couch. *Nice*, I think as I peel my face free. *Falling asleep in front of the TV is a lovely, life-affirming habit.* This morning the living room looks less rosy and more depressing than yesterday. I hear familiar music playing in the background, and clutch the blanket to my chest when I realize it's the *Pretty in Pink* DVD menu playing again. Which is odd, since I'm positive *The Breakfast Club* was still on when I fell asleep last night.

Not only did I reject *Pretty in Pink*, I seem to remember threatening to crack the disc in half when Mom kept pressuring me to re-watch it. I can't imagine why she'd sneak back in and put it on after I fell asleep.

Dad whistles as he walks down the stairs into the living room. "Good morning, sweetheart. You up for pancakes?"

"Pancakes won't work," I say. "Uprooting me my senior year is not the type of misery that can just be griddled away."

Dad gives me a double take, like his body has a stutter, and heads for the kitchen. He's stopped whistling. As a therapist, he should be glad I'm sharing how I feel, but now that I've hurt him, my feelings have all shifted to guilt.

Mom bustles in and spreads her arms wide. "Happy first day at your new school, Andie!"

"Not funny, Mom." I lie back down and pull the blanket over my head in an attempt to block out yesterday. "I don't get a do-over."

I hear her mutter, "Somebody woke up cranky," as she heads into the kitchen. "Maybe you should get some more sleep, sweetheart."

With a sigh, I fling down the blanket and, *What the . . .?*

I'm wearing the pink polka-dot dress again.

My mouth refuses to close. I stop breathing, and my eyes feel like they're about to pop out of my head as they take in the pink sea of floating polka dots. I toss off the blanket, and the skirt springs free in victory.

Scanning my brain, I definitely remember changing into comfy flannel PJs last night. The ones with the flowers. Did Mom do something insane, like sneak in and put this dress back on me while I slept? *Why on earth would she do that?* Did I do this in my sleep? Maybe I'm so distraught over epically blowing things with Colton that I've taken up sleepwalking. And sleep DVD changing. And sleep dressing.

I have terrible taste in clothes when I'm asleep.

Picking up my phone, I quickly open my social app. I scroll all the way down, but the picture I posted yesterday of Colton and me is gone. Which is something that's never happened before. Sure, I *may* have exaggerated how hard I was rocking Punxsutawney High, and the photo *might* have implied that Colton and I were together when we're not, but it's not as if lies are automatically deleted from the Internet now.

My phone must be having updating issues. I check the settings and restart it, but the most recent image that will load is a close-up shot of an unfortunate zit someone from my old school posted early yesterday morning with the caption, "First day of school. Huzzah."

And then I look at the date. September first. Which was yesterday. Just what I need; a wonky phone to deal with on top of everything else.

Spotting Mom's camera sitting on the end table, I pick it up and scroll through the recent pictures. The last one shows me posing dramatically in this stupid pink dress in a photo I remember Mom taking during our try-on session the other night. I guess she decided to delete the pictures of me with Colton so I wouldn't get upset. But while she unquestionably cares about my feelings, that doesn't really sound like her. I mean, she was fully stoked about those photos.

I head into the kitchen, and Mom turns from the sink. When she sees what I'm wearing, her face opens wide with a hopeful, toothy smile. "Oh, *Andie*. Perfect choice. That dress is so lovely on you."

Gathering up the skirt of the dress, I angrily hold it out toward her. "This dress? Needs to be burned. I'm never wearing it again."

"Sorry." Mom turns back to the sink. "I thought you maybe decided to dress up for your first day."

"What's with all the 'first day' crap?" I slump into a chair. "You know I already wore this stupid dress and had the worst day of my life. I hate Punxsutawney High."

"Language, Andie, and what on earth are you talking about?"

Mom furrows her brow. "You've never been to Punxsutawney High. You were looking forward to getting a ride there with Colton this morning."

"What the *actual* crap?"

"*Andie*. I said *language*." Mom firmly believes the word *crap* is a swear.

I catch myself and take a deep breath. "Um, did anything strange happen last night? Like, maybe I talked in my sleep or was dancing around the living room? Possibly wearing fishnet tights with this dress?" I don't dare hope that all of yesterday was just a dream.

My father glances at Mom. I can tell by his look that his therapist senses are tingling.

"Oh, no." I point my finger back and forth between the two of them. "You are not going to start acting like I'm the crazy one here. I am *not* the crazy one."

"Who said *anyone* has to be the crazy one?" Dad uses his counseling voice as he slides a plateful of steaming pancakes onto the table.

"Nobody has to be the crazy one," Mom says in a way that implies I'm definitely the crazy one.

The two of them look at me as if I'm a science experiment that might bubble over at any moment. Faking a laugh, I grab three pancakes off the stack and say, "I just didn't sleep very well on the couch."

Mom asks how I liked *Pretty in Pink* last night, and I just shrug and take a giant bite of dry pancake to avoid making eye contact with her. My mind is reeling. Unless I sleep-watched *Pretty in Pink*, and dreamed up a horrible first day of school for myself, and then sleep-watched *The Breakfast Club*, none of what's happening right now is possible.

An awkward silence settles around the three of us as we sit at the kitchen table, eating our breakfast. But these pancakes have not been whistled over. And I can taste the difference.

● ● ●

I head upstairs to get dressed for school, and root through my drawers until I find my flowered PJs. I sniff the flannel material as hard as I can and smell . . . nothing. Or rather, the slightest twinge of fabric softener. According to my sense of smell, I haven't worn these flowered PJs since they were washed.

But I have. I wore this awful dress to school and had a horrible day, and when I came home I changed into these exact PJs and fell asleep on the pink couch. I know I didn't dream everything.

I suppose Mom and Dad could just be messing with me to test my resilience or as twisted research for some new book, but my parents are not this good at lying. They tried throwing a surprise party for my fifteenth birthday, and the two of them were a wreck. Mom kept getting the hiccups and acted so frazzled I knew something was up, and Dad couldn't stop giggling. It was downright creepy. There's no way the two of them are behind this.

Could the universe really be handing me a do-over? Maybe each of us gets one do-over day in our lifetime. Is it possible I blew things so spectacularly yesterday that someone with a *lot* of authority decided I should get another shot? I can't imagine no one ever mentioning this can happen.

On my laptop, I type in a search for "repeating same day" and get some ads for "next day delivery," plus a bunch of links to various science fiction stories and a few romantic comedies that look sort of fun. Of course, the epic Bill Murray movie *Groundhog Day* pops up, and I stop to consider the Punxsutawney Phil connection. Unfortunately, I have to start getting ready before I can determine if the town mascot is some sort of mystical creature who's controlling my life.

I try taking a hot shower, but that does nothing to change the date on my cell phone. Whatever the date, at least I can wear a less outrageous outfit today. I style my hair in long, loose waves, and I'm just lacing my favorite black boots over my best-fitting jeans when I hear the doorbell ring downstairs.

"Andie!" Mom calls in a singsong voice. "Your ride is here."

Giving myself a quick once-over in the mirror, I head downstairs, barely daring to hope it could be Colton here to drive me to school.

As I make my way down the steps and the living room comes into view, there he is: looking as handsome as ever and wearing the same comfortable jeans and tight T-shirt he wore yesterday.

This time he and Mom are still standing by the front door when I get downstairs. I glance out the window, half expecting to see Kaia sitting in the passenger seat of his car, but it's thankfully free from the glare of her glossy hair.

"Cool shirt." Colton points to my T-shirt with a line drawing of a daisy on the front. I have to agree, it represents the perfect degree of irreverent charm.

"Thanks." I'm dying to ask him if he's here because he feels bad for ditching me yesterday, or if he's here because yesterday never actually happened. But there's no need to *advertise* the fact that I'm probably crazy now.

Dad comes out of the kitchen just then, wiping his hands on a dish towel.

Mom tells him, "Honey, this is Colton."

I can't hold it in any longer and ask, "Didn't you guys meet yesterday?"

"How would we meet? I've never been to your house before." Colton looks at my dad. "Have you been to the movie theater, maybe?"

"No, Andie gets her love of movies from her mother." Dad gives me a look of concern. "Are you okay? Starting at a new school might be more of a strain than I anticipated."

I stand there dumbly, feeling like I've just plunged headfirst into the setup for some wacky situation comedy. I try to decide what to do, but my brain comes up with zilch. This is unexplored territory as far as I'm concerned.

Colton smiles and grabs my hand. "Don't worry. I'll take good care of her."

He pulls me over the threshold, and I'm left holding on to the hope that things will at least go better than they did yesterday. I mean, well, today. That last time.

● ● ●

When we pull up to the school building, I jump out of Colton's car ready to figure out what's going on. Maybe here at the high school, time will catch up and things will go back to normal.

It isn't until I witness the same students from yesterday,

repeating their identical greetings to each other, that I allow myself to believe this is really happening. I stand in the doorway to the school, turning slowly amidst the uneven harmony of "Welcome back" and "Hey there" and "How was your summer?" and "I can't believe we're finally sophomores/juniors/seniors!"

This is real.

All of my wishing I that could go back and say or do the right or cool thing after saying and doing so many wrong and uncool things must've finally paid off.

I'm getting an actual do-over.

And I'm determined not to screw things up this time.

As we enter the school, Colton's admirers greet him enthusiastically, just like they did yesterday. Except that now people are giving me looks that are less confused and more curious as I project a semi-attractive-seeming red-haired new girl wearing the perfect first-day-of-school outfit, who may-or-may-not be dating Colton.

We walk past the same athletic guys as yesterday, but now a number of them eye me like I'm a girl rather than some freak of nature.

My hopes are soaring as we walk through the giant doors leading to the cafeteria. I've been trying to plot how I can fix the way things went yesterday and decide I really need to get Colton to myself for lunch. Looking back, that was the point where I completely lost him.

When he points out the table in the corner and tells me to meet him, I ask, "Is there anywhere we can drive to for lunch? A Taco Junction or Burger Palace? Or can we maybe just sit outside someplace?"

He wrinkles his nose and looks out the window. "I'm really looking forward to hanging with my friends, and it's a little over-cast today."

"No problem," I say. "I was just hoping to get a few insider tips for life here at Punxsutawney High."

He smiles. "The gang will be happy to help you get around. You're going to fit in here just fine."

Right. If I can only figure out a way to fit myself in-*between* him and Kaia.

As we leave the cafeteria and walk down the hallway, I imagine I detect fewer flirting signals flowing from other girls toward Colton. It's as if my appropriate first-day attire has cre-ated a force field of date-ability that is transmuting Colton and I into a more obvious couple who . . .

"Hey there, Colt baby!"

Colton is immediately engulfed by the three manic blonde cheerleaders from yesterday. I curse myself for thinking he could be taken off the market so easily.

This time, when one of the lesser-blondes asks me if I'm planning to try out, I tell her yes, which makes Colton's eye-brows jump in a good way. Of course, no human beings can ever witness me trying to act like a cheerleader. Or even clap, for that matter ... But at least for this moment, I have Colton's attention. Once I've pretended to memorize the details of tryouts, I easily pull him away from the blondes and their cheerleading skirts.

When we pass the people wearing black underneath the stairwell, I laugh at Colton's warning and even place a flirty hand on his arm. Once again, I get a dark look from one of the girls, and I fear that maybe all I'm doing is repeating my same mistakes. But Colton gives me a secret smile that causes every other thought to vanish from my head.

Next, my heart starts beating as we approach the door to the choir room, but I remind myself that today I'm not dressed in a way that will make them want to adopt me. Or even inspire them to be particularly nice to me.

But just to be certain, when Colton gestures to the room and says, "And here we have . . . these people," I grab his arm and pull him quickly out of the doorway.

Too late, I realize Tom was in the middle of greeting us with a friendly wave. So now it seems like I've purposely dissed him.

Tom turns the back of his slicked hair toward me and starts talking to the guy next to him who's wearing suspenders. I'm hit with a pang of guilt over how nice he was to me yesterday, but today I remembered my wallet, so it's not like I owe him anything anymore. Besides, he was probably only nice to me because I was wearing that bizarro pink dress.

As we walk away from the choir room, I can't resist the urge to go for another selfie with Colton. I'm much more casual about it today, and ask him, "Is it still called a selfie when it has more than one person in it?"

"I always wondered the *same thing*."

I take the photo super quick, and he has a genuine smile in this one.

I'm walking while posting it, but there's something nagging at me. Something I'm forgetting about . . . and *bam*, I remember. Or more precisely, I'm reminded about running into Goth Guy yesterday when I run directly into him again. Hard. Clearly, walking while typing isn't my thing.

This time, I mumble "sorry" as he bends down to pick up his Sharpie and I keep walking. If I don't look directly into his darkly lined eyes, I can forget I was ever rude to his friends, thus ignoring the whole am-I-possibly-a-horrible-person debate. I also avoid eye contact when we pass the cluster of brainiacs, but I can't resist a quick glance at the girl hugging her textbook to her chest. As she moves past, I wonder if she has a headband to perfectly match every outfit or if it's just a special first-day-of-school thing.

Despite my best efforts to detour Colton away from Kaia, that girl must have some serious tracking skills, because it isn't long before I'm cringing at the familiar nasally greeting ringing down the hallway toward us.

Colton looks nearly as happy to see her as he did yesterday, but not quite. And I'm encouraged when he glances at me before catching her dramatic hello hug.

But then I'm subjected to witnessing their reunion all over again, which was bad enough the first time. And yesterday, I didn't even know that he'd be driving her home instead of me. Now it's even worse, except for maybe the way her assessment of me in much cooler clothes sets her lips into a sharp line.

I wasn't a threat yesterday in my goofy pink dress and my unwashed hair, but I'm a serious one now. I smile at her sweetly. "You must be Kaia. Colton's told me so much about you."

Colton gives me a look of surprise. "I don't remember even *mentioning* Kaia this summer."

"Oh, yes. That's right." I give her a smug smile. "You never even mentioned her."

Kaia's smile turns sour, and Colton shakes his head. "What just—?"

I break into a fake laugh. "I'm kidding, of course."

But Kaia continues looking at me as if I've just spit on her kitten heels. She has no idea how I even know her name. Before I can truly enjoy her reaction, however, my tactic backfires. She turns to Colton, trails her maroon manicure through his hair, and purrs, "So, *were* you thinking of me this summer?"

She puts her face so close to his, there's no need for him to respond. Clearly, he's thinking of her now. *Great.*

When the two of them pull apart, Kaia coldly asks for my last name again, and this time I lie and say it's Walsh, because a) Walsh is the last name of the *Pretty in Pink* Andie I was named after and b) Walsh starts with a *W*, which will group me with Colton and *Vogel* instead of Miss Hair Gloss and whatever her last name happens to be.

"You and I are in the same homeroom," Colton says brightly.

I give him a wink. "Hope you don't mind showing me the way."

Kaia practically has steam coming out of her ears as I fling my arm though his outstretched elbow and the two of us head merrily down the hallway. In the *opposite* direction of what I know to be my actual homeroom.

As we walk, I try to engage Colton in a conversation about the action flick we watched repeatedly at the theater this summer. My goal is to remind him just how much time we've spent together, and just how helpful I was when he was working behind the counter for long hours.

He says, "There's something soothing about watching the same movie over and over. I only saw, like, two other movies in bits and pieces all summer long, but I caught that one at least sixteen times."

Which surprises me, because despite watching the action movie with Colton several times, I still managed to view a wide variety of films over the course of the summer. Actually, in between helping out and hanging out, I basically saw *every* movie that came through the theater since we moved here.

I'm all for re-watching movies. In fact, I completely agree with my mom that you can't truly know a movie until you've watched it multiple times . . . but sixteen viewings of one action flick over one summer? It sounds a bit excessive, even to me.

I shake my head and refocus on the fact that I'm here to make Colton fall in love with me, not the other way around.

When we arrive at his homeroom, he guides me directly up to the teacher standing behind the desk at the front of the room. Before I can stop him, he introduces me as, "New student, Andie Walsh."

The teacher smiles pleasantly and says, "I didn't realize we had a new student to greet this morning. Hello, Andie Walsh." Looking down at her list of names, I watch her expression shift to perplexed. I wonder just how much evidence is required to verify me as *New Student, Andie Walsh*.

Probably quite a bit. Plus, someone will likely notice that a new student named Andie Knedman was also supposed to be transferring in today. I imagine a call to my parents to investigate the misunderstanding. If my mom answers the call, she'll do her part to support my pursuit of true love, but then I imagine my dad picking up the phone and me ending up in some sort of juvie rehab program for forgetting my last name.

I say, "Oh, I'm sorry, that's my *other* name."

Colton and the teacher both watch me as I sheepishly look back and forth between them while avoiding actual eye contact.

"I mean, that's my *middle* name." I smile at Colton. "Do they not sort the students by middle name here?"

The teacher shakes her head and talks very slowly. "No, we go by regular last names here at Punxsutawney High School."

"Oh, well. That's the way they did it at my old school," I say. "My bad."

"What sort of middle name is Walsh?" Colton asks, and I shrug.

"Well then, what *is* your last name?" the teacher asks.

"My last name's Knedman," I say. "Guess I'm not in this homeroom after all?"

The teacher rifles through her desk. Handing me a small booklet titled *Student Handbook*, she opens the back flap to a map of the school.

"We're right here." She points to a spot inside the parallelogram and then draws her finger slowly along the shape to the opposite side. "*This* is your homeroom." She's one room off from my actual homeroom, but I'm not about to get busted by correcting her.

One of the lesser-blonde cheerleaders traipses into the room, and when she spots Colton, she immediately flings herself onto his back. He starts galloping in playful circles, and I realize that Kaia isn't my only competition for his affection after all.

It isn't until the teacher repeats Colton's full name three times that he finally stops and the cheerleader dismounts. Fortunately, the woman must assume I'm a complete idiot who can't find my way around a closed polygon on my own, because she asks Colton to please show me the way to my homeroom.

As we reach the door, I blurt out, "It's a family name."

The teacher and Colton both look at me.

"Walsh," I say. "It's a traditional middle name in my family." Colton gives a wide-eyed smile and steps into the hallway. As I follow him out the door, I realize that getting a second go-around only means more opportunities to humiliate myself in new and spectacular ways.

The hallways are almost empty now, but as we pass open doorways, the scattered calls of "Colton!" and "Yo, Colt!" make it hard for me to keep his attention.

As we approach our destination, I'm horrified to realize that the homeroom the teacher mistakenly identified as mine is actu-ally Kaia's. When we reach the door, I feel as if I'm delivering a perfect bouquet of Colton to her, but what else can I do? I'm supposed to be acting clueless about my homeroom number. Not to mention my own name.

When we enter the classroom, I immediately spot Kaia sit-ting in a seat by the window and laughing at something someone has just said. She could be posing for a shampoo ad, and despite the overcast day, a beam of light manages to glint off her hair, nearly blinding me.

"Can I help you?" the male teacher asks us when we approach his desk. I see Kaia's smoky eyes swing to Colton like a cat's.

I quickly blurt out, "I'm *Knedman*," while attempting to block my nemesis from her prey. But I'm too late. By the time I force the teacher to connect the dots and figure out that I belong across the hallway, Kaia has pounced.

"What's up, guys?" she trills warmly, addressing Colton only.

I answer, "Oh, there was just a little confusion about my proper homeroom, but Colton is helping me and I think we've got it now, thanks."

He and Kaia are looking at each other as if I'm not even there.

"What time do you have lunch?" she asks him, and I want to dive between them and cover Colton's face with both of my hands. But there's no way to stop this. The two of them establish what I already know: they will be sharing a table in the corner of the lunchroom in the not-too-distant future.

The teacher finally points me to the room across the hall. "Knedman would probably be over in room 124, or, wait . . ."

"Thanks, got it," I interrupt, putting a hand on Colton's arm. "I feel so silly, but can you point me in the right direction for room 124?"

With a grin aimed at Kaia, Colton finally drags himself away from her force field. But not before giving her the slightest wink, sealing my defeat.

Unless I can figure out a way to keep them apart for the rest of the day, Kaia will be riding home in the passenger seat of Colton's Honda Element for the second time in a row. I'm sure of it.

Even worse, when we make our way across the hall to my real homeroom, I see Tom perched beside the only empty desk. He gives Colton and me a cold, "Hey there," and I feel another pang of regret over ignoring his wave this morning.

Kaia says, "Well, you appear to be in good hands." She's standing at the door smiling at Colton, and I want to chase her back to the homeroom where she belongs.

Colton tosses a "Later, Andie" to me over his shoulder, and I watch him slide an arm around Kaia's waist as he escorts her back across the hallway. *Now* that's *the way to see a girl to her classroom*, I think with a sad sigh.

"Morning not going as planned?" Tom asks coldly.

"No." I turn to him. "Listen, I'm sorry about earlier. I didn't mean to ignore your wave."

"Little advice," he says. "You might want to think about making friends with a few people besides Colton."

"I'm making friends," I say defensively.

He shrugs. "I came to this school in seventh grade, and I'm still considered *the new kid*. Just be prepared to be seen as an outsider."

I say, "I'm not an outsider."

I check to make sure the pink dress hasn't magically reappeared and say a silent thank you that I'm still wearing my normal outfit. Then I look around and realize a number of people are trying to hide the fact that they're staring at me.

I tell Tom, "Okay, so I may be *the new kid*, but I'm a perfectly normal girl of average height and above-average intelligence. I'm sure I'll have no problem fitting in."

Tom laughs. "Well, then. Good luck." He turns around so he's facing the front of the classroom, and I feel yet another dip of shame. To be honest, I'm slightly below average in height, and he's right—I'm in no position to turn down friends right now.

"Thanks," I whisper to Tom's back as the teacher begins to make announcements about which clubs are meeting on which days.

I'm sure my folks would love it if I joined a few special interest clubs, but the only one that would get me closer to Colton would be the football team. Or possibly the cheerleading squad. They're meeting after school today, but as my aforementioned lack of rhythm can attest, I'll need to find another way to get close to Colton.

If I don't, I can say good-bye to ever getting that perfect first kiss I've wished for.

chapter 6

A t least I have less trouble finding my classes this time around. Although I'm still late to most of them since I choose to run the long way around the hexagon between each bell so that I have a better chance of seeing Colton. I end up jogging all six sides of the building in under four minutes after science, just so I can get a glimpse of him talking to another athletic-looking guy at his locker.

"Hey, Colt!" I try to hide the fact that I'm breathing heavily.

He smiles and holds up a hand. "Hi, Andie," he says, before turning back to his conversation. As if I'm one of the anonymous fans who've been greeting him all day. The fact that I'm sweating profusely probably isn't helping my cause.

I can feel myself blowing my big shot at a redo but don't know how to stop it from happening. I try paying closer attention in all my classes. My teachers repeat the same introductions verbatim as I search for some clue about how to change my destiny.

I remember my English teacher, Mr. Demers, explaining that we would be covering the Greek gods and goddesses this semester. I'd stopped listening since we already spent a lot of time studying mythology last year at my old school and I was just psyched this meant an easy A for me.

Yesterday, or rather Today 1.0, while Mr. D yammered on about Greek god nonsense, I'd distracted myself with daydreams about how I was about to see Colton at lunch the next period.

Today, version 2.0, I listen closer while Mr. D places his hands on his hips and asks loudly, "Who here has an Achilles' heel?"

A few hands fly into the air and one girl yells out, "Chocolate!"

Mr. Demers laughs and says, "Someone says chocolate every single class." He widens his eyes and looks around at us. "Same thing. Every time. What would that type of situation be called?"

Nobody raises a hand, and the awkwardness settles in around our desks. I know the answer, but I'm not about to get involved. I'm just an observer here.

Finally, he prods, "I hear the same answer, over and over and over . . ."

I'm feeling so much second-hand embarrassment, I can't take it and need to save us all from this discomfort. As I raise my hand, my heart clenches at how excited Mr. D looks when he points to me.

I say, "That would be a Sisyphean situation?"

His whole face opens up with happiness and he holds both hands in the air, calling out, "Bing! Our old friend Sisyphus. Can you tell us all what he was forced to do?"

I have everyone's attention now and want to crawl underneath the desks, but remind myself that I'm dressed as a normal teenage girl today and none of these kids know about yesterday's pink dress fiasco. I say, "He's the guy who had to push the boulder up the hill every day, only to have it roll back down every night."

Mr. D calls out, "Bing!" and I can't help but smile at him. He points to the desk behind me and asks, "Yes? Tom, you have a question?"

I spin around. I had no idea Tom was sitting behind me in this class and now I wonder if he followed me to the lunchroom last time.

"But why would the guy keep doing that?" Tom looks at me. "I mean, why doesn't he just stop pushing the stupid boulder up the hill?"

He stares me down as if he expects me to answer. I widen my eyes at him. "How am I supposed to know?"

The class laughs and Mr. Demers moves on to discuss the mythology behind the myths, but I'm left thinking about Sisyphus and what we learned last year. I remember one version of the story where he'd been a trickster, and when Hades came for him, Sisyphus outsmarted Hades and basically kept Death handcuffed in his closet for a while. It caused quite the ancient chaos, and that was the reason Sisyphus was cursed with pushing the boulder up the mountain every day.

For eternity. I shudder at the thought.

When it's finally time for lunch, I'm glad I remembered to bring my money today. I dash out of the classroom before Tom can stop me, still spooked by the way he looked at me when he asked about Sisyphus.

Like I have any choice in what is happening to me.

I stand in the food line, holding my tray and staring at the same pizza slice I ate yesterday. The grease from the melted cheese gleams underneath the heat lamp, and I'm reminded of the way it disagreed with my stomach last night. The brown goo that's being dispensed by a tired-looking woman in a hairnet suddenly seems like it could quite possibly be delicious.

Glancing over to the corner, I spy the table where I plan on staking out my position to wait for Colton today. I can't very well have a scoop of brown goo on my plate when he specifically told me (twice now) that pizza is the only acceptable school lunch. I grab the slice behind the one I ate yesterday, promising myself I won't finish the whole thing, and then I pay for it myself with a flourish.

I'm much earlier today, and my hair isn't nearly as poufy without the extra time spent stalling in the bathroom. I slide over to the still-empty table where Colton and Kaia fell in love with each other yesterday and casually position myself in the center of their spot.

Take that, I think, picturing Kaia deciding to sit elsewhere and maybe giving up on Colton entirely.

I'm still arranging my pizza "prop" attractively when I glance up and spot Miss Hair Gloss. There's no sign of the other girls I saw sitting around her yesterday as she scans the slowly filling lunchroom. Her eyes narrow when they land on me.

She strides in my direction, and I run a nervous hand through my hair to smooth it down even more. I make a mental note to figure out how to boost its shine factor. Furniture polish, perhaps?

"You're sitting in my seat," Kaia snaps when she reaches me.

"Colton told me to meet him here." I'm trying to be confident and assertive and maybe even a little territorial, but I'm pretty sure she catches the tiny waver in my voice.

Her full lips slide into a feline smile. "Colton is so nice, isn't he? But here's the thing: he and I are spending lunch together. We have a few things to *discuss*." She makes air quotes with her long fingers, and I picture the two of them nuzzling each other just like yesterday.

I can't let that happen again and so keep my butt firmly planted. Smiling sweetly, I make my voice go high and non-threatening. "He's a grown boy. We can let him decide where to sit."

She puts her face so close to mine, I can smell her hair. I catch a vague waft of coconut, and make a mental note to buy myself a vat of coconut oil. Kaia lowers her voice. "I can appreciate that you're figuring out where you fit here at Punxsutawney High. Really, I can. But you aren't going to *physically* fit right here." She gestures to the empty seats. "We have friends who sit with us, and I'm afraid we have no room for someone new."

I look around and see the lunchroom is now bustling with students. Tom's friends are filling up their table, the brainiac girls are congregating two tables down, and Kaia's model buddies are making their way toward us with trays of food.

"There's no place else for me to sit." I try to keep the desperation out of my voice. But it's there.

The first of Kaia's friends arrives, and she gives me a confused look. "Who's this, Kaia?"

"This is Andie, but she was just leaving." Kaia gives me a look that says she's considering dumping my pizza into my lap.

I spot Colton giving a high five to one of the guys I saw him with earlier. Apparently, it is customary to greet each other numerous times throughout the day here at Punxsutawney

High. I think of his shift from practically holding my hand at the movie theater to barely greeting me in the hallway earlier.

I'm suddenly not at all confident Colton will even remember my name a week from now. That is, if I ever get through today.

Kaia is watching me with her hands on her hips, and her friends are already sliding my tray out of their way.

"Colton told me to wait for him right here." My voice sounds firm, but I'm standing up to go as I say it.

"Are you sure about that?" Kaia asks, neatly shredding what remains of my confidence.

I look up to see Colton walking toward us. He's giving people casual waves as he crosses the cafeteria. Like he's famous or something. I see an underclassman actually sneak out her phone and snap a picture of him.

His gaze shifts over to our table and locks onto Kaia. I missed out on witnessing the two of them cozy into smooching position yesterday, and I don't exactly want to watch it unfold in real time now. I know how this ends.

I consider the table of smart girls and catch the eye of the one with the tight hairband. Another girl has a book open on the table in front of her, and I can see from here it's not a schoolbook. She's genuinely reading for pleasure. And it's not because she lacks a smartphone—I can see her phone right there beside her tray. Maybe they really are my people. Which makes me wonder whether Colton is worth trying to get past Kaia.

As he draws close, I feel panic rise from deep in my chest. He still hasn't noticed me, and I'm half standing at the table with my hands on either side of my tray. A tray on which sits one greasy slice of pizza bought only so I could prove to him what a good listener I am.

I tell myself that eating in the bathroom stall again is not an option, but as Kaia and Colton embrace, I quickly grab my tray and slide around behind them.

"Hey there, Andie. Where're you going?" Colton asks.

I turn and see Kaia already has an arm draped across his shoulder. She's glaring at me as if I'm a stray dog and she's protecting her favorite chew toy. Even if I do stay here, watching them will make for a very long lunch period. I scowl at the thought.

"I think I see someone I made friends with in my science class." I gesture to the nerd table. It's a lie, and yet it's not really a lie. I haven't had science class yet in this version of today, but "yesterday" afternoon I did share a quick eye roll and smile with a girl with a short black bob, who is sitting at the table I'm headed toward.

Kaia purrs, "Isn't it wonderful that she's making friends already?" as she bares her straight white teeth at me.

When Colton looks in her direction, Kaia repositions her lips into her patented pout and innocently blinks up at him. He says, "Good for you, Andie," but he doesn't even glance my way. He's wholly under Kaia's spell.

I can't believe I was handed some strange, supernatural second chance to make things right with Colton and I'm failing again. As I make my way toward the safety of the nerds' table, I purposely avoid eye contact with Tom and his rakishly tilted fedora. Also to be ignored: the sense that I might be a horrible person after all.

A guy slows down as he walks by the table I'm headed toward. He's wearing yellow suspenders attached to his dark jeans in an ironic way, and it looks like he may snag the last open seat at that table. The girl with the bob who I *will* meet in science gives him a shy small smile, and he blushes.

As Suspender Dude draws closer, the girl with the open book raises her head and pointedly stares at him. He freezes a moment before wordlessly retreating toward Tom's table.

Black Bob Girl looks disappointed, but as soon as I get closer, she smiles at me standing there with my tray. "Is this seat taken?" I ask her.

"Sit. Sit." She gestures to the empty seat.

"Yes, might as well." The reading girl rolls her eyes and tips her head toward Colton's table. "It's not like we're above accepting the meatheads' rejects."

"I'm not . . ." I start to protest, but when she gives me a full-on glare, I bite back my response. It appears there's a very nonexclusive club labeled "Colton's castoffs," and I'm the newest member. I wonder if he's rejected any of the other girls at this table. Or possibly all of them.

As I humbly place my tray down, I consider the half dozen females who are mostly on their phones. They seem far more subdued than people at other tables. These girls carry an air of maturity that makes them seem like undercover agents who are only pretending to be high school students.

The reading girl I slide next to has on jeans and a T-shirt, but the shirt is so new that it still has fold marks. I smile and say I like the emo band that's pictured on the front.

She looks down at the image of floppy-haired boys making

goofy faces. "Thanks. I'm wearing it ironically." She goes back to reading. *Ouch*. If she is undercover, she's amazing at it.

As the girl with the black bob introduces herself as Petra, I give my pizza a poke. I wonder if only eating half will have the same bad effect on my stomach as a whole slice did yesterday. I mean today, but that first time.

I lose my appetite.

I realize Petra just asked me a question, and I mutely stare across the table at her a moment before snapping back to reality and asking her to please repeat it.

She asks, "Where did you live before moving here?"

I attempt a smile that feels more like a grimace and tell her we're from a tiny little speck on the map called Jaytown.

"What's it like?" she asks.

"It's, well, it's just normal, I guess. Everyone knows everyone. The days move on in a linear pattern without repeating." She gives me a confused look, and I'm suddenly feeling very homesick. "Just kidding. You know, Punxsutawney. *Groundhog Day*."

There's an awkward silence.

Finally, Petra laughs. "Right. Because of the *movie*. I love that movie!"

I want to both slap her and hug her at the same time. She's mocking my situation unknowingly, and yet I must admit she has splendid movie taste.

Without looking up from her book, the girl beside me says, "Nothing like a movie that parodies our whole town for its *Groundhog and Pony Show*." She lifts her gaze to mine. "It's like we only exist on February second, and Punxsutawney Phil is the only living creature who matters."

"Don't mind Anna," Petra says. "She has this thing against the groundhog celebration and blames the movie for making everything worse."

Anna shakes her head and goes back to her book, mumbling something about Colton loving that stupid celebrity groundhog. I find the connection strange, so I blurt out the first thing that pops into my head.

"Did you and Colton *date* or something?" I ask, and everyone freezes. Anna intently stares at the page of her book, and hair-band girl pauses with her forkful of brown goo poised midair. I look at the tableful of mannequins around me. "What?"

Petra makes a slashing motion across her neck and hisses, "Abort, abort."

"Oh, um, I mean . . ." I widen my eyes at her. "Did you? . . . What were we talking about?"

"Do you have any special interests?" Petra saves me, and continues filling the air with questions to deflect Anna's attention. "What clubs did you belong to? Any photography experience? Surely you play a musical instrument."

Anna finally snaps her head up from her book. "She is not joining the band."

The two of them stare each other down hard. To break the tension, I blurt out, "Sorry, I don't play any instruments."

"Doesn't hurt to ask," Petra says, and turns to me. "We really need someone to play the bass."

"Your marching band needs a bass drum player?" Anna rolls her eyes again and I mumble, "Sorry. I'm not really a drumline sort of girl—missing the rhythm gene."

With a sigh, Anna goes back to reading, and the girl with

the tight headband chimes in. "How about photography? We could use someone on the yearbook staff."

"I'm not too bad with a camera," I say, and it's true. All the years spent studying movies have given me a decent eye for setting up a shot. At least, I know enough to pay attention to background composition and make sure it doesn't look like a tree is growing from the top of someone's head.

"That's great!" Petra tucks her bobbed hair behind both ears. "Listen, we're meeting in the library after school. The yearbook committee needs to get started now with selling ads and collecting baby photos of the seniors."

Anna gives Petra a look that clearly says, *Stop talking now*, but Petra ignores her.

The girl with the tight hairband says, "Yearbook is the best. Anna already got a very unflattering photograph of Princess Kaia over there scarfing down a bag of chips like a gavone."

Anna smiles for the first time. "It's going on one of our 'candid collage' pages."

I think of Kaia making herself throw up in private and feel a wave of empathy for what must feel like an endless cycle of eating and purging. It sounds even worse than Sisyphus's curse.

I turn around in my seat to look at her, and most of my warm, empathetic thoughts go cold. I didn't even manage to slow down her luring of Colton. They're on the same trajectory as yesterday.

When I turn back to my table, everyone is watching me with obvious pity. I shrug and try sounding casual. "Hey, I heard the pizza here is pretty good."

Picking up my slice, I take a tiny bite. *Nope*. Still horrible.

• • •

As the lunch period winds down, I excuse myself from the table and head to the one spot where I know Colton and Kaia will be after lunch: the entrance to the girls' bathroom. It's my final chance to make this do-over worthwhile and win Colton back.

Parking myself beside the swinging door, I stand guard as if I'm a bouncer collecting a cover charge from underclassmen.

Finally, I spot Kaia and Colton walking arm in arm down the hallway, and it's as if Kaia has some sort of radar that can detect my plan to steal Colton away from her. She eyes me up and down as I lean against the wall, pretending to consult my phone.

I look helplessly at Colton and ask him which direction room 305 is in. Since I've now spent a day and a half wandering around these hallways, I'm actually pretty confident the room is to my left, but acting helpless seems like the most efficient way to get him away from Kaia. Colton can't seem to resist playing superhero.

Before he can respond, Kaia displays an amazing capacity for quick thinking. Placing a hand delicately on his chest, she says, "Colton, honey, I forgot my planner in my locker—would you be a dear and grab it for me?" She looks me directly in the eye and adds, "It's pink."

Colton grins at her. "Sure, no problem. I'll grab it on my way back from dropping Andie off at her class. What's your locker number and combo?"

She turns her back to me and quietly gives him the information, making it clear she doesn't trust me. I try to give her a confident smirk of victory, but as soon as I catch her eye, she smacks her head with her palm as if she's just remembered something else.

I figure she's going to tell him to skip the whole locker scheme since it didn't get him away from me anyway, but instead she doubles down on her lie. "I forgot that I *really* need it before class so I can get back to Casey about our plans later on." She smiles at him. "Any chance you could meet me back here with it? I'm sure Andie can find her way once she's pointed in the right direction." She aims her smile at me. "Isn't that right, Andie?"

Man, she's good, I think as I involuntarily nod my head yes.

Colton points me down the path I already know I need to take, which is, of course, the opposite way he's heading. As I walk away, I kick myself for allowing Kaia to dissect me from Colton's life so easily.

The rest of the day plays out basically the same way it did the first time: Kaia convinces Colton to usher me onto the bus, where I ride home like the friendless mutant I am. The pizza I ate disagrees with my stomach, and I'm reduced to eating Puffs 'o Oat cereal for the second night in a row. Too late, I remember the yearbook committee meeting I was invited to and think, *Well, there's another bridge I've burned.* Just more evidence in my horrible-person casefile, since Petra seemed really nice too.

I can't even think about facing the pink couch.

Mom's clearly disappointed when I turn down her invitation to watch a movie.

"I'm heading in early," I tell her when she enticingly waves a DVD case. On the cover is Mathew Broderick as Ferris Bueller, leaning back with his hands behind his head as he takes his day off. I didn't share as many details of my day with Mom this time, so I guess she arrived at a different movie suggestion.

"You sure?" Mom grins and recites the movie's tagline about how fast life can fly by. She quips, "You need to make sure you don't miss it."

No danger of that. "I'm okay with fast-forwarding through tonight," I say, but then I get an idea. "Let me just see what else is left in the glass case."

She slides out of my way, and I start poking around the shelves of her collection. When I'm positive she's not looking, I open the pink plastic case to *Pretty in Pink* and snap the DVD neatly in half, fake-coughing to cover the sound. I close the pieces back in the case before she notices.

"Sorry, I thought something might catch my eye, but I'm just really tired." I turn and give Mom an exaggerated yawn. "We'll watch something cool together tomorrow night, I promise. Maybe *The Breakfast Club*."

She looks so happy at this suggestion, I want to cry. As I make my way slowly up the stairs, I feel bad for deceiving my mother and for breaking one of her precious movies, but that *Pretty in Pink* DVD had to go.

chapter 7

I hear the music playing and I don't even need to open my eyes to know where I am. On the enormous pink couch, with the DVD menu from *Pretty in Pink* playing on the television. And it's the first day of school.

I sit up and look around at the rosy morning light. I really thought today would be different. When Dad comes whistling in to ask if I would like pancakes, I say, "I really, really don't feel well," and I'm not lying.

He walks over and takes my temperature, using the very scientific method of holding the back of his hand against my forehead.

"Cool as a cucumber," he cheerfully announces. "Nothing a nice, hot stack of pancakes won't fix. Do you mind turning that music off?"

"Sure, no problem." I walk over, hit eject, and snap the DVD in half again. I shove the broken pieces underneath one of the cushions of the pink leather couch, wondering if I should try burying them in the yard. Or perhaps I should be digging a couch-sized grave.

When Mom walks in with her unbounded excitement over

this endless first day of school, I repeat the news that I'm not feeling well. To take my temperature, she uses the much more accurate method of touching her lips to my forehead, but her assessment is the same as Dad's.

"You feel fine, sweetie. Probably just nervous about your *big first day*." She grins. "Are you planning on wearing that dress?"

I flip the stiff pink skirt into the air and it happily floats back down and settles around my thighs. "It doesn't matter." I sit down hard.

When Dad waves a plate of pancakes in front of me, I just stare at them. "What is causing this?"

I don't realize I've asked the question out loud until Mom pats my head. "Don't question it. Just enjoy it. Your dad's guilt over moving you your senior year of high school won't last forever."

"What?" I look at her dumbly.

Mom furrows her brow. "The pancakes? You asked what was causing them."

Could it be something as simple as the pancakes causing my . . . whatever this is? Hallucination? Time loop? Mental breakdown? I shove the plate away from me. "I'm going upstairs to lie down for a little while before I have to get ready for school."

"So exciting," Mom says. "First day!"

"Yup." I walk away. "First day."

As soon as I close my bedroom door, I rip off the crazy pink dress and pull on my flannel flowered jammies. *This is insane.* There is zero chance I am mentally okay right now.

I jam my fingers against my neck to take my pulse and confirm my heart is beating quickly. This is the extent of my health examination know-how. *Heart beating? Yup, I'm alive.*

I start pacing around my room, and think about asking my dad for a diagnosis. The image of myself sitting in a straitjacket fills my mind, and I shove the thought away. My mother would be more likely to believe me. But even her creative mind won't be able to wrap itself around all this and come up with a reasonable explanation. She'll just tell Dad, which leads us right back to the straitjacket scenario.

I look to my phone for help, but there's no one I can think to text. I can't even consult Rhonda, since I've been awful at staying in touch with her over the summer. First, I was busy with the move, and then I discovered the joys of stalking Colton at the movie theater. She even accused me of sounding like I'm obsessed with him. I *hate* it when best friends are right. If I write to her now, she'll just say Colton's the problem.

Which reminds me. I look at the small white clock on my end table. He'll be arriving in a little while to drive me to school. Flinging myself onto my bed, I roll over and face the wall. I can't go through this again. I'm staying in these jammies.

Mom calls up, asking how I'm feeling, and I call back down, "Tell Colton to go ahead without me when he gets here. I'm not going to school today."

I can hear Mom quickly stomping up the stairs to my bedroom, and feel the breeze as she flings open the door. "What are you talking about, Andie? You can't miss your first day at the new school." Looking at my jammies, she adds, "And where's that pretty dress you were just wearing?"

I gesture to it lying in a heap in the corner. "I've already done this. I'm not doing it again."

Mom comes over to sit on the edge of my bed. "Honey, I

know this is hard, getting to know all new people. But you were so excited last night. What happened? I thought you were hoping Colton might be your first kiss."

First kiss . . . I sit up like I've been struck by a lightning bolt. "We did wish for that together, didn't we?"

She laughs. "I just wished for your first kiss to be with your true love."

My mind is busy whirring as I nod to Mom in response.

She stands up and moves toward the door. "You still have some time." Her voice goes firm. "But even if you're wearing those jammies, you *are* going to school today."

I lie back down in aggravation, and she laughs as she closes the door.

But the first kiss idea won't leave me alone. I try to remember everything that happened back before this time-loopy thing started. We were definitely talking about my first kiss being with my true love, and I wonder, *Could that really be the answer?* Like some sort of fairy tale story where the kiss from the prince awakens the sleeping/poisoned/brainwashed/time-repeating girl?

Maybe Colton doesn't even need to fall in love first. Maybe true love's kiss will be *how* he falls in love with me.

I sit up and grab my laptop. Since I skipped the pancakes, I have an extra while today. A search for "power of true love's kiss" leads to a bunch of scientific stuff comparing kissing to taking drugs where the chemical dopamine gets released through the system. Which gets boring pretty fast, but it makes me think I'm on the right trail.

Next, I learn all about a group of prairie dogs who do this thing called "greet kissing" to say hello. Apparently, the way they recognize each other is by first making out. After watching an adorable video of two prairie dogs kissing at the zoo, I check to see if prairie dogs are the same things as groundhogs (since Punxsutawney Phil is still high on my list of suspects). They're not—groundhogs are bigger and less social, with fluffier tails—but I do discover that groundhogs are sometimes called "whistle pigs," which is kind of perfect.

But also not at all helpful to my situation.

I head down the path of Internet movie trivia about the movie *Groundhog Day* before deciding that even if the movie is secretly based on true events, it is still true love that breaks Bill Murray's character free. True love must be the key.

Finally, I discover a page devoted to true love's kiss as a trope in stories, which I find fascinating. I'm surprised to learn that in Grimms' original version of "The Frog Prince," instead of kissing the frog to turn him into a prince, the princess threw him up against the wall. I laugh, imagining the flattened frog turning into a prince with a concussion, who in the story goes ahead and marries the princess anyway.

Reading through the list, I realize that magical true love's kisses really are everywhere. Besides Disney franchises and fairy tales, they're in a ton of live-action movies as well. Even *The Matrix* uses one. Spoiler: after hours of fighting and violence, the most kick-butt female ever, Trinity, saves Neo with a simple kiss. Actually, not simple. It is clearly *true love's first kiss*, and it is all-powerful.

Eventually, my research devolves into watching the twenty-five top kissing scenes from movies including *The Princess Bride*, *Clueless*, *Lady and the Tramp*, *Spider-Man*'s epic upside-down kiss in the 2002 movie version, and finally the very last scene in *Sixteen Candles*.

Mom already had me watch that Molly Ringwald classic, and I remember Molly's character, Sam, barely said two words to her crush, Jake, through the whole movie. Yet that final scene of the two of them sitting across from each other on top of a table feels so right and true. And then Molly and her guy leaning over her birthday cake to share their first kiss is one of the very best movie happy endings of all time. (It's *nearly* epic enough to make people overlook the inappropriate way the prom queen gets treated, as well as all the offensive Asian jokes. Nearly.) Still, that romantic kiss softly lit by burning birthday candles convinces me I must be onto something big here.

Molly Ringwald is apparently a sage who holds all life's wisdoms, both real and scripted. And I'm convinced that winning true love's first kiss will be what sets time moving forward for me again.

I'm getting that kiss from Colton today if it's the last thing I do.

But if I'm going to make a real impression, I'll need to shake things up a bit. When Mom pokes her head back in to check on me, I'm already busy, slicking my hair back and securing it into a bun. It's the style Molly wears at the end of *Sixteen Candles*.

"That's the spirit, Andie." Mom smiles, then can't resist asking, "What are you planning to wear?" She eyes my flannel PJs.

"No worries, Mom. I've got this."

"Well, I'm not sure what you've been doing up here all this time, but you'll need to hurry if you want to be ready on time."

"I just had to watch a few quick movie clips," I say.

Mom shakes her head. "Andie, you really don't have time now—"

"Molly Ringwald has helped me figure out *everything*." I innocently smile at her. I have all the time in the world.

"Okay, well, then . . . Good, I guess." Mom gives me a puzzled look before closing the door. After a beat, she calls, "I'll be downstairs if you need me." Which is code for she's going down to talk to Dad about my worrisome behavior.

I go back to the mirror and turn my head from side to side, noting how shiny my hair looks when it's plastered this tight against my head. Not to mention the fact that my face is suddenly all cheekbones. I don't know why I haven't tried this hairstyle before. I suppose I've never felt the need to make a drastic change in my appearance in the hopes of breaking free from a painful, never-ending day. But there's a first time for everything.

Giving my head an extra healthy dose of hairspray, I move to my mother's room to borrow her cosmetics. If I'm going to win Colton's heart, copying Kaia's makeup just might help. Leaning toward the mirror above Mom's dresser, I go to work with the shadow and liner.

It does not go well.

Applying a smoky eye is difficult—but making my two smoky eyes *even* is the real challenge. In my quest for symmetry, I keep adding liner and shadow to one side and then the other again and again. By the time Dad comes upstairs, I look like I've been double-punched in the eyes.

"Is there something you'd like to discuss, pumpkin?" he asks.

I project my anxiety back onto him by wailing, "I've told you that calling me pumpkin makes me feel like I'm a freak with red hair."

"You have *literally* never told me that." Dad looks more annoyed than upset.

"Well, think about it." I scoop up Mom's makeup caddy and make my way to the bathroom.

"Andie—"

I give him a dripping-with-teen-surliness "I'll be fine" before I close the bathroom door.

After quickly washing my face, I try again, using the handy-dandy color map that came free on the back of Mom's eye shadow package. The results are better, but not by much. I still resemble a feral raccoon.

After a third failed attempt, I give up and go with several coats of mascara. Then I emphasize my lips with Mom's bright pink pencil. I'm surprised at how cool it looks with my slicked-back bun.

I pull a fitted black T-shirt from Mom's pile of castoffs and cut the collar from it, creating a casual yet cleavage-emphasizing top. I pair this with a pair of her stylish, mid-sized heels and my great-fitting jeans.

When Mom calls up that Colton has arrived, I cringe over how clompy I must sound in her heels overhead. "I'll be right there," I shout, trying to cover the clamor of my wobbly footsteps down the hallway.

The shower is running when I pass the bathroom, but Dad's not singing the way he usually does. Which would make me feel bad if it weren't for the fact that he's an awful singer.

I can hear Mom talking to Colton downstairs, but I take a

moment to consider my efforts in the full-length mirror by my door. I must admit I'm kind of looking like a knockout. Molly's hairstyle and Kaia's outfit may have been my inspirations, but I've made the look all my own.

My reward is Colton's undivided attention as soon as he sees me walking down the stairs. It's too bad my ability to climb downstairs in heels has not been helped one iota by my repeating this same day twice now.

Recovering from a quick, life-threatening right ankle roll, I hold on tight to the bannister the rest of the way down to the living room. I realize my biggest mistake thus far has been ignoring opportunities to make myself better with my extra time. I mean, I could be a pro at both applying a smoky eye and walking in heels by now, and wonder if I should spend today in my room practicing both skills.

Colton asks, "You look ready, doll. Shall we go?"

I smile at him. My goal today is not about self-improvement. It's about somehow getting Colton's lips on my pink ones before sundown. Judging by how attentive he is as he ushers me into his trusty Honda Element, I think I've got a decent shot at taking Kaia's place this time around.

● ● ●

The best benefit of walking poorly in heels is the fact that Colton takes my arm for this whole round of the school tour. I can't be sure if it's because of my slamming outfit, or the fact that when I attempted to exit his car I ended up sprawled facedown on the blacktop, but he sweetly took my hand and placed it on his forearm to steady me as we headed through the front doors together.

Today, when people greet him, it is with added interest toward me, and I realize everyone now assumes we are together. As in: a couple. As in: all my dreams are coming true.

Maybe the third time really is the charm. I even remember to avoid running into Goth Guy this morning.

When we approach the gym, where the gaggle of cheerleaders awaits, I lean closer and whisper into Colton's ear, "Thanks again for the ride." He smiles at me, not even noticing the girls watching us as we walk past.

Now that we've been through all of this a few times, I'm able to steer Colton away from some of his more attention-hogging teammates. More importantly, I manage to completely avoid Kaia. In fact, throughout the day, I quickly derail every attempt she makes to come into contact with the boy who seems more and more mine by the moment.

At lunchtime, I wait in the hallway so I can intercept Colton on his way to the cafeteria and ask if we can please eat outside alone. "I have a few questions about the building's layout." I let my voice go so high I sound almost baby-like. "What shape is this building even called?"

He laughs. "I know it can be a little confusing. Come on, I'll get us some pizza and we can sit in the *hexagonal* center court-yard with a map." I spot Kaia pouting at the table in the corner, waiting for Colton to come and fall in love with her. I give her a smug wave of victory. Since we were never introduced today, she slowly returns my wave with a look of confusion.

Her confusion turns to frustration when she watches me

steer Colton directly out the side doors to the courtyard. The benches are mostly empty since it's still overcast today, but I use the opportunity to snuggle tightly into Colton's side as he shows me how to access a pdf of the school's map on my phone. He dips his head close to mine, and I smile at how well I am girling right now.

I flirt my way through our lunch together, which unfortunately involves ingesting yet another slice of pizza. As I swallow the last bite, Colton makes a comment about how much he likes it when a girl really shows her appetite.

I happen to be a master at eating, and realize this is a chance for me to really shine. Despite my knowledge that the pizza will turn on me later, I boldly announce, "I'm going back for dessert."

Colton gives me a dreamy look, and I'm sure to give him a sultry over-the-shoulder glance as I wobble back toward the cafeteria. Hopefully, he doesn't notice the way I need to lunge for the door and cling to its handle to avoid falling again in these heels.

I step inside and am happy to see the line has gone down. I won't be away from Colton for too long. When I approach the dessert counter, I realize Tom is standing directly in my way.

He takes in my outfit and turns his attention back to the rows of plates holding slices of cake. It seems he thought I looked better in my pink dress from Today 1.0. "Careful," he says, and catches my arm as I nearly stumble in my heels.

"Thanks," I say. "Any recommendations?"

"Yes." He laughs. "Stick with footwear you can actually walk in."

I slap his arm, trying not to smile. "I meant *dessert* recommendations."

He's holding up a slice of carrot cake and nods to the row of plates. "I'd steer clear of the pudding, especially if you ate the pizza. I think the two are chemically formulated to create a hazardous reaction." He holds his stomach dramatically.

"Thanks. I'm pretty sure the pizza does that all on its own." As if in response, my stomach does a quick flip.

Tom says, "Guess you got your wish." I give him a strange look, and he shrugs. "You and Colton? Together? It's obvious you were hanging around the movie theater all summer just to get close to him."

I look down at my impractical shoes. "I like movies too, you know."

"Yeah." He laughs. "You like them more than he does. Why do you think I never really minded you being around?" He hands me what appears to be some sort of lemon square with powdered sugar on top, straining to escape its plastic wrap. "These are always a safe bet. My treat."

I look up at him with surprise. "I remembered my money today," I say.

"Okaaay, good for you." His lip gives a twitch. Of course; he knows nothing about my actual first day, when he bought me lunch.

I point toward the courtyard. "Really, I've got this. Colton's waiting for me."

"Don't want to keep you two apart."

"Thanks for the valuable pudding and pizza toxicity warning," I say. "The stomach you saved could be my own."

Tom nods and moves so I can grab a second lemon square and head to the register in front of him. On impulse, I grab two bags of cheesy puffs and stuff one under each elbow. If Colton likes a girl with an appetite, I will show him a girl with an appetite.

"Good luck," Tom says as I carry a dessert plate in each hand and teeter toward the doors with the *crinkle* sound of chip bags ringing out from my armpits.

I reach the doors, push my way outside, and—too late—am horrified to discover Kaia has joined Colton where he was waiting for me on the bench. On *our* bench.

I'm speechless at the way she is snuggled up beside him, in the very same position they've ended up in for the past two days. Being outdoors has actually increased the coziness quotient of their cuddle. He has such a gooey look on his face, I realize Kaia is much better at girling than I can ever hope to be.

The door closes behind me, calling attention to the fact that I'm standing here, teetering on too-high heels with junk food in my hands and tucked under my arms.

Just as Colton and Kaia look up, I spontaneously stumble, landing facedown and popping the snack bags of cheesy puffs under both arms. The lemon squares go flying in opposite directions, and one of the dessert plates shatters when it hits the ground.

When the cloud of cheese dust finally clears, Colton looks like he'd love to get up and help me, but Kaia has her long denim legs flung possessively across his lap.

I sit up fast and call out, "I'm fine. Don't worry."

Awkwardly, Colton says, "Kaia, this here is Andie, who I was just telling you about."

My soaring thought that he was telling her about *me* gets

grounded by her lipsticked smirk. "Nice to meet you, Andie. The bathroom is out the cafeteria doors and to the right if you'd like to get yourself cleaned up."

I lift myself off the ground and look down to see my chest is covered in orange powder from the dual bags of cheesy puffs. So much for trying to show a little cleavage.

I stand up and let out a squeak before escaping the stares of Colton and my snuggle stealer. Flinging open the glass doors to the cafeteria, I rush inside, running smack into Goth Guy, who was busy returning his tray. It falls to the ground with such a loud ringing clatter that everyone in the cafeteria stops to look at me, now covered in both cheese dust and Goth Guy's leftover brown goo. *Perfect.*

All hope has officially left the building for the rest of the day.

chapter 8

fter yet another ride on the awful, smelly school bus and another night of cereal for dinner because of wicked stomach cramps from pizza that I can't seem to stop eating, I spend the rest of the night in my room. There, I practice walking in heels while watching video tutorials on how to properly apply a smoky eye.

Apparently, until I get true love's first kiss, I'll be stuck repeating this same day. I might as well work on getting better at a few things.

Dad bangs on the ceiling at my tromping back and forth, but I merely stomp even harder. He likes writing psychology books so much, let him live one. I'm effectively channeling "teen train wreck" right now, and if he sorts me out, he'll probably have a bestseller on his hands.

The next morning, after waking up on the couch and getting myself all ready, I'm, well . . . I'm still pretty spazzy at walking in heels, but my eye makeup application is starting to improve. And since things with Colton continue to go about the same as usual, with Kaia intercepting him at different points each day, I get a few more evenings of stomping about my bedroom in heels.

Eventually, I kind of get the hang of it.

One morning, I take my position at the top of the stairs and my brain tells me, *This is it.* I've perfected my morning routine, and my smoky eyes are picture-perfect and smoldering. I stride confidently down the steps in my mother's patent leather four-inch heels and stop to strike a solid pose at the bottom.

Mom stands in the center of the living room staring at me in shock, and Colton lets out a long whistle.

"Let's do this," I say, confidently, as I stride over and take Colton's arm. By now I feel so comfortable with him, knowing exactly what he'll say and when he'll say it, that I take charge.

Which sort of backfires.

"Are you okay, Andie? You seem . . . *different.*" He says it in a way that makes it clear different may not be such a good thing.

I'm so sick and tired of inching closer and closer to getting a kiss from him. A few times I've even considered just grabbing him and pressing my lips against his simply to break this blasted curse once and for all. But kissing Colton in my living room in front of my mom is not the version of reality I'd like to break the cycle with and stay stuck on.

"I *feel* different," I say. "Excited to get to Punxsutawney High and check out what my new school has to offer."

"That's the spirit, honey," Mom calls, and snaps a photo as I lead Colton out the front door.

I can tell by the way he half-heartedly opens the passenger car door for me that I've overplayed my self-confidence. He doesn't seem to be interested in what must have come across as "arrogant Andie." I just can't seem to pull off Kaia's poise and confidence without turning Colton cold.

By the time we get to school, it's obvious another day has been blown. Colton is polite, but so distant I don't even bother trying to direct our path as I numbly cruise-control my ride through this tour. I'm nearly Colton's height as I stomp silently beside him, passing rows and rows of identical lockers and thinking to myself that I'll try again tomorrow. The word reverberates in my mind with every step. *Tomorrow. Tomorrow. Tomorrow.* And I'm hit by the truth.

Tomorrow isn't coming.

I feel a wave of depression over the idea of puppeting through this day yet again. "I'm not sure how much more of this soul-crushing sameness I can take," I say out loud just as we pass Anna sliding a heavy book into her locker.

"You can say that again." She slams her locker closed with a *thunk* and walks away.

Colton and I find ourselves in the gymnasium, interacting with the cheerleaders. I notice Colton is utterly fascinated by their uniforms, and wonder for the first time if the key to getting a kiss from him and freeing myself could be as simple as becoming a cheerleader.

And by "simple," of course I mean "impossible."

But maybe, instead of trying to out-Kaia Kaia, I should be reinventing myself, incorporating all Colton's favorite features into one Amazing and Utterly Irresistible Andie. After all, nothing has been working so far, and I'm willing to try anything. Even becoming a cheerleader.

So what if I can't clap in time to save my life? I have the greatest power of all in my possession. I *own* time. I've got time handcuffed in my closet and I can do anything I want.

I tune in just as one of the girls is asking if I plan on making practice for cheerleader tryouts later. It feels like fate when I answer her with a wide smile. "What time and where?"

● ● ●

Cycling through the endless number of days it takes for me to learn how to become a cheerleader is a unique and exquisite torture. I know just how Sisyphus must have felt with his heavy boulder as I show up for practice after school again and again and again.

I'm so naturally off beat that it takes a full week's worth of humiliating afternoons just to get me clapping somewhat in time. The girls laugh at me behind my back as well as to my face, but they continue trying to teach me. They seem to have infinite patience, calling out, "Ready? OKAY!" over and over until I am saying it to myself anytime I'm about to do anything.

Time to climb into the shower: "Ready? OKAY!"

Time to get on the sad yellow activities bus and go home: "Ready? OKAY!"

Time to get up from the giant pink leather couch and try again: "Ready? OKAY!"

Progress is agonizingly slow, but as I begin to pick up the routine, I start to get what can only be described as respect from the other girls. Treating me like more of a peer, the cheerleaders show a different side of themselves. A side that could be called . . . nice.

I am forced to consider the possibility that these girls were never really my enemies.

"That sweater looks great on you," I hear repeated often enough that I know it's a genuine compliment. And Mom's vintage Mary Janes never fail to garner a stream of praise from the blondes. "You really should try wearing your hair in a high pony," one of them tells me. "The bounce of it will emphasize the sharpness of your moves."

As days cycle through, I get fleeting glimpses of the girls' bond with each other. There's a cool Sharpie cartoon on the back of the bleachers that must've appeared over the summer. It's a stylized drawing of two little kids talking about how exhausted they are from stress. The blondest-blonde, whose name is Tammy, calls the gang over at the beginning of practice each day to show it to everyone.

"I found this this morning and had to share it with you guys. It sums up how I feel sometimes," she says. "The pressure is so intense, it's like we don't have permission to just be young and have fun and *play*!"

At that, the least-blonde blonde always calls out, "Same! I want to play!" and the whole gaggle of cheerleaders bursts into rowdy high kicks as they disperse to finish warming up.

One afternoon, after admiring the cartoon, Tammy asks me, "What are you doing tonight?" I've apparently won her approval by nailing a particularly difficult cheer the first time. I mean, the first time this day. I've probably been working on it for over a month by now.

"I really need to spend some time practicing tonight." This is the truth. The only reason I'm getting good at this is because I spend hours each night working on my own.

"You sound like Jacynda. She practices obsessively, even

though she doesn't need to." Tammy points to a short African American girl with dark curls, who is busy doing a gravity-defying backflip.

"Trust me," I say. "I need the practice."

Tammy flings an arm over her head and bends into a deep side-stretch. "Jacynda thinks she needs to worry about tryouts too. Isn't that right, Jayce?" Jacynda must be listening in, because she gives Tammy a big thumbs-up with the hand that's not holding one of her own legs straight in the air.

"Okay, if she needs to worry, I may as well just give up." I try miming Tammy's stretching moves, but despite endless hours of practice, my inner awkward klutz still shows up often.

Tammy laughs. "You may not be at Jayce's level, but based on how quickly you picked up that last cheer, I'd say you're a shoo-in to make the squad."

"Thanks." I give a tense smile. The only way I'll ever advance to tryout day is to convince Colton I'm full of surprises and cheerleading talent, and hopefully get that first kiss. I've come up with a really good plan that I hope I'll be ready to execute soon.

Tammy tells me, "Well, if you decide to stop obsessing over your performance, we're heading over to Maya's house after practice. You'd be a welcome addition."

"Yeah, you should come!" the least-blonde blonde named Casey says with so much enthusiasm, it's as if she thinks I'm a whole football team in need of encouragement. She even punches both arms in the air for emphasis.

I shake my head. Spending the evening at some house party with a bunch of cheerleaders doesn't sound like very good use of my time. "I can't, but that's cool you guys all hang out together."

"Well, it's good to give back," Casey says, which is a strange thing to say about going to a house party. I haven't met anyone named Maya yet, but she must not be very popular if everyone here acts like going to her house for a party is some form of charity.

Casey bounces off, literally, and I ask Tammy, "What got you into cheerleading in the first place?"

"To be completely honest? I thought it would make me more popular." She twists back and forth with her hands on her hips.

Jayce walks over, falls into a split, and begins stretching. "That and you're a crazy-good gymnast."

Tammy folds herself neatly in half, hugging her straightened knees. "Yeah, that too."

I glance at Jacynda, who is now arching backward, the top of her head nearly touching her back leg. "So, I guess joining the squad worked. I mean, you guys seem pretty popular."

As if to emphasize this point, and right on schedule, a group of guys walks by the doorway calling, "Hey, girls," and, "Yo, Jayce," and, "Looking good." The girls don't react.

"We stopped caring." Tammy stands and calmly turns to me. "It's nice to be liked, but we learned pretty quick that most people think cheerleaders aren't much more than football player arm candy."

"We're part of a real sisterhood," Jayce adds. "We're here for each other."

"Sweat is thicker than water," Tammy says. "We all push each other and practice hard."

"Yeah," Casey chimes in. "Not all of us can just pick up new routines as fast as you can, Andie."

"The matching skirts are cute." Tammy gives hers a flip. "But we're bonded by our commitment to become the best squad we can possibly be."

I look around and realize that she's right. These girls come here every day after school, push back the tables of the cafeteria because the basketball team practices in the gym, and together they work on their routines, day in and day out. This goes deeper than wearing cute skirts.

"From the top," Tammy calls out, and even though I've practiced these moves more than anyone, everybody groans at this repetitiveness. "Ready? OKAY!" At her perky countdown, we all automatically move into formation, and I realize why people play team sports.

Connecting with a group and trying to do something really well together can make anyone feel less alone. Even someone as fundamentally alone as me.

● ● ●

Finally, it's time to execute my plan. From one of Mom's massive clothing bins, I dig out a vintage cheerleading skirt and top for this first day of school. I secure my hair into a high ponytail and add a looping ribbon that matches my yellow-and-maroon uniform. Mom acts supportive despite seeming confused by my new look. As I said, she did witness what's known as the Great Zumba Debacle. But Colton nods approvingly when he sees the way I'm dressed.

"I didn't know you were into cheerleading," he says as he helps me into his car.

"There's a lot you don't know about me," I say teasingly and think, *A whole lot.*

At school, Colton gives me the usual tour, and as we get to the gym, the cheerleaders accost us, *oohing* over my outfit and asking if I'm trying out for the squad. I look at Colton and shrug. "I have a move or two." Casually, I ask, "What kind of routine are you gals working on?"

"Well, I'll be teaching a tryout routine tonight," Tammy says. "It goes a little something like this . . ."

She calls out, "Ready? OKAY!" and the three of them move into an aggressive V formation. Music starts up from somewhere, and the trio begins to move to the beat, performing the routine I've been working to learn this whole time.

"So, I guess you're saying it goes something like this?" I smile at Colton as I move into position beside the girls and start punching my arms to the beat, joining right in.

Everyone freezes in amazement as I nail the routine. Even a couple walking past the open gym doors slows down to watch me perform. I kill every move . . . right up to the point where I stumble while trying to execute a very complicated kick into a split and end up falling on my tush. When I jump back up, my mind goes completely blank and I stand in an awkward pose, waving spirit fingers and grinning like a fool.

The following day, I make it successfully through the whole routine.

I do so well that when the music stops, Tammy asks me, "How much time are you willing to devote to cheerleading?"

I shrug. "I've got all the time in the world. Why?"

"We pick one of our co-captains based on leadership ability

and the other based on natural talent. You could easily be in the running for talent if you're interested."

I look at Colton and he smiles at me. "Oh yeah, Andie is absolutely interested in that." He turns to Tammy. "As co-captain of the football team, I'll even vouch for her."

I blush. "I'm sure there are other girls who are more qualified. I'll just be happy to make it onto the squad."

"Oh, you'll make it onto the squad all right," Tammy says. "You picked this up so fast, I can't wait to see what you come up with on your own."

Casey chimes in, "Hey, yeah. That's a great idea. Let's see what else you can do."

With a big, fake smile, I launch back into the same routine we just did, and the energy in the gym drops off dramatically.

I slump away. That afternoon, after Kaia snags Colton for the umpteenth time, I grab Tammy during cheerleading practice and begin the long, slow process of having her help me come up with something completely original.

It feels like it takes forever, and meanwhile I've memorized every single sneeze and sneaker-squeak that happens each school day. I know what everyone is going to say before they say it, and I especially know precisely where Colton is every moment of the day.

One morning, just for kicks, I wear my comfy flannel jammies to school, which of course inspires Tom to talk to me.

"Just not feeling the day?" he asks me with a grin in homeroom. His tone makes it clear he thinks wearing flowered pajamas for the first day of school is the ultimate in cool behavior.

I hug myself. "I was all snuggly and didn't want to leave my house."

Tom laughs. "So this was the compromise you came up with?"

I smile and nod. "I drew the line at bringing along my pillow, but it was a difficult sacrifice."

"You are a surprising girl, Andie." Tom smiles appreciatively and clears his throat. "Plus, you have great taste in jammies."

I surprise myself then, feeling a blush rising. It must just be the heavy flannel material, but my voice is the tiniest bit horse when I tell him, "Thanks."

Nobody else seems to share Tom's positive view on my jammie-wear. Even his oddly dressed friends give me a wide berth as I walk down the hallway. In fact, nearly everyone avoids me on pajama day, and I'm happy Colton will have zero recollection of me in this outfit.

His level of popularity dictates that he really shouldn't be seen with me wearing head-to-slippers flowered flannel, but he's very sweet and even gives me a chaste hug before lunch. I think he can tell that I need it.

Of course, he still turns around and falls for Kaia, same as always.

● ● ●

At last, my dance routine is ready, and I don my cheerleading skirt once more. When Casey chimes in with her usual, "Yeah, let's see what you've got," I bust a move so hard I render everyone speechless.

I'm executing dance moves from every decade, including a

pop and lock sequence that ends in a breakdance head spin that, well, makes everyone's heads spin. A crowd begins to gather as I shake my butt like that's what it was made for. Hours and hours and *hours* of hard work and dance video tutorials are all melting together in one mind-blowing dance routine. As I swing and kick and twist, someone in the audience starts clapping to my rhythm. Others join in, and the echoes of the beat shake the bleachers.

The energy of the crowd rises until my insides are soaring.

I end with a backflip into a full split, and grin as the whole gymnasium breaks into roaring applause. Colton is looking at me with stars in his eyes, and I can feel it. This will be the day he falls in love with me. I'm getting my first kiss, I'm sure of it.

Word of my performance spreads like wildfire throughout the school. Suddenly I'm known as the redheaded cheer master. By the time English class rolls around, even Tom knows about my new reputation. He says, "I heard you really knocked the socks off everyone in the gym this morning. I had no idea you were a killer dancer."

I've learned from experience that engaging with Tom reduces my chances with Colton. It might be some sort of inverse probability factor that is beyond my mathematical ability to grasp. Or it could be the fact that Colton doesn't like Tom being his boss at the theater, or maybe it's just some basic high school popularity algorithm. But even though everything is riding on today, I can't help but smile at Tom now. "Guess I'm just full of surprises."

Tom smiles back. "Especially since you came off like such a klutz at the theater this summer."

"Well, it made for a decent meet-cute anyway, didn't it?"

"It definitely did do that," Tom says, and I detect a small bite of bitterness in his voice.

My mind wings back to that first day at the theater. I remember Tom's eyes going wide when I shoved that first handful of malted milk balls into my mouth. I picture him covering his mouth with his hand, and wonder for the first time if he and I could've been headed for a meet-cute of our own. Once Colton showed up, I didn't really give Tom another thought.

Thinking of Colton gives me a surge of happiness over how well things went this morning. My plan has been going flawlessly, and I have our next encounter already mapped out in my mind, down to the smallest detail.

If I really want to seal that lip lock, all I need to do is avoid any uncertain factors for the rest of the day. Again, I think back to cramming my mouth full of Whoppers and the look of surprise on Tom's face. I should probably steer clear of Tom for the rest of today just to be safe and keep everything predictable. Tom has a way of catching me off guard.

For the first time ever, Colton is the one who suggests the two of us meet outside in the courtyard for lunch. I've been resorting to locking the doors behind us as well as positioning myself so that Colton can't see Kaia pounding on the glass. I've even perfected the act of timing cute little kitten sneezes to cover up the sound of her knocking.

The best part about this tactic is that Colton thinks my little sneezes are adorable, and he always says "bless you" in a high-pitched voice that makes us both laugh. Of course, I've made the mental note to never sneeze for real in front of him, since my actual sneezes are earsplitting and borderline violent.

I manage to execute my lunchtime interaction flawlessly, and throughout the day I respond to every one of our exchanges just right. By the time the final bell rings, Colton asks me, "So, you ready to get out of here?"

"You're driving me home?" I try to sound cool about it, but I'm sort of freaking out inside. I feel like the moment I've been working toward for an eternity is finally happening. I'm getting back inside that Honda Element and changing my destiny.

"I'm happy to drop you at home, unless you'd like to head someplace else. The mall, maybe?"

I don't know what mysteries the Punxsutawney Mall may hold in store, but I do know that heading anywhere with Colton beats the insane level of monotony that is waiting for me at home.

"The mall sounds great." Down the hallway, I see Kaia moving toward us with a look of determination on her face. "Let's go!" I practically shove Colton out the door.

"Oh, wait, I forgot." He stops, and Kaia moves even closer. "Don't you have cheerleading practice after school?"

I want to scream in frustration. I have spent way too much of my never-ending life in that practice room. And now Kaia is nearly upon us. "I think I'm good," I say. "I mean, I know the routine already. I'll just pick up where they leave off tomorrow."

Colton looks skeptical, and I know I am risking blowing things with him right now, but I seriously need to get him out of Kaia's range if I ever hope to get my first kiss and break myself out of this endless time loop.

This is still, technically, the first day of school, but I'm so sick of it that I'm ready for the holiday break. And that's not getting any dang closer.

Finally, I manage to throw Kaia off Colton's scent by angling so she can see me put my hand on his shoulder. I seductively lean into him as if I'm whispering something private and personal into his ear. She stops and stares a moment before turning on her heel to leave.

Colton is looking at me expectantly, and I realize I haven't said anything to him. I smile while trying to think fast. Finally, in a low voice, I say, "Maybe after we go to the mall, we can hit a movie, just you and me."

He wrinkles his nose. "Tom's working tonight, so we'd have to pay full price for our tickets. Seems nuts, don't you think? Maybe this weekend?"

I would give *anything* for it to be the weekend. Two new movies are being released that I've had my eye on for a very long time. One of my favorite young actors, who's nearly as good-looking as Colton, is starring in a romantic comedy, plus there's a big-budget action flick that, according to early reviews, hits every emotional note perfectly.

Mom and Dad always say I have an uncanny ability to predict what's going to happen next in movies. But it's usually easy to anticipate what's coming if you've seen as many films as I have in my lifetime. And knowing what's coming doesn't mean I can't enjoy watching it unfold.

But as I climb into Colton's car, I must admit that *not* knowing what's coming next feels pretty good for a change. For the first time in a very long while, I'm heading into new and unknowable territory.

And to be perfectly honest, I cannot wait to see what happens.

chapter 9

The mall looks nothing like it did the one time I came here
with my mother over the summer. On that day, it was basically empty, with only a few scattered gaggles of girls wearing
flip-flops and an elderly couple speed-walking together in their
thick, white sneakers.

Now, it's packed due to what appears to be a ritual of congregating in various social groups to celebrate the first day of
school ending. *Please, please, please let it really be ending.*

I'm guarded as Colton leads me toward the food court,
watching for Kaia or anything that could thwart me from reaching the target that's been placed on Colton's lips. If I remember
correctly, my archnemesis has mentioned plans for the mall after
school on several occasions, so depending on whatever version
of a day she's had, there's a decent chance she'll be here.

At least she's not here with Colton this time.

"Hey, Tom," Colton says as we pass Tom and his colorful crew.

The kid from the lunchroom—the one who seemed interested in Petra yesterday, or today, or a year ago—adjusts his
yellow suspenders and smiles awkwardly. He's standing next

to Tom, whose gaze follows Colton and me as we walk by. Thinking of our meet-cute discussion earlier, I place my hand on the crook of Colton's arm in a way that shows he and I are together and I'm happy about it.

Tom turns back to Suspenders Boy with a furrowed brow, and I wonder what they're discussing so intently.

"Here we are. Care for Szechwan?" Colton gestures to the Chinese food place in front of us, and I remember how much he likes girls to have an appetite. I've been adding our lemon squares and cheese puffs at the same time Colton gets our pizza, so I'm seriously not at all hungry.

"I'll just have a little rice," I tell him, hoping that might soak up some of the pizza grease, sugar, and orange cheese dye #9 from earlier. I could honestly just go for a nice long nap about now.

I wonder for a moment if taking a nap will reset the whole day, and make a mental note to try it. Then I realize that I may not need to. This could be my last time through the cycle—if I can only get Colton to kiss me before the day ends.

With a hearty nod, I follow him over to the food counter. He orders for us, but he's still in the process of paying when a guy comes swooping in behind us and violently grabs Colton around the neck. I scream.

A few other very large guys join in, shoving and hitting my semi-boyfriend. They all start chanting, "Woodchucks. Woodchucks. Woodchucks!"

And I finally recognize them as Colton's teammates.

I instinctively put both arms up to protect my head as they all beat each other on the backs and shoulders. Finally, Colton notices me and admonishes the group. "Hey there, easy, guys. Andie and I are grabbing a bite. Catch up with you later?"

With a few friendly punches and one ringing heinie slap, the crowd moves on down the mall.

"Hey, Motko," Colton calls, and one of the guys turns and walks backward a few paces. "Make good choices."

Motko is tall and wiry, and he jerks his head quickly to the side to force the bangs out of his eyes before giving us a salute.

Colton watches his team go before paying the bored-looking girl behind the counter who's wearing a red hat made of paper. She slides him a tray piled high with chicken and rice. Carrying it, Colton finds us a table located off to one side of the food court. "How's this?" he asks.

"Looks great to me." I smile, and the two of us sit down across from each other.

Colton leans forward and starts digging in as if he hasn't eaten in days. I marvel at the metabolism he must have to stay in such good shape.

Looking around, I spot a cluster of goths standing outside a card store. Not all of them go to our high school, and I ask Colton if there's another school in the area.

He nods, and between bites gives a muffled, "Catholic school."

I take a closer look and see one of the girls I don't recognize is, in fact, wearing a plaid, pleated skirt underneath her black jacket. She also has on combat boots, and her white shirt is filled with safety pins, but *technically* I guess she's wearing a school uniform.

Colton playfully offers me a bite of rice, and I try my best to eat it daintily. But no matter how much extra time I've had to practice acting graceful, I'm still me. I bite at his fork like I'm one of Jim Henson's puppets with a single hinge for a mouth.

Fortunately, Colton smiles at me as if he finds my snapping at his fork adorable. He dips his head forward, and I wonder if my first kiss is about to happen here in the middle of the food court at the mall.

"Ugh, get a room," I hear in a disdainful voice on our right, and look over to see Kaia gliding by with her crew of girls—who I still haven't managed to put names to.

Colton looks surprised to see her. "Where were you hiding all day, girl?"

She sidles up to our table and traces a manicured finger along the edge. "I could ask you the same thing, Colt. I was hiding in plain sight."

I just sit there with my Muppet mouth hanging open. I wait for the two of them to put together the fact that I manipulated the entire day to keep them apart, but Colton only shrugs. "Yeah, I was in plain sight too. Showing Andie, here, around the school."

"Hi, Kaia," I say, giving a feeble wave.

Her airbrushed features collapse into a scowl. "Have we met?"

Shoot. I realize too late that she and I obviously didn't meet today. It's just so hard to keep track when everything is so repetitive. "Sorry, I thought I heard someone call you Kaia just now." I point in the general direction of her friends.

She looks at me suspiciously.

Colton must pick up on the tension between us. He grins and says, "Andie and I got to know each other during the summer at the theater."

Kaia rolls her eyes. "You and those stupid action movies."

Colton looks at me. "Andie's a hardcore movie buff."

I laugh. "Understatement."

"I heard she's a bit of a performer too." Kaia is clearly not happy with the way Colton is continuing to look at me. I could squeal with triumph. Obviously, I've finally won his affection, if not his love. *Could he possibly love me?*

"She was amazing in the gym this morning." His dazzled gaze answers my question. He may not love me yet, but he's definitely on his way.

And Kaia can see it too. She gives Colton a huffy good-bye and struts away, her friends faithfully following her wake.

I'm glad to see her go, even though I realize that without the benefit of the extra time spent working on a dance routine, Colton would be with Kaia right now. In fact, it's not entirely fair that he's with me.

But none of that should matter because I'm *in*, right? I won. I just need to get Colton to follow through with a kiss, and my life should start moving forward again in a nice, chronological fashion.

With a smile, he scoops up another bite of rice and says, "My buddy has this house party that's sort of an annual tradition to celebrate going back to school. It's always a blast. You want to come along?"

I'm not sure if him asking me to "come along" to a house party is quite the same thing as asking me out on a date, but this sounds like my big chance to snag that first kiss.

"I'm in," I say, and snap open my jaw hinge as he shoves another mouthful of rice toward me.

• • •

After I change out of my cheerleading outfit, Mom has the time of her life trying to help me decide what to wear to the party. Of course, she thinks I should be rocking that stupid pink polka-dotted dress I woke up in.

I've never been to a high school house party that had more than three people and less than one mom present, but I have seen many teen movies. So I know for a fact that the vintage dress would be all wrong for the party. Not to mention another small detail—the thing seems to be the bane of my existence.

I reject Mom's advice to "stand out, not blend in" and wear the jeans, black top, and high heels that mimicked Kaia's outfit. I remember Colton liking it almost as much as my cheerleading getup. Plus, I did work *super* hard figuring out how to walk in high heels, so I might as well exploit that skill.

When we pull up to the house where the party's taking place, my first thought is that it could be straight out of a movie. Spotlights illuminate the bushes in front, decorative bricks line the oversized windows, and the grass is so smooth and green that the yard looks practically carpeted.

Once Colton cuts the car's engine, we can hear the music blasting from where we're parked on the street. It gets louder as we get closer, and as soon as we enter the front door we're greeted by a wall of sound. I start thinking maybe it would be better to have my perfect first kiss somewhere private and quiet.

"Colt!" The call rises above the din of music, and Colton responds by punching both arms up in victory, which initiates an even louder cheer.

As we make our way through the living room, a cluster of football players crowds around and chants. I work to get my energy up to match the room by thrusting my hands in the air a few times. I even give a little "Woo," but nobody even seems to notice.

After about six minutes of this, I make a quick, silent wish to be back home on the couch with the DVD remote in my hand. Of course, the fact that this is my natural reaction probably explains why it has taken me months of reliving the same day over and over to finally get invited to this epic social gathering.

And by "epic" social gathering, of course I mean "over-crowded and loud."

Unlike the mall, there are no social outliers present. Everywhere I look there are either jocks, or wannabe jocks, or girlfriends of jocks, or wannabe girlfriends of jocks.

It's strange, because most of the teen house parties I've seen in movies have a diverse cross-section of types.

This must not be Maya's house either, because there's no sign of a single cheerleader, and Petra and Anna clearly didn't get an invitation. Also not present are any of the goth kids I've run into, and I can't even picture Tom's zany crew crashing this party. A quick sweep of the room shows no sign of Kaia or her glossy-haired friends, and I wonder if she'll show up here in this version of today.

Colton takes my hand and leans close to my ear. "Did you have parties like this back at your old school?" he asks over the music.

I grin at him. "This is a first for me."

He laughs. "Well then, I'll be gentle, I promise."

I laugh back, but for the first time since I met Colton, I feel slightly uneasy. I have been so focused on getting my first kiss with him, I haven't considered what else he might expect from a girlfriend. Suddenly, I'm wondering where on earth the parental supervision is at this party.

Colton leads me into the kitchen, where red Solo cups are being filled from a big, silver keg in the sink. I do realize that underage drinking is a common trope in teen movies, but I didn't think it happened in reality. Especially not on a school night.

When Colton grabs two cups filled with beer and tries to hand one to me, I give the first excuse that pops into my head. "Sorry, I'm on antibiotics."

He frowns and takes a step back. "I hope it's not for anything serious."

"Oh, just an ear infection." I stick a pinky in my ear and wiggle it around to really sell it. A few people from the small group in the kitchen are watching me, and they look a little grossed out. So does Colton. *Great.* But I'm definitely not drinking that beer.

With a shrug, he takes a sip from each of the cups he's holding. "More for me." We begin to circulate, and I can't help but notice that despite the manic tone of the music, nothing much is really happening here. There are some people taking selfies that I'm sure will look great online, but just because they are all perceived as cool does not mean that this party is necessarily a *cool* party. I'm pretty sure I attended better birthday parties when I was, like, eight. In fact, introducing a piñata might help right now.

Colton guides me into the living room, where a rather unruly crowd is gathered around an enormous television hanging on the wall. Onscreen, a female acrobat is busy giving a round-house kick to a soldier wearing a beret. He retaliates with three rapid-fire punches to her face, and the crowd reacts with a cheer.

The guy who answered to Motko at the mall food court earlier is standing beside a cute brunette, and the two of them are manically working over the buttons on two large controllers.

"Whoa!" someone cheers. "Now finish him, Shana."

I realize Shana's character is the soldier, and she's undeniably winning this match. The one loop-through when Shana and I spoke, her voice was soft and she seemed a bit on the shy side.

Now her face goes red as she screams, "Die, you meat bag. Die!" Apparently, I'm really bad at reading people. But it also shows just how much different settings affect how people act.

For instance, I happen to know that Motko is whip smart when it comes to calculus, since he's in my class and has known the answer to the first difficult question every time the teacher asked it. But right now, he's either drunk or half asleep, because he's grunting illegibly while jabbing at the remote control with both thumbs.

"I play winner," Colton pipes in.

When Motko finally dies onscreen, Shana takes his remote and holds it out toward Colton. "You sure you can handle this?" She is clearly flirting with him, and my jealousy level shoots to DEFCON 5. Or maybe that's DEFCON 1; whichever is the high one. I make a mental note to look that up.

But I've worked too dang hard to get to this point just to lose Colton to another girl because she's awesome at playing video games. I can be awesome at playing videogames too.

"Let me give it a shot," I say, plucking the remote from her hand.

Her eyebrows shoot up in surprise when we begin, and my Asian fighter instantly wallops her soldier with a few good kicks to the face. The crowd presses in expectantly, but my luck runs out after two roundhouses.

Within moments, my character is bleeding profusely as the announcer describes my beating in new, creative ways, calling out things like, "Spectacle!" "Failure!" and finally, mercifully, "DE-feat-ed!"

Colton eases the controller out of my hands. "Let's try that again."

I whisper to myself, "Let's try that again, *indeed*," and step back to make room. In my mind, I'm already figuring out how many loops it will take for me to become an expert gamer. Skipping school to practice playing seems like an excellent plan.

Colton uses the remote to change his character into what looks like an adorable little white squeaky toy. Next, he switches the background to a boxing ring, and the announcer declares, "Free for all!" and counts down from ten to "Go!"

The whole crowd in the living room begins cheering at the television as Colton and Shana's characters ruthlessly attack each other.

It is immediately obvious that Colton is even better at the game than she is, and he seems to take great delight in beating her soldier senseless. Once the announcer confirms his victory, Colton gives a satisfied grunt and punches both arms victoriously in the air.

The room erupts into cheers as if we're at a major sporting

event and the home team just scored. Colton smiles, keeping his hands up as he turns to me.

"What do you say, Andie?" He asks loud enough to be heard over the noise, "A kiss for the winner?"

I widen my eyes at him. This is an odd and awkward and *extremely public* way to get my first kiss.

On one hand, I'm happy that I do *not* need to become an expert gamer after all, since that wasn't something I really wanted to spend the next few weeks or possibly months doing. But on the other hand, I have no idea what's about to happen. I mean, this isn't an ordinary physical attraction/dopamine situation. This is some advanced-level space-time continuum stuff.

Will there be a flash of lightning when our lips touch? Is levitation a possibility? Maybe I'll pass out and realize this was all a dream when I awake. Can I be instantly whisked into the correct point of time in the future?

I try to figure out the proper timeline since school started and estimate we would probably be well past the holidays if time hadn't stopped working on day one.

As I've been debating whether to kiss Colton, a forceful chant has been rising up. People are calling out, "Kiss! Kiss! Kiss!" as if Colton and I are an old rock band my dad still listens to.

It would be easy enough to simply ignore the group, go home, and cycle through tomorrow. Maybe angle for a more secluded moment. Now that I know the layout and players of the party, I'm pretty sure I could redirect all this action. But then, I don't really want *more* action. I'm thinking a public kiss will at least keep things respectable.

This is it. *I'm going for it.*

I give a small smile and lean toward Colton. The private way he smiles back makes me realize right away I was wrong about the whole "respectable" part. He snakes both arms around my torso, and dips me backward in one smooth motion.

I can feel my face heat as the blood runs up my neck. While my blush gains force, Colton stands over me, mugging for the chanters. Who are now wildly hooting and hollering at us.

"Go for it!" someone calls, and next thing I know, Colton's lips are sealed to mine as he holds me firmly in my uncomfortable backbend.

There are no lightning bolts. There is no levitating. No waking up from a dream.

As Colton makes a big show of mashing his lips into mine, what I experience is the feeling of his hand boldly working its way from my back toward my bottom.

I try to squirm free as the crowd's *Ooooohs* grow louder and louder, but Colton holds me fast. With both wide hands. Including the one that is now fully *cupping my butt*.

I go blind with rage.

Breaking free, I channel every bit of my cheerleading training to deliver a powerful flex kick, nailing him right between the legs.

Colton goes down so fast and hard, a unanimous "Oh!" sounds from the crowd surrounding us.

In my mind, I see a montage of movie clips showing numerous cheap groin kicks and pain-filled, comical reactions as Colton curls into the fetal position on the floor.

Everyone stands silently gawping as if I've just hit the pause button on the gaming control. Time seems to have frozen completely. Like, now instead of rewinding and looping on me, everything has just stopped.

Finally, Shana unpauses to give a brief giggle.

Colton yells out a nasty endearment in my direction, and I turn on the stems of my high heels and make a dash for the door. On my way through the living room, I knock into someone's red Solo cup and beer splashes onto my jeans. I run from the house without looking back.

I've pictured how my first kiss would go many, many times, but I never in my wildest imagination ever envisioned it like this.

● ● ●

My calves burn as I walk the three miles home, and I can't even call my mom because I reek of spilled beer. But, hey, at least I'm totally preoccupied by that awful image of my very first kiss. I can't believe Colton publicly groped me in the middle of a house party. And true love or not (and obviously *not*), now that we've kissed, I'm pretty sure I'll be stuck living with this version of today.

I would've been better off with my very first do-over. In fact, I'd almost prefer the original, humiliating pink polka-dot dress version. Almost.

All my hard work to establish myself as Colton's girlfriend has been a complete waste. Plus, of course, I'll be living out the rest of my senior year as a social pariah.

I find an empty soda can and stomp on it with the front of my toe, flattening it so I can kick it along the road as I walk. Each time a car drives by, I tense up, afraid that Colton or one of his friends will come after me, but nobody does.

It's just me, and my used-up, flattened, empty soda can slowly making our way home. By the time I hobble in the front door, I'm feeling just as raw and scraped up as the crumpled can.

Mom is sitting on the giant pink couch, and turns to greet me with an excited, "Did you have fun?"

Her raised eyebrows drop fast when she sees my expression. "I kicked my date in the groin and had to walk home in these heels. So, ya know, not such a great night overall."

Mom holds both hands over her mouth. "Did he try something?"

I nod my head. "He got a little too friendly, but don't worry. I knew just how to handle him."

"You . . . kicked him in the groin?" Mom slides her hands down, and I see she's smiling proudly. "I suppose that's one way to send a clear message. Do I need to get involved?"

"No. I took care of it." I'm just mad at myself for not paying enough attention to whether I even liked Colton after spending so much time with him. I was so smitten over the summer that I didn't really look at the way he treated me, let alone other people. I have started to feel very, very stupid for spending all these endless days doing everything I could to impress him.

"Well, at least you only wasted one night," Mom says brightly, and I resist the urge to burst into tears. She looks at me with sympathy, and gives one of her typical responses. "I already queued up a good movie, in case you came home early."

"Of course you did." I sigh and fall into the pink leather couch beside her, pulling the blanket over my jeans. The beer smell is mostly gone by now, but it's better to be safe.

"It's okay if you don't want to watch it." Mom sounds a little hurt.

"What's the movie?"

Her excitement is immediate, like I've just flipped her switch to On. "Well, I really wanted you to see this before your first day at the new school," she says.

"It's fine," I say, dully. "I'll simply rewind today."

Mom gives me a slight shove and laughs, but I can't.

"Well, what movie is it?" I ask. Her suggestions have changed based on my moods and our interactions after school.

Mom slides the DVD case resting on the end table into my hands. On the cover is the iconic eighties gang of teenagers. She whispers in my ear, "*The Breakfast Club.*"

Obviously, she can't remember watching it with me the first night I looped. I slide it back to her. "Sorry, Mom, but I saw this last year when it was streaming."

Her face falls, but quickly recovers. "Well, you're seeing it again with me. Right now."

"It's actually a little late to be starting a movie," I say, but my mother acts like she's deaf in one ear.

She aims the remote at the TV and says conspiratorially, "We'll just watch the *beginning*." Her familiar tactic to suck me into a film.

With a sigh, I slump down deeper into the pink leather. It may have taken me a bunch of tries to get to this point of social exile, but I certainly made it. And thanks to my first kiss, this could be my new reality.

If so, I might as well get used to sitting under a blanket on the sofa, rewatching old movies with my mom.

Onscreen, the five teenagers arrive at Saturday detention one by one, and I want to cry and tell Mom everything that's been happening to me. But she looks utterly enthralled by the familiar film, so I snuggle down and allow the sharp dialogue to comfort me.

When Molly Ringwald's Claire Standish greets her obvious social equal, the athletic Andrew—played by Emilio Estevez—I remember rooting for the two of them to get together the first time we watched this. Which I now see would've made for zero character arcs and a really super-boring, non-iconic movie.

The weird and crazy Allison must've been a fantastic role for the actress to play, and the geek, Brian, is so perfectly awkward, he's almost painful to watch. I wonder for a moment why modern directors don't use truly geeky adolescents to play adolescents anymore. Bender—the roughest character, and played by the actor who's clearly the farthest from high school age—reminds me a bit of the goth guy I used to run into every day.

Mom and I silently watch as the social walls between the characters are taken down brick by brick. As the nerd and the athlete open up, and see that they both have similar pressures, they begin to change the way they view each other. *We are not all so different.* I think of the goth guy again.

And I get the tiniest seed of an idea.

It is obvious I've ruined my chances of getting in with the most popular kids at Punxsutawney High. In going after the hunkiest of the hunky boys, I have flown too close to the sun. But maybe I can infiltrate one of the other cliques and survive the rest of high school with some other group instead of as a friendless freak.

None of the other groups were at the party tonight. Maybe nobody else will remember me and I can reinvent myself. As soon as the movie ends, I tell Mom I want to watch just a few special features, and tell her goodnight.

"I knew you'd come around," Mom says, smiling. "There are some good cast interviews on this one, but don't stay up too late. It's a school night."

As soon as she disappears upstairs, I start digging through the bags of clothes beside the couch that hold her latest thrift store scores.

Mom must've already started preparing for her favorite holiday, Halloween, because I pull out a pure black dress fit for a witch. I hold it up to my front. Maybe just as Splenda-sweet Claire ends up with big, bad Bender, I'm meant to be with Goth Guy or someone equally misunderstood.

I immediately begin assembling an outfit. As well as a plan.

chapter 10

When I wake up on the couch with the *Pretty in Pink* DVD playing on the television screen, for the first time I feel relieved.

It's nice that I won't have to deal with being a social outcast, but erasing that awful first kiss with Colton is what makes me truly happy. Now that I've realized I don't even like him, getting him to go away will be my first order of business this morning.

Thankfully, as soon as he sees my outfit, he nearly backs out the front door.

Mom gives him a commiserating nod. "I couldn't talk her out of it. You must be Colton."

I grin from underneath my mini black veil. I made it using a swatch from a layer of netting in one of Mom's puffy fifties skirts. It's very Winona Ryder circa *Beetlejuice*.

"If you want to run ahead to school without me, Colt, I'm really fine with catching the bus. I'm sure you have friends to meet up with, and I need to add another layer of eyeliner anyway." I blink my kohl-rimmed eyes at him. I've even trimmed my bangs into short spikes as a show of commitment to this new direction in my appearance.

Colton can't seem to stop staring through the black veil at my bangs.

"It might not be a bad idea for you to learn the bus schedule," he concedes. "Are you sure you'll be okay?" He already has his hand on the doorknob.

"I'm good." I give a fake smile and wave energetically. I couldn't be happier to watch him walk away. In fact, I don't even bother watching him walk away.

As soon as the door closes behind Colton, Mom gives a growl. "What a jerk."

"Guess he's not a fan of *Beetlejuice*." I shrug.

"Well, I may not love your outfit either, but I guess you're better off discovering the guy's a superficial creep now, before you invest a ton of time."

I laugh so hard and so long that inky tears stream down my face and I fall onto the couch with the hiccups.

Mom looks like she's ready to call upstairs for Dad to give me a quickie psych evaluation, so I pull it together. She asks, "Are you positive about that outfit?"

Wiping the black laughter tears from my eyes, I remind her, "You're the one who said I could be anyone I want to be."

"I did say that, didn't I?"

"Repeatedly." I smirk.

My dad makes his way down the steps and Mom hurries over to put one arm around his shoulder. She gestures to me with the other. "What do you think of our daughter's new look?"

Dad lets out a long, low whistle. He hasn't seen me since I went upstairs earlier to get ready. He grins. "She's certainly making a statement, isn't she?"

"Perhaps." Mom wrinkles her nose. "But what is she really *saying* with this outfit?"

"I'm saying that my new favorite *Breakfast Club* member is Allison." I hold out my arms dramatically, and add, "Pre-makeover, of course."

"You watched that without me?" Mom looks stricken, and I realize my mistake. She doesn't remember me watching *The Breakfast Club* with her twice now, because those nights never happened.

I let my arms drop to my sides and dip my head so I'm looking at her through the black tulle material. "It was streaming last year and I caught it after school one day. Sorry, once it started, I couldn't stop watching it."

Mom sighs. "Well, I suppose there are worse movies to draw inspiration from. But why couldn't you have gone with something from the movie last night? Something maybe *pretty* or something *pink*?" She laughs, and I feel a tremor run up my spine.

"Mom, please don't . . ."

"Oh yeah, what did you think of *Pretty in Pink* anyway?"

I close my eyes and take a deep breath. "To be honest, Mom? I loved it at first, but after thinking the whole thing over a few times, I'm not a huge fan."

Her eyebrows shoot up, but before she can ask me any more questions I head upstairs to finish getting ready, mumbling quietly to myself, "Not a fan of that movie *at all*."

● ● ●

The curdled looks I get while walking into the school remind me of my true first day when I wore the vintage pink polka dots.

At least that time I was being seen with golden boy Colton, so people treated me like a human person. Now, I'm completely on my own.

I'm looking-acting-sounding-feeling 100 percent goth, and it is oddly liberating. From the small nod the goth girl gave when I climbed onto the bus to the guy wearing eyeliner who held open the school's front door, the only people making eye contact with me today are those dressed in all black.

The rest of the students I pass either avert their gaze or cringe the tiniest bit away from me. I stride down the familiar hallways with my head held high, proudly showing off my black fingerless gloves by pulling them up higher on my wrists.

When I nearly collide with my goth guy, he stops and greets me with a smirk. "Nice gloves." He's weaving his Sharpie between his fingers. "I'm Czyre. You must he new here."

Grinning, I say, "Something like that."

Czyre invites me to follow him with the gruff command, "Come on."

I follow him to the space underneath the stairs, marveling at how much changing my look has changed our interaction. He usually seems vaguely horrified by me when we run into each other, although the worst time by far was that first day when I wore the pink polka dots.

Once my eyes adjust to the dim light, the goths' lair isn't nearly as scary as I imagined. And I finally get a closer look at the cartoons drawn on the back walls.

There's one of a cheerleader that's clearly supposed to be Tammy, standing in her cheer skirt and shouting with all her strength for onlookers to "CARE!"

The crowd is yelling back at her, "WE CAN'T!"

The other drawings consist of ironic observations about the various teachers and a few prominent students from the other cliques. I move in close to one that shows two circus freaks facing each other. They're both wearing giant clown shoes and one is saying, "I thought it was my turn to wear big shoes today. Now everyone is going to look at us funny."

They're obviously drawn by the same artist who drew the stressed-out toddlers on the bleachers. I point to the cartoons and ask, "Who does these?"

A girl whose eyes are swimming in eyeliner looks me up and down. "They're Czyre's. But nobody can know he's the artist."

Czyre gives me a big grin and points to a knotted symbol at the bottom corner of one of the cartoons. "This is my signature."

The girl pulls up the cuff of her tight black pants. Pointing to a small tattoo on her leg, she says, "He's good. He designed this one for me."

"Very cool." I'm honestly impressed. I've never been much of a tattoo person, but the Celtic-looking knot peeking out from above her combat boot is small and artful.

"It's a trinity symbol," she says proudly, and Czyre looks embarrassed by all the compliments.

He grumbles, "Yeah, well, Bridget is a preacher's kid, so of course she would choose the holy trinity symbol for her big act of teenage rebellion."

Bridget gives Czyre a punch. "Seriously? That's how you introduce me?" Turning my way, she says, "I like people to get to know me better before finding out about the whole PK thing. They always assume I'm going to shove a pamphlet in their hands or start flinging holy water on them or something just because I'm a Christian."

Czyre rolls his eyes. "Bridge has a bit of a complex, but she's pretty cool."

"Yeah," says a guy leaning against the back wall. "Her dad just happens to work for Jesus, that's all."

I laugh. "My dad's a psychologist, and he devoted a whole chapter of a book he wrote to examining my behavior when I was younger," I say. "It made me a little bit paranoid about being judged."

"Yeah, I know that feeling." Bridget smiles. "Like I'm part of an exhibit that's open every Sunday."

"Well, it's safe here," Czyre says. I glance up just in time to catch Colton peering into our lair. He does a double take when he sees me, but then heads up the stairs without giving any indication that the two of us know each other.

The guy leaning against the wall must have seen him too, because he says, "Just the usual zoo display here under the stairs at Punxsutawney High."

Czyre says to me, "We're not the mindless animals. They are."

Everyone in this school seems to have a distrustful "us vs. them" mentality. I just want to figure out where the goths I'm speaking with fit into the whole picture of me and my never-ending first day here.

A girl in all black with matching black lips and a nose ring appears at the entryway. "Hey, guys," she calls into our cave. "I can't hang out this morning, need to get my schedule switched. But wanted to get this to you before I forget, Bridget."

She reaches a hand into her bag, and I picture her pulling out cigarettes or drugs, and feel my whole body wince. I'm glad it's too dark for anyone to notice, because when her hand emerges it's holding a large can of bean soup.

"What do you guys do with those?" I ask, trying to remember the drug warnings I learned back in health class. I know people do stupid stuff like sniff glue and drink hand sanitizer, but I can't think of anything they can do to get high using a can of bean soup.

I realize everyone is looking at me, and feel more claustrophobic than I did a moment ago.

"What is that supposed to mean?" Czyre asks.

Bridget laughs. "Leave her alone. You have to admit bean soup is a strange gift." She gives the big can a mini toss in the air and tells me, "My dad runs a food pantry at the church, so people are constantly handing me nonperishable items."

She thanks the girl, who is apparently named True, and shoves the big can into her black bag. "These guys right here are the most generous group in the entire school." She looks around with obvious affection for her fellow goths.

"Oh," is all I can think to say, because becoming one of them is not at all what I expected.

I wish there was a way to show everyone else that surly first impressions aren't always accurate. And that even a marginally horrible person (*cough* me *cough*) is capable of changing her perspective.

● ● ●

When I get to homeroom, Tom peeks under my little veil. "Andie? Is that you?"

"Hi, Tom." I start rooting through my black leather bag. Not looking for anything in particular, just trying to maintain my aloof goth persona.

He asks, "Are you okay? I mean, your dress is great, but all summer at the theater, I never saw you wear eyeliner even once."

I turn my kohl-rimmed eyes toward him, and he looks at me so earnestly, I can't help but smile. "Yeah, sometimes I like to color outside the lines." I bat my lashes at him.

He laughs. "This Tim Burton aesthetic isn't really what I pictured when I was encouraging you to be creative."

"Oh, I see," I say. "You have something against *Beetleju*—"

His eyes go wide and he puts a finger to his lips. "Don't say his *name*!" He holds in a smile as he looks around pretending to be paranoid.

I laugh. "Oh, what? You mean I shouldn't say *Beetlejuice, Beetlejuice, Beetle*—"

He lunges across his desk and puts a hand over my mouth, and the two of us dissolve into laughter. In the movie, saying the name three times conjures up Michael Keaton's wacky titular character (and if you haven't seen the film, you might want to take a serious look at your own life's priorities).

Tom is still grinning at me when he drops his hand from my mouth, and I realize too late that half the class has turned to watch us. We both disengage and face forward.

"I think I got lipstick on your hand," I say quietly.

He pulls out a purple bandana and holds it out to me. "I think I smeared you a little there, sorry."

I take out my phone and use it as a mirror to fix my lips. When I'm done, I say, "Nice hankie" as I toss it back to him. "Why purple?"

"Embrace the strange and unusual, Andie." He wipes his hand on it and repeats, "Embrace the strange and unusual."

Which, in case you didn't already know, is from the movie. (And again, if you didn't; take stock of your life.)

As I make my way through the morning, I enjoy the anonymity of being invisible to most of the people I pass in the hallways. It's a bit counterintuitive that I also like that instant connection I feel with the other goths when we cross paths with each other.

Every time I run into Tom, he starts miming the conga dance they do in *Beetlejuice*. I finally give in and join him right before English class, putting my hands on his hips and allowing him to lead me through the door. As we work our way around the classroom together, his movements get more and more exaggerated. Since I'm not participating in very goth-like behavior, I try to keep my head down so my veil covers my smile. But I can't hide how much fun I'm having.

Finally, Mr. Demers enters the room. "Ah, how nice to see students so thrilled to be here," he says. "*Apollo* would certainly enjoy this dance. We'll be learning about Apollo shortly." Louder, he calls out, "Can anyone guess what we'll be studying this semester?"

Without raising my hand, I call out, "Mythology!" at the same moment Tom says, "The Greek gods."

Mr. Demers chuckles and tells us to both please take a seat. Under his breath he says, "Looks like Cupid may have some easy targets."

If Tom hears him, he pretends not to, which makes sense. Tom could never think of me romantically. He's literally the only person who witnessed me throwing myself at Colton all summer long. I can erase every mistake I've made since school started, but I can never go back far enough to undo that. Though now I sort of wish I could.

At lunchtime, Bridget cuts in the food line beside me like we've been friends for ages. Once we've gotten our matching scoops of brown goo, she brings me out to the center courtyard, where the rest of the gang sits around a table.

They're laughing and arguing in a way they probably wouldn't if their table wasn't situated behind a wall of bushes growing out of cement buckets. I never would've found them on my own, but now that I think about it, I vaguely remember hearing noise coming from this corner of the outdoor hexagon.

I suppose I was always so focused on Colton that I never even wondered who was making the ruckus behind the bushes. I kind of imagined it was some teachers letting off a little first-day-of-school steam. It's almost comical how much more subdued and bored-seeming this group is in public. Here, they're acting downright rowdy.

When Bridget and I reach the oversized table, True is busy taunting one of the purple-haired guys.

She's saying, ". . . and *this* from a guy who's willing to eat chocolate that tastes like *dog poo*!"

"That was in a game of '*would you rather*'!" he yells. "You can't take that out of context! The alternative was eating *dog poo* that tastes like *chocolate*." The smile in his voice tells me the two of them are either a couple now, or they will be soon.

Czyre is busy working on a drawing that features an assembly line rolling out identical copies of football players. A guy with a clipboard and a badge that reads "quality inspector" is facing the woman running the machine. He's saying, "Careful there. You nearly made that one unique." The look of horror Czyre has drawn on the woman's face indicates this would be an unforgiveable offense.

I look around at the group. It needs to be said. "But from the outside, don't you think people assume *we're* all the same? I mean, we're all dressed pretty much alike, aren't we?"

I'm suddenly being studied by a half dozen pairs of glowering eyeballs. The eyes slide from me to consider each other. For the first time since kicking Colton in the groin, I'm worried I'll need to defend myself. Uniqueness is clearly sacred here.

Finally, True gives me a small smile. "Hey," she says, "I'll stop wearing black when they come up with a darker color."

The rest of the group murmurs their agreement, but Czyre studies me more closely. "What were your friends like at your old school?"

I try to hide the panic in my chest by shoving it down as far as it will go. "My best friend and I were, you know, sort of outsiders. Although our school was so small, we were also kind of insiders too."

Bridget says, "I think Czyre's trying to ask if you decided to dress the way you're dressed out of the blue this morning."

"No, give her a chance to talk," he says. "You obviously have some sophisticated ideas about social groups, Andie. I'd like to hear more about your definition of outsiders versus insiders."

I consider trying to tell them the truth. If there's any group that might believe the incredible reality I'm living, it would probably be this one. Instead, I come only partially clean to them and admit I didn't always wear this type of outfit.

"There weren't enough of us to have cliques at our old school," I say. "So no one really bothered dressing differently. I usually just wore jeans and a T-shirt, and so did the rest of my classmates."

Bridget squints at my face. "So, then, how did you get so great at doing eyeliner?"

"By spending a LOT of time practicing." I laugh. "Actually, I got the idea from watching the movie *The Breakfast Club*. I decided I liked Allison better before her big makeover, so I copied her look." For a moment, everyone stares at me, and I'm afraid I'm going to have to retry getting to know this group tomorrow, but then Czyre laughs.

"Do you make all your decisions based on movie observations?" he asks.

I grin. "I can think of worse places to seek wisdom."

As we eat lunch, I share more about my favorite movies, but quickly realize I'm the only movie-obsessed person at the table. Bridget and I shift to comparing notes on our dad's professions and how much they affected us growing up.

"My dad had an office at home where he would meet with patients," I say. "I remember wishing he worked at a normal office when I was younger. I would wonder what each person's damage was as they came through our front door."

Bridget shrugs. "I've always thought it was kind of nice having my dad around in the mornings, sitting in his prayer chair and sometimes making us breakfast. But then when I started going to school, everyone began seeing me as some sort of Jesus freak."

Czyre says, "You are a *total* Jesus freak, Bridget, always talking about how much God loves us all, and how we can lean on him and ask him for help when we're hurting."

"He does love us!" She laughs. "So bleeping much! If pointing that out to people makes me a Jesus freak, I guess that's what I am."

"Watch those bleeping 'bleeps,' Bridge," Czyre teases, and I decide that *bleep* is my new favorite swear.

"Isn't she adorable?" True says.

The purple-haired guy she's been flirting with wraps an arm around her from behind and says, "You're adorable," and kisses her on the cheek. Apparently, they're already a couple.

Bridget says, "I tried to fit in with the other social groups, but really this is the only gang who accepted me just as I am."

"We *like* freaks here," Czyre says with a smile.

She rolls her eyes. "I started dressing like this to make my mom mad, but it turned out she loves this whole group."

"We all call Bridget's mom, 'Mom,'" says the guy hugging True, and a few others call out, "*Mom!*"

Bridget says, "She's driving some of us to the mall later. You're welcome to join us."

I nod. "I'd love to come."

Czyre has been working on a new drawing, and he turns it around to face me. It's a sketch of a movie reel with a winding ribbon of film curling in a dramatic loop.

Bridget's face spreads into a wide smile. "Now *that* would make an amazing tattoo."

I pull the picture closer so I can get a better look. "That is fantastic," I say. "Too bad I'm underage, or I'd definitely get that tattoo on my foot someplace."

Bridget makes a face. "Your foot?"

"It seems like it wouldn't hurt as much," I say.

"It also doesn't show as much." She pulls up the leg of her jeans to admire her trinity symbol. "My next one is going right on the back of my neck, no playing around."

Czyre says, "Nice. But not all of us have parents who are fine with visible tattoos."

I turn to Bridget. "Your dad doesn't mind?"

She shrugs. "Both my folks have tats. My mom loved this design so much, she got us matching tattoos for my sweet sixteen. Hers is on her inner wrist."

"I can see why your mom is such a hit. It's cool that she gave her permission before you turned eighteen."

Czyre's eyes actually sparkle a little as he leans in close. "Well, if you're serious about getting a foot tattoo, I think I can help you out."

I look at the design he's drawn and swallow. If I'm being completely honest, I was mostly getting into the whole spirit of talking about tattoos here. I've never really considered getting one beyond deciding the foot would be a cool spot. But when I look up, everyone around the table is watching me. There's no graceful way to punk out now. "Help me, how?" I ask.

Czyre says, "My guy works out of the basement at the mall, and he'll be happy to do your tattoo without special permission."

"I, uh, don't have any money. Aren't tattoos kind of expensive?"

Czyre says, "He's actually an apprentice who needs the practice. It'll be totally free."

There are lots of things that are awesome to get for free. I do not think tattoos are one of those things, but I'm pretty much out of excuses, except for, "I don't think I can get a ride to the m—"

"I'm giving you a ride, remember?" Bridget cuts in before I can even finish stating my excuse.

"Right, thanks." I try to smile, but my face doesn't feel natural.

"It's settled," Czyre says with a very natural-looking grin. "One other thing, though." He puts a hand over mine. "Foot tattoos actually hurt the worst of all."

My unnatural smile falls completely. "Great."

chapter 11

"Woodchucks! Woodchucks! Woodchucks!"

We're walking inside the mall when the familiar chanting rises from the direction of the food court. I look over and see the football players surrounding Colton, practically lifting him onto their shoulders as Kaia and her friends look on.

I stop a moment and watch as the guys pound each other's backs a few more times before all sitting down at the table piled high with food.

Colton grabs Kaia into a playful headlock and kisses her on the cheek as she laughs and feigns resisting. Everyone is obviously having a great time, and I realize something: Kaia fits in perfectly with Colton and his life and his friends. The two of them were clearly meant to be together. *And she was never my nasty rival at all.*

"Andie? You okay?" Bridget's hand on my arm makes me aware of the fact that I'm standing in the middle of the mall, openly gaping at my sort-of ex-boyfriend kissing his perfect-for-him new girlfriend.

"I'm good. Really," I say, and scamper a few steps to catch up.

Bridget and I are on our way to meet Czyre and the rest of

the gang at the shop where his friend is an apprentice. Three of us are planning to get tattoos, but I'm clearly the most terrified.

We all rode together in the van, but she and I stopped to buy me flip-flops so I don't have to put shoes over my new tattoo right away. Of course, I'll still need to cover it up before my parents see it, but there's plenty of time to worry about that after I've dealt with what promises to be an excruciatingly painful visit to a not-quite-ready-for-paying-customers tattoo artist. *Awesome.*

The rest of the mall isn't as filled with Punxsutawney students as I'd expected. Bridget and I have walked from one end to the other, and the only people I've seen besides Colton and his friends are Tom and his odd tribe. Today, he gives me a friendly wave and mimes a few conga dance moves.

I mimic his conga from across the mall, but then Bridget looks at me as if I've lost my mind. "What are you doing?" she asks.

I shrug at Tom and keep walking.

As we enter the glass elevator, I ask Bridget, "Do you really think getting a tattoo at the mall is a great idea?"

She punches the B button and leans against the railing as we head toward the basement. "This is perfect," she says. "Kind of like an ironic twist on the cliché of getting your ears pierced at the mall."

"Not sure if that counts as irony, or if it's just a plain bad idea."

"It can't be as bad as getting a tattoo at a carnival," she says. "Or, I once saw a tattoo van that traveled around. This is way better than getting your tattoo in a van."

"You speak truth," I say.

"This guy is really nice. You have nothing to worry about."

The doors slide open on the lower level, and Czyre is waiting there with the rest of the group. Bridget tells him, "I think she's getting cold feet."

"Well, then," he says, "I guess we'd better get a little ink on those footsies to warm them right up."

As soon as I see the entrance to the shop, two things become very clear to me. 1) Ironic or not, getting a tattoo at the mall is not remotely related to going to Claire's to have my ears pierced, and 2) There is a good reason parents need to give permission for their underage offspring to get tattoos: so they can intervene and save them from themselves.

Or in this case, save them from severe peer pressure. I'm still trying to figure out how to extract myself from this situation when a young man covered in ink walks through the swinging doors that lead to some unknowable dark lair.

"Hey there, George!" he calls to Czyre, and I give Bridget a questioning look.

She tips her head toward mine. "Czyre is actually George's middle name. Just go with it."

Which seems to be today's ongoing theme.

I "just go with it" as the tattoo guy introduces himself as Rodney and has me hop up into the red leather chair.

I "just go with it" as George/Czyre draws his design directly onto my foot.

And then I "just go with it" as I admire the movie reel image on my foot, which in truth does look sort of fantastic.

Trying not to think of the buzzing needle heading my way, I lie back with my knee bent so my bare right foot is set flat against the leather cushion. My toes wiggle in anticipation of the pain and Rodney tells me to relax.

"Here," he says, handing me a pillow. "Hug this, and maybe George can hold your hand. Squeezing something will help you keep your foot loose."

"Ha," I say. "*Footloose.*" But nobody else seems to get the reference.

I sit up and wrap both arms around the pillow. Czyre hands me a stick of gum and I say, "Thanks," and take his hand. I chew quickly and give a practice squeeze of his hand. He doesn't flinch, and so I amp my grip up to a death hold.

The very first poke of the needle stings so much that I curl my toes and kick my whole leg out in shock. *Bleep! that hurts.*

"Whoa!" Rodney yells, and I nearly start crying. He rubs my foot and apologizes for his outburst. "That was my bad," he says. "I should've warned you that I was about to start, and maybe do a few practice pokes to make sure you were ready."

I squeeze Czyre's hand even tighter and nod. "I'm ready for real now." I want to get this over with.

Resisting my natural reflexes, I focus on holding myself still while Rodney leans in so close, his face is nearly touching my foot. I wonder for a moment if Rodney is half-blind or something, then decide I don't really want to know.

As the tattoo needle works its way over the top of my foot, I gradually become numb to the pain. Though every time Rodney passes his needle over a bone, my pain level spikes—so at least my foot is completely *filled with bones.*

I say to Czyre, "I guess all the bones in the feet are what make this extra painful."

He nods while keeping his eyes glued to what Rodney is doing. "Locations that don't have much muscle or fat can be quite uncomfortable."

I squeeze his hand and the pillow simultaneously. "Yeah, *uncomfortable*. That's just how I would describe this feeling."

"You're doing great," Bridget tells me from down by my foot.

To which I respond, "*Ow, ow, ow.* I need a break."

"Hold still," Rodney says. "I'll give you a break in a minute. Just need to finish this outline."

"Wow, you're nearly finished with—" I look at my foot. "Oh." Beneath the spots of blood and spilled ink covering my foot, I can see he's not quite done with the thin, round outline of the movie reel. He hasn't even started on the winding ribbon of film, not to mention filling in and shading the whole thing.

"Sorry. I'm new to this, so I move a little slow."

"Oh, that's cool," I say. "Better than making a mistake." My lip trembles as I try to smile. *This is one way to dramatically slow down time.*

When we finally take a short break, I notice Czyre is shaking the blood back into the white fingertips of the hand I've been squeezing. When it's time to start again, he offers it back with a grimace.

"Are you sure?" I say. "You might need use of that hand again at some point, and I don't want to cause permanent nerve damage."

He laughs. "No worries. This isn't my drawing hand."

As Rodney continues making progress on my movie reel, I try to distract myself by going over the details of today's time loop.

As a fresh stabbing pain emanates from my foot, I come to the not-so-startling realization that I am not a tattoo type of girl. This whole thing hurts way more than any benefits I can envision. It is taking every ounce of my considerable self-control to not kick Rodney in the teeth and run for my life right now.

I picture Czyre's reaction to that and can easily envision him protecting me from Rodney's wrath. He is a great guy, but as he gives me an encouraging smile, I come to yet another realization. One that *is* slightly startling.

This whole first-kiss plan to stop myself from time looping is turning into a total bust. Czyre is not my true love. I stave off a fresh wave of pain by squeezing his hand again, and he confirms everything I'm feeling by kindly brushing a lock of my hair out of my eyes. It feels like I'm being comforted by a brother or a cousin. Czyre is sweet, but there is zero chemistry between us, and I know he feels it too. Or rather, doesn't.

"Breathe, Andie," he tells me. "You can do this. Visualize the pain as something with limits that you can control."

My eyes widen at him as I pump out short breaths like I'm a woman in labor. My mind wings back to Tammy telling me almost the same exact thing while she encouraged me to push through exhaustion at cheerleading practice. The two of them are similar in other ways too. They each lead their respective groups through gentle encouragement, wrapped in a steely, tough outer layer. In fact, the girls had called Tammy "the egg," and Czyre seems to be just as soft on the inside.

"Don't hyperventilate or you'll pass out," Rodney warns.

Czyre positions himself so he's looking directly in my eyes, and he breathes slowly until I'm able to find his pace and match it. Which just confirms how much he and Tammy are alike, since she was always all about breathing properly while cheerleading.

I try to envision the two of them together, but know that

under the current social conditions at Punxsutawney High, it could literally never happen. Maybe *that's* my purpose in this whole thing. To break down the walls between cliques so that people like Czyre and Tammy can realize that they're perfect for each other.

Maybe I'm supposed to Breakfast Club Punxsutawney High.

I give a whimper of agony that gets Czyre rubbing my arm with the hand I'm not crushing. Again, zero romantic sparks.

While I'm trying to manage the pain I'm feeling, True and her boyfriend, Zepher, walk up to Czyre with an open binder filled with tattoo drawings.

"Do you think you could maybe give this pair a little flair?" True asks, holding out a page of his-'n'-hers tattoos.

I lean up to get a closer look at the design she's pointing to. Beside a drawing of an owl is a tree with an owl hole in it. I grin.

"That is so sweet." I loosen my grip on Czyre's hand.

Despite the opportunity to regain circulation to his fingertips, he doesn't pull away as he considers the drawings. "I think I can add some nice detail to these. Who's getting the owl?"

"I am," True says. "Maybe you can girlie up the design. Make her pretty."

"And I'm going to need some more masculine roots on my tree," says Zepher. "The branches already look pretty cool, though."

As the two of them excitedly discuss placement options that would hide the designs from their parents, I feel something close to happiness for them despite my current state of agony.

They are clearly soul mates and were lucky enough to end up in the same social clique. But now I can't stop wondering about all the other couples who are meant to be together.

Those true loves who are star-crossed because of some stupid, arbitrary social barrier separating them. Like Czyre and Tammy, others may not even realize they're going to the same school with their could-be one true love.

Bridget has been standing down by my foot, confirming that Rodney is doing a good job by saying, "*Oooh,*" and, "*Wow,*" and nodding at me with wide eyes. I try to picture her with Motko or one of the other football players. I could be wrong, and my someone-for-everyone worldview proves I've clearly watched too many romantic movies, but doesn't Bridget deserve to find out if her true love could be hiding in plain sight?

Czyre is already drawing a detailed owl on an index card with his free hand, while Zepher holds the binder Czyre is leaning on and True holds the card still. The three of them are working so hard to support me right now, and I only just met them.

I really wish Colton and his gang of friends could see this side of the goths. They are more alike than different.

I let go of Czyre's hand. "I've got this. Thanks."

Between flinches from needle pricks, I try to formulate a plan for knocking down the school's social walls. I realize that despite my many journeys through the hallways of Punx High, I still don't know all that much about the student groups beyond Colton and the cheerleaders. And now kind of the goths.

I think back to the lunchroom and the carefully segregated tables. Picturing the day I sat with the brainiacs, I remember Tight Headband Girl and Petra talking about the yearbook committee meeting taking place after school in the library. Petra really wanted me to join them.

I may not understand much about the ins and outs of the

different social cliques, but that yearbook meeting could give me a decent overview. If tomorrow is the first day of school again— and I have no reason to believe it won't be—I know exactly where I'm heading after final bell.

When Rodney finally announces he's finished with my tattoo, the group gathers around to admire my foot. It looks so cool that they actually break into applause.

"You rocked that," Bridget says. "I was such a wimp when I got mine, and the leg isn't nearly as painful as the foot."

I feel so warm and delighted, I wonder for a moment if maybe this could be it. *Maybe I am right where I belong.*

True and Zepher have their arms around each other and seem like the happiest two people with matching piercings and black lipstick I've ever seen. But when I look at Czyre now, all I can think of is how much he and Tammy should at least get a chance to know each other. I wish I could somehow make that happen.

At the end of *The Breakfast Club*, the nerd, as played by Anthony Michael Hall, writes a missive to the teacher, Mr. Vernon, chastising him for the way he views the students—as cliques and clichés instead of unique individuals. The kids are sick of being reduced to basic terms like "princess," "brain," and "basket case." AMH eloquently says it may be convenient for the teacher to lump kids into narrow categories, but he is not really seeing any of them for who they are.

And I realize this is still happening with students today, and we're doing it to ourselves. Judging each other based on appearances. Divided by assumptions. Blind to how desperate we all are just for a place to belong.

I still may not know where I'm supposed to fit in, but maybe I'm the one in the right position to make everyone else see the truth. Even if it's only for one day.

chapter 12

When I get home from the mall, my parents greet me at the door together. The way the two of them are holding hands makes it seem like they were just about to report me missing.

"Are you guys okay?" I ask, and they look at each other.

Finally, Dad says, "We're worried about you, Andie."

I can't help but laugh. Which makes Mom look even more horrified. "I don't know what happened, sweetie," she says. "Last night, the two of us were having fun trying on dresses, and then today you're all . . ." She gestures to my goth outfit as if it confirms I've lost my mind.

"I like what I'm wearing." I shift weight off my throbbing foot. After walking around the mall in my flip-flops, I covered my new tattoo with the plastic wrap Rodney gave us and crammed it back into my combat boots. Now it wants to be set free.

"Is this some sort of cry for help?" Dad asks.

I hold in another laugh. "Guys, I can't even get started on how much help I need. But don't worry, I'm working things out."

"But we want to be here for you," Mom says. "You don't need to work things out on your own."

Dad says, "Andie, please let us in."

I envision sitting down and telling them everything that I've been through. Reliving the same day over and over. Learning to become a cheerleader and wear high heels and do a killer smoky eye. Kissing and subsequently kicking Colton. The trips to the mall, the tattoo, all of it. But as I take in the stress on both their faces, I can't justify making them more upset right now.

I'm probably going to reset in a few hours anyway. And if this was my last day looping, then I don't want to kick off the rest of my life with a field trip to mandatory therapy.

"I was trying out a new look," I tell them. "Don't worry, I just need to figure out where I fit in. Things at this school are a bit . . . different."

Mom says, "Well, I know you said you were copying Allison before her makeover in *The Breakfast Club*, so maybe tomorrow you could copy Andie from the movie last night. Now *there* was an outcast who had style."

Ugh. "Please, Mom. I do not want to talk about *Pretty in Pink*. That movie ruined my life."

Mom and Dad look at each other, and I turn and start running up the stairs.

Dad calls after me, "Wait, Andie, I'd like to hear more about your life feeling ruined."

I ignore him, continuing with my escape, but can hear him say to my mom, "See? This is what you get for using movies as a parenting method."

When I get to my room, I immediately drop to the floor to take off my boot. I peel back the plastic wrap protecting my tattoo and see that the thick salve Rodney rubbed into my foot has given the tattoo a glossy sheen. The design is pink and irritated-looking around the edges—but it is beautiful.

Impulsively, I dig out the black pumps I've trained in and pull them on. Expertly, I stride directly toward my full-length mirror, admiring the way the shoes perfectly frame the cool tattoo.

I've nearly reached the mirror when my mom bursts into the room.

"Don't you ever knock?" I ask as I fall to a crouching position, trying to cover my foot from her view.

"Andie!" she says. "When did you learn to walk in pumps that way?"

I pretend to tip over, with my foot aimed strategically *and painfully* underneath me. "I'm just starting to learn, and thanks for making me *fall*."

"I'm sorry," she says. "Your dad and I are just really worried about you."

"Yeah, well, I'm worried about me too." One hand covers my foot as I slide awkwardly toward my closet. I hide my foot under the pile of clothes that permanently occupy the floor there and I get a great idea to distract her. "What do you think of me wearing *this* to school tomorrow?" I hold up the pink polka-dotted dress that I tossed in here when I took it off this morning. I may have given it a couple of kicks too.

Mom grins. "Oh, Andie. I think that would be just *perfect*."

I try to look sheepish. "I just thought the heels would be a nice touch."

"I'll leave you to practicing, sweetie." Mom takes a few steps into my room and kisses me on top of my head. "Walking in heels is all about spending time practicing in them."

I try not to wince as I shift to cover my tattooed foot with the dress, scratching my tender skin with the edge of crinoline. "Thanks, Mom."

If only she knew just how much *bleeping* time I've had to practice.

● ● ●

When I wake up the next morning on the pink couch with music playing, the first thing I do is fling the blanket off my foot.

It's completely blank.

As cool as that tattoo looked, I have to admit I'm pretty relieved. The thought of having to hide my foot from my parents for the rest of my natural life comes with the image of me wearing tube socks to go swimming.

Still, getting a tattoo was oddly empowering after feeling zero control over everything happening to me, and I decide to keep taking control. Today is not about permanent body art— today is about the yearbook club, and, most importantly, getting to know the ins and outs of the social groups at Punx High.

Of course, Mom doesn't remember my promise to wear the pink polka-dot dress, but she's nearly as happy when I walk downstairs modeling a sleeveless yellow sweater with matching headband and pencil skirt.

I ride to school with Colton, but immediately let him know I feel more comfortable making my way around the school alone. "Besides," I tell him, "you don't need me slowing you down."

"Are you sure?" He's genuinely surprised, and I prefer this

friendly, considerate version of Colton. I'll just pretend I never got to know him any better.

"I've got this," I assure him with a grin. "And I'm thinking I should ride the bus home so I'm familiar with that too."

He pats my shoulder, and his handsomeness tries to suck me in. Of course, the image of me flex-kicking him in the groin still sits fresh in my mind, so I'm able to resist.

I say, "I'll see you around." But I'm pretty sure I won't.

At lunch, Petra is as nice as ever, and I learn that the girl with the tight headband is named Katy. Even Anna is less aggressive toward me, probably because she no longer sees me as one of Colton's castoffs.

When Petra asks me about my interests and if I play bass, Anna doesn't give a single eye roll.

"I really enjoy photography," I say.

Petra grins. "You have to come to the library after school for the yearbook committee."

Katy tells me about the unflattering picture of Kaia eating again, and I say, "Listen. I got to know her a tiny bit, and I realize she may seem like pure evil in kitten heels from a distance, but the girl isn't a bad person."

The table goes immediately silent. Apparently, sticking up for Kaia is not going to make me very popular with this crew.

Finally, Katy adjusts her headband and says, "She used to bully me back in sixth grade."

Anna says, "It got so bad, the school psychologist had to get involved."

Petra leans closer and tells me, "Katy was so upset, she got a bald spot from pulling out strands of her own hair."

Katy looks down at the table and adjusts her headband.

I glance over my shoulder at Kaia and Colton cozying up to each other. I picture her as a mean middle-schooler, then think of her in the bathroom, forcing herself to purge her own lunch. Turning back to the girls, I say, "Well, I'm sure she has her own burdens to carry."

"Good. She deserves them," Anna says. She reaches over to rub Katy's arm, and I realize that she's just feeling protective of her friend. I can't blame her for that.

I ask, "So, where's the library we're meeting up in after school?"

Of course I already know the answer—at this point, I could teach a master class on this building's full layout—but it feels like a good time to change the subject.

● ● ●

I'm the first one to arrive at the school library after class, and when Petra walks in she looks surprised to see me.

"You came," she says, her face opening into a wide smile.

"Yeah, I told you I would."

"Well, lots of people say they're going to join our club and get involved, but the follow-through isn't always so great."

I feel a pang of guilt over blowing this meeting off the first time I was invited. "How big is this yearbook staff?"

Petra shrugs. "We've been putting the word out, but I'm pretty sure it will just be our same little circle doing a ton of work again this year."

"Wouldn't it make sense to have one representative from

each social group on staff?" I ask. "That way, everyone could just submit the pictures they're probably taking of themselves anyway."

Anna must've been standing behind us, because she chimes in, "Yeah, you'd think so, wouldn't you? But you're the first recruit we've gotten in two years." She looks me up and down pointedly. "And I'm pretty sure you're going to be hanging out with *our* friend group in the end."

I cross my arms. "I actually got to know a few of the goth kids, um, earlier, and that girl Bridget is pretty cool. You never know, she and I could become friends."

Petra and Anna look at each other and simultaneously break into laughter. Finally, Anna gets it together enough to tell me, "Good luck. Let us know how that works out for you."

"She's nice!" I insist.

"That girl is a preacher's kid who is looking to get into as much trouble as possible," Anna says.

Petra whispers, "I hear she goes out drinking every night, and that her torso is completely covered in tattoos."

I think of Bridget and her tiny trinity symbol artfully inked on her leg. "I'm pretty sure she just has one little tattoo," I say. "And I know for a fact that she doesn't drink or do drugs. She doesn't even really swear."

Anna dismisses me with a wave of her hand. "Believe what you want, but don't expect the goths to teach you their secret handshake or anything. You'd have a better shot getting in with the cheerleaders or jocks."

I cross my arms. "The cheerleaders are nicer than you'd expect." Anna and Petra don't look convinced, so I add, "And

I'll have you know I spent some quality time hanging out with Colton Vogel this summer."

Anna's face flushes. "What do you even know about him?"

"He's . . . Well, he's kind of overly flirty, to be honest."

"Ya think?" Anna says sarcastically. When she turns away, Katy and Petra draw closer to me.

Katy says, "A few years ago, Colton asked Anna to go with him to the Groundhog Day celebration at Gobbler's Knob, and she started crushing on him so hard."

Petra says, "She bought a pure white coat and matching ear-muffs and everything."

"She had weeks to prepare," Katy says, "which only made everything worse once February second came around."

"He completely ditched her," Petra says. "It turned out he may have been doing it to make some cheerleader jealous, because that's who he hooked up with instead. Anna believes the whole thing was all a prank, especially when one of the cheerleader's friends *accidentally* spilled red punch on her new white coat, but I think Colton is just a big flirt."

"Thanks, Petra," Anna says. She's apparently overheard everything. "Tell my pathetic story to the whole world, why don't you."

"Sorry." Petra shrugs. "It's ancient history." Maybe, but obviously Anna is still really bothered.

Anna says, "Fine, so it felt like we shared a real connection, and I got stuck liking him even after he ditched me. It is humiliating enough without you making it sound like I was already registered for our wedding gifts or something."

"You *did* practice writing your married name a few times,"

Petra says, and gives a sing-song "An-na Vo-gel" as she mimes signing a signature.

Anna releases an aggravated growl. "Can we please just let it *go* already? We should be working on a plan for getting more candid shots for the yearbook, not reliving my mortifying eighth-grade year."

As we make our way toward the bank of computer tables near the back of the library, Petra leans in to whisper to me, "And ninth-grade year."

"I heard that," Anna says. But she doesn't correct her. It sounds like I'm not the only girl to fall for Colton hard.

But I bet I'm the only girl whose stupid, ill-fated crush somehow caused a fallout with the space-time continuum that has given new meaning to existential crisis.

● ● ●

As two other students filter in, Anna opens a file of photos that run as a slideshow of candid shots of various students. At this point in my tenure here at Punxsutawney High, I recognize nearly every person onscreen, but Petra is helpfully telling me all the names as they appear.

"There's that boy who goes by the name Czyre, but I don't think that's his real name." She pauses the slideshow and zooms in on him glaring at the camera through his eyeliner.

"Czyre is probably just an alias so the cops can't find him." Anna pretends to shudder and the two of them laugh.

I bite back the temptation to tell the two of them that he's the anonymous artist who draws the clever make-you-think cartoons in out-of-the-way places around the school. They'd probably just consider it further evidence that Czyre is a straight-up criminal, which he isn't. I mean, besides the *technical* vandalism. And, of course, the underage tattoo ring he's privately overseeing.

I say, "I talked to him today, and to be honest, he seems pretty nice."

"First Bridget, now him," Anna says. "It sounds like you've interacted with the goths more in one day than I have in all my years of going to school with them."

I give a big smile. "Guess I'm just really friendly."

Anna looks at me a moment before unpausing the picture slideshow with a grunt. "Yeah, well, knock that off, would you? People will think you're on drugs or something if you're seen hanging out with the wrong classmates."

The screen fills with an image of Tom's face, and his big, cheesy grin makes me release a small laugh through my nose.

"What a dork," Anna says, apparently missing the point that Tom was just clowning around for the camera.

I close one eye as I consider the photo. "I don't know," I say. "I've talked to Tom, and he can be pretty funny."

Petra smiles at me, and I feel myself blush.

Photos continue to scroll by, showing students in every imaginable state of mid-sentence. It's almost as if the goal of the photographer was to catch candid angles of students with their mouths twisted and their eyes half closed. When a photo pops up showing Kaia unattractively shoving a bite of food into her wide-open mouth, I reach over and click the pause button.

Anna laughs. "Yeah, I'm thinking this should maybe be on the front-cover page."

Looking at the humiliating picture, I think of how happy I would've been to see it during my first few cycles through. Back when I thought Kaia was stealing Colton from me. Then I think of her kitten heels facing the wrong way inside the bathroom stall.

"I have to be honest, Anna," I say. "I don't think sharing this picture with the whole school is a good idea."

"You're kidding, right?" she says. "Kaia is a *terrible* person. The only reason I haven't posted this photo online is because I'm saving it for the yearbook. Then everyone will see it at once and it can spread faster and live on longer."

"I understand she was awful to Katy a few years ago, but this is super harsh." I squint at her. "Is this maybe about Colton liking her? Because I can tell you for a fact that those two belong together."

"Are they officially together now?" Petra whispers scandalously. "There's been a will-they-or-won't-they tension building up between them since the end of last year."

Anna's straight, even hair swings as she snaps her head to glare at Petra.

"Sorry," Petra says.

Anna shakes her head and stands up. "Okay, I'm calling this meeting to order." She raises her voice. "Thank you *all* for helping to make this the best turnout ever, guys."

I look around. It's not a very big group. I'm pretty sure that putting together a yearbook and writing captions and double-checking names will be more work than this small handful of students can manage.

Anna asks, "What do you guys think of a layout where we

dedicate one photo collage and section to each clique in the school? It will be a more honest way of organizing the yearbook, since that's how everyone usually hangs out anyway."

"What about fringe people?" Katy asks. "Will they get their own separate page?"

Anna thinks a minute. "We'll either round them all up for one group photo together, or else sort them to be included within the established groups."

Half to myself, I say, "*Sort* them?" We are not at Hogwarts. This is only going to reinforce the walls between the groups. It's the *opposite* of Breakfast Clubbing them.

"I don't know," Petra says. "I think the jocks and cheerleaders will expect a bigger portion of pages since they obviously participate in more things."

Anna says, "Which is just one more reason why an even number of double-page spreads for each clique will be better. Look, I have a few shots laid out to help give you guys the idea."

What she really means is that she's done a mock-up version of the yearbook with each group segregated into their own giant multi-page section. I shouldn't have worried about this project being too much work, because Anna has basically completed the whole layout already.

"This is an impressive amount of progress," I say. "When did you do all of this?"

"I wanted to finish the more intense structure work before we get too deep into the semester. There's always so much grinding away to do once classes take off."

I look at her a moment, trying to figure out if she's still on the first day of school with the rest of our peers, or if she's actually into it months deep the way I am. She just stares back at me blankly. It would seem she's genuinely already stressed out about schoolwork. On day one.

The first page she shows us has the one image of Czyre brooding, surrounded by pictures of vampires from a popular television series. "For the goths," she proudly announces.

Petra says, "Um, most of these people do not go to our high school."

"Yes." Katy pretends to fan herself. "Believe me, I would've noticed."

Anna rolls her eyes. "It isn't easy to get photos of the goths at this school. The lighting underneath the stairs isn't exactly con- ducive to taking candid photographs. I just used these as fillers."

"We can handle getting the photos." Petra laughs. "But are you seriously going with that font?"

"Forgot the font, what's up with the caption?" I point to where big red letters dripping with blood label the page *Goths Gone Ghastly*.

"It's a work in progress," Anna says with a sly grin. "Wait until you see the rest of the layouts."

The only page that has been fleshed out to look like an actual yearbook page is the one with the people who are here on the committee. They're pictured smiling and laughing, with words like *friendship* and *joy* sprinkled generously in the margins. It's as if they're the only ones Anna sees as real people.

For the rest of the pages, she's basically done a caricature of each clique, and given them harsh labels and quotes. I'm almost positive it's meant to be satirical, but it's clear to me that Anna is a girl in need of a hug.

"We'll obviously be swapping out pictures of our actual student body for these stand-ins," she says, pointing to a photo of a famous wrestler in a flex pose on the jocks' page. "But this should give everyone the general idea what sorts of shots we're looking for."

"I'm pretty sure you're going to want to change this label too," I say, pointing to the bold blue collegiate lettering that reads *Muscle Heads*. "And this," I say when she turns to a page titled *Circus Freaks* that features a few of Tom's friends. Anna has filled in the extra spaces with carnival sideshow people who are colorfully dressed and performing acrobatic stunts. I can almost envision Tom being proud of the pages, and it makes me wonder how he and his clique-mates see themselves.

Anna has even dedicated a bright pink page to the cheerleaders, with a swirly font that reads *Mean Girls*. I think about the girls I got to know as they helped me learn the routine with painfully slow deliberation. I picture Jacynda working obsessively to perfect each of her routines, and the fact that Tammy clings to the squad as a way to feel a part of something. They're about the farthest things from mean girls in this entire school.

I watch as Petra and Katy point to Anna's pictures and laugh. Clearly, I'm not the only one who made unattractive assumptions about the cheerleaders before I got to know them.

And I'm shocked to realize that despite everything I've learned by watching teen movies from the 1980s, the cheerleaders at Punxsutawney High just might be less snobby and elitist than the school's resident nerd girls.

Anna describes the types of photos we need to start capturing in order to swap them out from her layout. Since it will take a few months to have the yearbooks printed, and she's so certain we'll all be too busy to function in the very near future, she has us going out two by two right after this meeting to search for the other cliques and get as many candid photos as we can.

She and Katy high five when she announces the two of them will be working to get super-sweaty and gross photos of the cheerleaders practicing in the cafeteria. Having my days repeat is nothing compared to this out-of-body experience as I watch Anna plot to humiliate the rest of the student body. But, as Katy cautions, "Just nothing bad enough to get us called out by the administration."

Anna is busy telling Petra that she's on mall duty. She asks, "Who do you want to bring with you?"

Petra smiles at me. "I'm thinking Andie here can be my assist. I'll show her around too, since she probably hasn't even been to the mall yet."

"Great." I try to look enthusiastic. "We can get photos of Colton and his buddies while we're there." I try to remember what Tom's group was referred to as. "And maybe the, um . . . circus freaks?"

"Who're the circus freaks?" Petra squints at me, and I flip back to their yearbook page so I can point to their label.

"Oh," Petra says. "Right."

I look up, and Anna has an annoyed expression on her face. But she's not upset about me messing with her yearbook. Instead, she asks me, "How do you know Colton Vogel's going to be at the mall?"

Whoops. "Oh, you know. Just sorta . . . *guessing*?"

Anna continues studying me. "Why would you specifically mention him?"

"I honestly don't have a crush on Colton, if that's what you're asking." I say it a bit too firmly, but that's just because I'm defensive about the fact that I once had such a huge crush on him.

Petra chimes in. "You and I are going to have a blast at the mall. Even if nobody from school is there."

I want to thank her for intervening with Anna, who is quickly distracted by people lining up to ask her questions. When nobody's looking, I sneak back over to the computer and click the back button through the photo slide show until I get to that unattractive shot of Kaia.

After making sure I'm not being watched, I drag the picture to the desktop trash and quickly click on "empty trash."

Because let's face it: Kaia isn't my favorite person in the world, but nobody deserves that level of public humiliation.

chapter 13

When we get to the mall, Petra leads the way. Again, I find myself walking near the food court just in time to catch a resounding round of, "Woodchucks! Woodchucks! Woodchucks!"

"Ugh," Petra says, using her long lens to capture some candid shots from across the food court. "What a bunch of Neanderthals."

"That Motko kid is actually pretty smart," I say.

Petra lowers the camera and makes a face. "Who, Mark? What makes you say that?"

Note to self: Motko's first name is Mark. I shrug. "He's in my advanced math class. From what I can tell, he's definitely good at numbers."

She raises the camera back up to her eye. "Yeah, well. Having a brain might make it worse that the guy acts like such an adolescent."

"I think he just wants to fit in, and likes to have a good time when he's with his friends," I say, instead of pointing out that we are, in fact, *all* adolescents.

I wonder for half a second if my looping could be some sort

of developmental thing. Like, everyone has one day to repeat over and over until they're mature enough to handle growing up. Then, I think of my mom and realize this theory doesn't hold up when there are grown-ups who seem like eternal teens at heart. In fact, Mom may have jumped *ahead* in time.

"Hey there, Andie." A familiar voice greets me, and I see Tom waving in my direction.

"Hi, Tom." I walk over to where he's standing with his eclectically dressed friends.

Petra hands me the camera. "Here you go—let me see what you've got."

"Sure." I turn to ask the colorful crowd, "You guys mind if I take a few shots?"

In answer to my question, one girl climbs on a guy's shoulders as they all gather into a spontaneous group pose. One guy leaps into a girl's arms so she's cradling him like a baby, and a few of them give sideways peace signs while making exaggerated duck lips.

"Okay." I laugh. "So this is happening."

Holding up the camera, I look through the lens at the over-the-top poses, and the first thing I realize is that the focus is off and I have no idea how to adjust it. I take a step back, examining the front lens of the camera and trying to remember what I learned in the photojournalism workshop I took at the community center. I remember writing down something about f-stops, but the tiny numbers running in rows around the side of this fat lens seem meaningless to me now.

"Sorry, guys," I say to the frozen group. The smiles grow fake and the positions sag and falter as people get too heavy to hold up. A wave of nervous laughter runs through the crowd as tired arms droop.

Things feel so uncomfortable that instead of focusing on the camera puzzle in front of me, my brain shuts down and a voice in my head just starts sounding the alarm, *Awkward! Awkward! Awkward!* over and over. Finally, Petra moves in beside me.

"Oh, okay," she says, making a few quick adjustments.

When I hold the camera back up I call out, "Ready," and the group revives itself, trying to recapture the initial spontaneous vibe with varying levels of success.

Petra says, "It's easier to start by focusing on one person at a time." Reaching over to the top of the camera, she pushes in the zoom.

"Uh, thanks?" I take a photo of a girl who's dressed like a fifties cartoon sweetheart as she blows a kiss at the camera, and I smile. Moving down the line, I zoom in on one person at a time and can see that they each very much have their own look happening.

The guy with the yellow suspenders hooks his thumbs around them and looks off into the middle distance. But I catch him glancing back at Petra when he thinks nobody's looking. I frame one of the acrobat couples and then the kissy-faced duck impersonators, appreciating how much fun they're all having.

There are a few hippie-looking standouts in the group whose bathing habits seem a bit "European," but even they're wearing authentic-seeming seventies clothing and detailed accessories. For the most part, the group members have put thought and effort into the way they look. Except it's as if they don't care what any outsiders might think of them, and they're not trying to fit into any particular mold. They each seem to have dressed to please themselves.

I continue moving down the line and find myself zoomed in on a familiar face: Tom. I lift my head in surprise. Looking at just his face, he's quite cute.

I tilt my head at him, and it's like he's framed by a whole new perspective. He stands with his arms spread wide, displaying drooping jazz hands, and I decide he is maybe more than cute. Tom might be *very* cute. Especially when he's smiling . . . and right now, he is giving me the biggest, most genuine smile.

Petra leans in to whisper to me, "You're doing great," which wakes me from my gawking at Tom.

I ask the fifties girl her name, and when she tells me she's Sue, I say, "I love your dress, Sue. Do you mind holding that pose, but moving just a half step to your left so I can get your full skirt into the shot?"

I reposition a few other people, zoom out so they're all in frame, and tell them, "Say, 'Punxsutawney'!"

In unison, they call out, "*Punxsutawney!*" and I click the shutter, rapid-fire.

Scrolling back through the pictures, I laugh at the twisted expressions I've captured. "Okay, so I got you all on the *p* and the *s* and the *w*. Maybe we can try that again."

Petra calls out, "But let's just go with the classic saying of 'cheese' this time."

The group obligingly calls out, "Classic saying of *cheese!*" holding out the *e* until I definitely get the shot.

Looking down at the screen display, I smile. "Okay, so I got one with everyone's lips all twisted on the *ch*, but the rest of the shots look really great." I scroll through the photos.

"We should really get going," Petra says. I follow her eyes over to where the guy in suspenders is half having a conversation with two girls, but over their heads his stare is mostly focused on Petra.

The way she continues looking back at him seems almost wishful. I ask, "Do you like that guy or something? Because I think he likes you too."

"What? Who? Chuck? No! How'd you even . . ." She grabs the camera from me and starts walking down the mall corridor. "Let's go. We've got to cover the rest of the mall."

Chuck turns to watch her go, and even without the zoom lens I see his dejection. I wonder if this could be another star-crossed-lovers situation . . . Social divisions in this high school seem to be even stricter than the family divides in a Shakespeare play.

Curious, I wave Tom over. He ambles up to me with his head dipped to one side, and I ask him, "Is there some sort of social barrier between your clique and the girls running the yearbook?"

He squints. "What?"

"I mean, okay, what are you guys considered?" I gesture with my arm and ask louder, "What would you guys call your social group if this was a movie?"

A few of them laugh and I hear a chorus of "Freaks!" and "Geeks!"

One girl calls out, "We're self-aware nerds!" and an approving cheer erupts.

I grin. "Self-aware nerds. I like it." I picture a fun layout in the yearbook using these photos, and realize Anna might be wrong about segregating by group for the yearbook, but she's right that students seem to keep to their own circles in real life.

I glance back at Colton and his friends, who appear to be drinking milkshakes in a competitive manner. I guess when you love sports, you turn *everything* into sports.

When I turn back, I realize Tom has been standing there, looking at me. "Do you really need to label everyone that badly, Andie? We're each individuals. How about trying to see us as such."

"Sorry." Holding up my hands in defense, I say, "I didn't mean to offend anyone. I'm just trying to figure out the social system here at Punxsutawney High. At my old high school, we didn't have enough students to group off separately."

"Yeah, well, sorry I can't Breakfast Club everything here for you with a tidy John Hughes bow." He raises his voice. "We will not be easily categorized for your convenience!"

"Let's go, Andie." Petra must've realized I wasn't following her, and she's made her way back to us. She adds, "We'll just label the photo 'Punx High's troupe of thespians.'"

"Thespians," one of the girls repeats in a snooty voice. "We are a *troupe* of *thespians*."

"Hello, Miss *Thespian*," a boy says as he dramatically bows before her, taking her hand. "How do you do?" He kisses the back of her hand, and the two of them dissolve into laughter.

Petra says, "Got it." She's holding the camera and has just covertly captured their awkward little scene. They seem delighted at the thought of their mini mall-play performance appearing in the yearbook, which makes me think that, as nerds, they're maybe a little less self-aware than they realize. In fact, they look rather over-the-top silly right now.

"Thanks, guys." Petra gives one last look to Chuck before walking away. I give Tom a wave good-bye and move to follow her.

"Hold on, Andie." He stops me. "I'm really curious. What were *you* thinking our group's label should be?"

I look around at the zanily dressed crew. My mind swims with suggestions, but after a quick pause I look Tom straight in the eye. "I think you're basically a collection of teenagers with eclectic tastes who have plenty in common with your peers from school, but you choose to focus on the ways you are unique."

Tom raises his eyebrows. "Nice." I turn to follow Petra, who's already halfway down the mall's main corridor, but stop when he calls after me. "And what do you call yourself, Andie?"

"Ha!" I turn and call back, "I'm a free agent." I punch the air the way Bender does in the final scene of *The Breakfast Club*.

"Yes!" Tom closes his eyes and gives a big open-mouthed grin as he mimics my punch. The two of us freeze frame like that.

After a moment, the girl in the fifties pinup dress asks, "What on earth are you two doing right now?"

I break my pose and cover my mouth in laughter, but Tom holds his steady until one of his buddies takes him by the shoulders and shakes him back and forth. He finally reanimates with a laugh.

I turn and walk away, but that image of Tom's smile framed by the camera's lens is still burned into my brain.

When I catch up to Petra, I ask, "So, what was the deal between you and Suspenders Boy back there?"

Her blush is immediate as she holds up the camera and starts scrolling through the photos I've just taken. She stops on the shot of Chuck's face as he dramatically gazes off into the middle distance, and she sighs. "Yeah, that's Chuck. We used to be close."

"Did you two go out? Did it end horribly? Why can you barely look at him without blushing?"

"I'm not blushing." She turns her beet-red face to me. "And Chuck and I didn't even speak today. How did you notice us?" she asks.

"It just seemed like he wanted to talk to you at lunch today, before Anna blew him off. And he was definitely watching you back there."

"Wow, you're pretty observant, Andie. Has anybody ever told you that?"

"I just sort of . . . see a lot, I guess."

Petra puts the camera strap around her neck and lets the device drop to her waist. "You're right. I do like Chuck." She goes on to tell me of how she ran a fund-raiser volleyball tournament last year that Chuck helped her put together.

"It was for autism, and he has a brother with autism, which meant he really wanted to get involved." She smiles. "He is absolutely *horrible* at volleyball, so he put together this team of really bad players who were just there to have a good time."

She describes how funny it was to have all these serious teams who were organized and super competitive coming up against Chuck's players. "They'd do crazy stuff like kick the ball and bump it off their heads, and then they'd cheer and celebrate each time they simply got it over the net." She laughs. "I ended up joining their team just so someone could return the ball once in a while. It was hilarious the way they'd all go wild when I'd get up to serve."

"Sounds good so far. What happened?"

Petra's face tightens. "Anna happened," she says. "I mean, you saw how they all acted just now. I'm not really like them, and Anna is a real take-charge person. She kyboshed things between Chuck and me before they even got started." She sighs. "Anna hates that whole group."

"How could anyone *hate* them? They're only having fun."

"Yeah, they like to have a little *too much* fun," she says.

I widen my eyes at her. "They do drugs?"

"Gosh, no." She gives a little chuckle. "Last year, a bunch of them started this challenge where they tried to get into as many yearbook group photos as possible." Petra rolls her eyes. "Anna didn't realize what they were doing, since she was in half the extracurricular activities photos herself."

"She is *quite* the joiner," I say.

"Nobody noticed all the photobombing until we were doing the layout pages, and by then it was too late."

"So they played a little prank," I say. "Anna can't forbid you from seeing a guy you like over it."

"Trust me. Anna takes the yearbook *very* seriously. In fact, I'm a little worried about the crappy job we're doing here right now. The shots I got of Colton and Kaia acting all cozy will just set her off, so I'm probably going to delete them from the camera."

"That's silly," I say, but Petra's brow is furrowed with anxiety.

She says, "All we've really gotten so far are shots of a bunch of students clowning around at the mall. All kids Anna has grudges against."

"Anna's grudges seem to spread far and wide." I don't point out that one of her grudges could be keeping Petra from finding true love.

She turns to me. "Anna puts an incredible amount of pressure on herself to do everything perfectly. It would make her so happy if we can just find a few classmates from a different clique to photograph."

"I'm pretty sure the goths are beneath us," I say, and she gives me a look of surprise.

"They're still *people*, Andie."

"No! That's not what I meant." I let out a laugh. "I only meant that I think they're on the floor below us. Getting tattoos. Unless it's still too early." I look at my phone and try to remember what time I got here with Bridget yesterday. Or maybe they only came for my sake. I picture my film reel tattoo again and smile.

Petra looks at me like I'm crazy. "What are you even talking about? Secret tattoo tunnels?" she says. "Have you been to this mall before?"

I think of cycling through with Colton, back when I thought he was the love of my life. "Once or twice," I say. "But I *have* been to the basement."

Petra's phone buzzes, and she looks at it. "Shoot. I forgot about band practice. Did you say you play the bass?"

I laugh. "Apparently, I do today." Petra gives me another strange look, and I add, "I mean, I'm in the early learning stages, but I'll give it a shot." After all, now that I know how to keep a beat, how hard can it be to march around on a football field banging a bass drum?

I text my mom that I'll be home later. She texts back, **Yay! New friends?** and I start to write, **Maybe**, but then delete that to write, **Yes I love it here!**, because, hey, why not make my mom happy?

Petra asks if I want to swing by the food court to get some dinner before we go. "I'm starving," I say. The brown goo I've switched to eating may not upset my stomach, but it's less filling than authentic sustenance.

Colton and his groupies are still at the same table when we go by, and I realize he must have left the food court early back when I was with him, probably because it was clear I wasn't enjoying myself. I can't believe I was ever so blind to our obvious incompatibility.

As Petra and I move past his table, he stops to greet me. "Hey there, Andie, I haven't seen you around. Hope you had a good first day."

"Yeah, thanks," I say. "It's been pretty *ongoing*."

Kaia is watching me intently, and I want to tell her to just relax with all the jealousy already. She may seem like she's perfect, and confident, and perfectly confident, but I've come to realize she's actually very insecure when it comes to Colton and other girls. Which is a shame.

I tell them, "Have fun together at the party tonight." Colton gives a strange look, so I quickly add, "I mean, I'll see you around," and I make a dash over to the Spudz World counter where Petra's busy ordering.

". . . and two cheddar bacon broccoli Spudz," she's saying.

"Three with just bacon. Oh, and cheese on those too. In fact, extra cheese on everything." It sounds like she's getting an insane quantity of cheesy Spudz.

"I'm not actually all *that* hungry," I tell her, and she laughs.

"Anna texted me everyone's order so we can bring dinner to the practice." She nods toward Colton and his crew. "So, what was that all about?"

"Oh, Colton and I know each other from the movie theater this summer."

"That's cool," she says, "but I'd play that down when you're around Anna."

"Are you afraid of Anna or something?"

"No," Petra says, and then shrugs. "Just afraid of upsetting her."

Once she and I are all settled in her car, surrounded by sacks of Spudz, she pulls out of the parking lot in the opposite direction of the school.

"Wait, I thought we were heading to band practice."

"Yeah, we are. It's in Katy's basement. It's the only spot with a full drum kit."

"Oh, wow. It's still in a kit? I'll probably need a little help putting it together." I'm thinking I should've looked up what being a bass drummer for a marching band entailed before opening my big Muppet mouth hinge about being able to play. Perhaps this isn't a skill I can fake with a little learned rhythm.

Petra looks at me strangely. "I thought you were on bass."

"Yup, that's me. Can't wait to start playing." I press my lips together so I'll stop speaking, since I have no idea what she's talking about. I'll just have to wait and see how this drum thing plays out.

chapter 14

I t turns out that the whole scene of me marching around with the band as I bang on a bass drum strapped to my front is very different than how I pictured it. Especially since Petra, Anna, and a few of the other girls aren't in marching band at all.

They're in a rock band.

I can't believe I'd assumed they were talking about the bass *drum* when in fact they meant the bass *guitar*.

They're already playing in the basement when we arrive at Katy's house, and I don't need to know very much about music to know that they are *loud*.

As soon as we show up, the band yells out "Food!" in unison, and abandons their instruments to launch an attack on the bags from Spudz World.

Anna smiles at me, which is so unexpected, it's almost unnerving. "I'm glad you joined us, Andie."

"Um, thanks?" I look at Petra, who hands me a Spudz and a spork.

"Our band's called Mad D Batteries." Anna points to a guitar leaning against an amp and says, "And we've desperately needed a bass player."

Uh-oh. "Right," I say. "I can't wait to get my hands on that guitar."

As we all inhale our Spudz, Anna shows us the pictures she shot of the cheerleaders at practice. "They're so gross and sweaty!" she says gleefully.

She must be good at hiding, because I never noticed her taking the photos when I was learning to be a cheerleader. But I do know how hard the girls in the photos are working. Looking at them, I can still feel it in my limbs. Their strained faces dripping with sweat aren't exactly model perfect, but I think they look amazing.

The next thing I know, Anna is strapping the bass on me and plugging it into the amp. I know almost nothing about guitars, but I'm thinking this four-stringed one's at least two strings easier to play than a regular guitar.

Petra sits behind the drums and starts rolling her shoulders and stretching her neck. I stand in position, holding the bass low and reminding myself I've played plenty of air guitar over the years. This should be a piece of cake to fake.

I look over at Anna tuning her guitar and start imitating her: strumming the strings and twisting the little knobs as if I have some idea what I'm doing. I oversell my tuning, plucking and twisting until I realize everyone is watching me.

Looking around, I stop what I'm doing and nod at the guitar in approval. There has probably never been in all of existence an instrument that is more *out* of tune than this guitar. One of the strings is actually hanging slack. Holding it in place before someone notices, I grin and announce, "All set."

"Let's rock," Petra says from behind the drums. "I'm pretty

sure you've heard this one." Banging her sticks together, she counts down, and everyone launches into a song I instantly recognize.

This song has been playing everywhere and constantly for the past few years. It was basically my generation's anthem when I was in tenth grade, and Rhonda and I even made up silly yet elaborate hand motions to the lyrics.

I'm faking my way through, mimicking a bass player in a rock band, but between my out-of-tune bass and my having no idea how to play it, the other girls gradually stop playing their instruments one by one.

Without the rest of them covering up my sound, it's truly horrible. I freeze and realize everyone's looking at me as if I'm shredding my bass. And not in the good way.

"That was awful," Anna says.

"Yeah, I know. Sorry," I say. "I've uh . . . never heard that song."

Petra says, "Seriously? That song is iconic."

"What is up with you anyway?" Anna squints at me suspiciously. "Are you messing around with us?"

I look around and try to come up with a reasonable excuse. "Actually, I ran off the road in my car and hit my head." I start talking before I have an idea what I'm about to say. Which never ends well. "I was on my way to pick up a pineapple!" I grin as if adding in a plot point from one of my favorite movies will make my lie more believable.

The girls all stare at me. I think about what happened in *Fifty First Dates.* "I got amnesia and, apparently, I've forgotten that song . . . and how to play the bass." I look at the guitar I'm still holding as if I don't know how it got into my hands or even what it is.

Finally, Katy says, "How do you know you *ever* played the bass?"

I nod. "Good point."

Petra says, "Wasn't Drew Barrymore on her way to get a pineapple in that one movie—?"

"Who's Drew Barrymore?" I practically shout.

Anna narrows her eyes and asks, "So, you don't have any memories from before your accident?"

I squint my face like I'm trying to remember stuff. Finally, I pretend to give up and shrug my shoulders. "Nope. It's all gone."

Katy widens her eyes. "Did you transfer here because you don't know who you are or where you really belong?"

"No, my parents moved here on purpose. We moved to, um, help me recover. I kept getting freaked out when people I didn't remember walked up to me like they knew me." This is going worse than I imagined.

Anna hasn't stopped studying me. "And you just *forgot* how to play the bass?"

I nod my head harder, willing her to believe me.

It's clear from her expression that she doesn't. "That's really strange, because the part of the brain that stores long-term learned skills is in a different place than the part that would remember things like people you've met and songs that everyone in the English-speaking world knows."

I give a weak laugh. "Yeah, it is strange, you know. I was actually hit on both sides of my head." Because, *hey*, why not dig myself in a little deeper? "It sort of knocked back and forth." I mime getting my head ricocheted around.

When I stop, Katy and Petra are giving me looks of pity, but I can't tell if it's because they believe me and feel sorry for me, or if it's because Anna is clearly about to bust me for lying.

A look of knowing passes over Anna's face. It's the second thing, I'm sure of it.

Thinking fast, I pull out my phone and hold up the screen. "Oh, look at that. It's my mom calling. I need to go home, since my condition means I need to get to bed at, uh"—I look at my phone—"eight o'clock."

"By all means then, you should *go*," Anna tells me.

"Listen, I promise you, my brain is seriously messed up." As the truth of that statement washes over me, I'm hit with sadness. I can feel my eyes start to sting with tears. "My whole life is like a surreal art film where the timeline is all messed up and you never know what in the world is going on."

Anna's smug expression falters, and Petra quickly moves around her drum set to put an arm over my shoulder.

"I don't understand," she says. "You seemed so super observant about things like me and Chuck."

"Oh yeah," I say. "It's weird, all right."

Katy says, "So your *medium* memory is extra good, but your long-term and short-term memories are shot?"

Anna puts her hands on her hips. "That is not the way the brain works, Katy."

I shoot back at her, "We have *no idea* how the brain works." And then I feel the tears spill past my lower lids, because I realize that everything around me may in reality be the same as ever, and I'm genuinely losing my mind.

Anna says, "Despite the numerous cases of amnesia on

cheesy soap operas and medical dramas, the phenomenon itself is very rare." She looks at me. "And the version you're describing is scientifically impossible."

"Did you forget other learned skills, like dressing yourself?" Katy asks. "Because it really doesn't make sense otherwise."

"It doesn't make sense period," Anna says.

I try to think. What I *really* have is some form of amnesia in reverse. I am remembering things that are impossible for me to remember, because they're all from a day that never happens.

It's as if I'm the only person on the planet who *doesn't* have amnesia.

I cover my face with both hands. Petra is rubbing my arm, but I feel so detached I might as well not even be here.

"Leave her alone," Petra says protectively. "She is crying real tears, you guys. Those cannot be faked."

"Sure they can," Anna says. "Come on, let's take it from the top. It's obvious we still need to find a good bass player, because this chick is just playing games with us."

"I'll drive you home," Petra says, and even I can tell when there's no point trying to backpedal anymore.

"Good luck with your *brain*, Andie," Anna sweetly calls as we leave.

And because I'm pretty sure this isn't my last loop and I'm feeling extra mean, I turn back and say even more sweetly, "Good luck trying to make *Colton Vogel* fall in love with you."

Petra claps a hand over her mouth, and her eyes are wide as she grabs my arm to make a dash for the door.

We climb into her car and she says, "Did you see that look on Anna's face? She's *never* going to forgive you."

"I'm pretty sure she'll get over it." I slump down low in the passenger seat. "By tomorrow, I'm predicting."

"That Colton is a true heartbreaker," she says. "Anna's crush on him really changed who she was."

"Heartbreaker doesn't even *begin* to cover it."

"Why? Did you have a crush on him too?" she asks.

I laugh so hard that I can't speak, and I don't stop for so long, Petra starts to look worried.

"Is your brain thing okay right now?" she asks. "Whatever it is, do you need me to pull over?"

I tell her I'm okay and hold in my laughter, which makes my eyes start tearing up again.

Petra reaches over to pat my arm. "It'll be okay, Andie. We can figure all this stuff out together."

Which just makes me start crying. Hard.

chapter 15

B y the time I walk in the front door, I've stopped crying and am starting to feel a little better.

"Oh, honey. What on earth's wrong?" Mom says the second she sees me. It's as if she can sense what I'm feeling, even when my feelings are running so wild I can't catch them myself.

I drop into the couch and slump down. "Nothing, Mom. Just a hard night."

"I thought you were having fun with some new friends. I would've been happy to come pick you up if you needed."

"Yeah, I know." I lean over and lay my head on her shoulder. "I'm just ready for today to be over."

"Wishing you could fast forward through your life is no way to live it, sweetheart."

I start laughing until I find myself crying all over again.

Mom just sits there, petting my hair until I calm down. Even once my breathing has stabilized and I've stopped hiccupping, Mom doesn't ask a single prying question about my spontane- ous emotional meltdown. Instead, she walks over to her video library, opens the glass door with her key, and pulls out a movie.

Without showing me what it is, she puts the DVD into the

player. The screen fills with the image of a corkboard with scribbled-on Post-its, a photo of teens joyriding in a red convertible, and a button that reads *Save Ferris*.

"*Ferris Bueller's Day Off*," Mom announces with a flourish. "It's about time we revisit the old classic." She looks so happy, I just nod and settle into the pink leather couch of doom. I have no fight left in me.

Onscreen, Ferris is preparing for his day off by tricking his parents into believing he's too sick for school. Breaking the fourth wall, he explains that secretly licking one's hands will make them seem clammy. He calls it a perfect symptom for a nonspecific illness.

He points out that the hand-licking thing is really childish, but then again, so is high school.

Ferris Bueller does not lie.

Mom and I smile together over the teacher's repeated, "Bueller. Bueller. Bueller." And when his friend asks what they're going to do that day, she nudges me as Ferris gives the classic response that it's more about what they *aren't* going to do.

And it hits me. I can do *all the things*. While the teens onscreen create havoc in a fancy restaurant and ride on a parade float, I start constructing a list of fun activities in my mind.

Maybe I've been viewing my situation wrong, and I'm not being punished like Sisyphus after all. Maybe this isn't a curse that I have to break.

Maybe this has been a gift all along.

● ● ●

The next morning, I start my school day by crouching on a toilet inside the boys' bathroom near the front office. I'm wearing a baseball cap and hoodie and holding the mop I've snagged from the janitor's closet. Listening, I wait for the president of the senior class to arrive to take his morning leak.

As soon as he's tucked inside his stall, I slide the mop pole through the door handle, effectively locking him in. I'm hit with a wave of guilt as I leave the tiled room. The boys' bathroom is beyond foul. In fact, if I'd ever tried to eat my pizza in there, I would've been immediately sick from day one.

Keeping my baseball cap low over my face and pressing my back against the wall, I sneak inside the announcement booth in the senior class president's place and commandeer the microphone. In an official newscaster voice, I begin politely reciting everything that's about to happen all day. And I do mean *everything*.

I've cycled through enough times at this point to include small details, such as, "Barry Helfeger will have so much trouble opening his locker combination, he'll resort to kicking open his door, only to discover he's broken into Kimberly Kessler's locker instead of his own." And, "The back two rows of Mr. Hoovler's third-period science class will want to secure their glass beakers to avoid unnecessary damage when Christopher Nolan creates an explosion at his desk using a chemical reaction he learned over the summer at science camp."

I go on like this for some time until, finally, the assistant principal breaks in and turns off my microphone. I apologize for the prank and am sentenced to detention for the rest of the week. She eyes me suspiciously when I accept my punishment with a bright smile, but doesn't hold me for further questioning.

Probably because she has no idea how impossibly accurate my predictions just were.

As I walk out of the booth and down the hallway, I spot two seniors I've announced will be breaking up today. I forecasted Jay and Jody's split because they've had a very public fight in the hallway after sixth period every single time I've looped. But right now, I see the two of them embracing in front of Jody's locker.

Smoothing back her hair with one hand, Jay says, "That announcement was crazy. I love you." Hearing me announce their break up must have somehow convinced them to rally and save their relationship.

Of course, my prophecy that Colton and Kaia will hook up before the day's end absolutely comes true. I obviously didn't say anything about her eating disorder, but I've checked in on the bathroom near the cafeteria after lunch here and there. Sure enough, her kitten heels are always facing the wrong direction. I wish I could help her, but I have no idea how.

Over time, I've worked a few public service acts into my schedule. For instance, I pace my walk down the hallway to fourth period just right so I can seamlessly catch a freshman's books for him before they go flying. His look of gratitude borders on outright adoration.

I leave my new school sneakers inside the locker of a girl I've noticed is insecure about having shabby ones of her own, and I surreptitiously spray air freshener into the locker vent of a kid who forgot to shower this morning. I consider leaving a stick of deodorant on the shelf inside, but I'd hate to have him feel like it wasn't from a friend. Hormones are no joke, and the same ones that have him stinking up the tenth grade could conceivably cause him to burst into tears if he realizes someone else noticed his body odor.

Sitting beside Petra in the cafeteria, I do a quiet countdown of, "Three. Two. One . . ." and a huge *clatter! crash! smash!* sounds out from the kitchen. I return Petra's shocked expression with a knowing look. Raising one finger, I mouth along with the lunch lady shouting out, "Crikey!"

Petra's eyes grow even wider, but I just shrug and go back to eating my brown goo. Which, by the way, is an acquired taste.

In all my classes and without raising my hand, I answer every single question posed by every single teacher. Sometimes, before they've finished asking them.

I even mime the English teacher, Mr. Demers, as he goes over the syllabus for our study of the Greek gods. Turning, I realize Tom is watching me with rapt attention.

He leans over and whispers, "Did you hack into the computer system and steal his notes or something?"

"Nope." I smile. "I've just heard all this before."

"Yeah, right." He laughs. "Nice trick."

"What? You don't believe me?"

"Did you already sit through this class by accident or something? If you can memorize lines that easily, you should try acting classes. That is some serious skill."

"More like, I've listened to this speech over and over every single day since the summer." I look up at the ceiling. "About four and a half months' worth by now."

"Summer vacation *literally* just ended yesterday," Tom says. "And you weren't even at this school before that." He gives me the look my dad gives me when he's deciding whether I'm due for a mental assessment and tune-up.

"Tom! Please." It's the first time I've heard Mr. Demers speak sharply. He consults his seating chart. "And Andie, is it? Do you two mind holding your conversation until after class?"

"Sorry," I say. "Please do *go on* about Sisyphus." My voice drips with irony that only I can understand.

When class ends, Tom asks, "So be honest, how did you know what Mr. D was going to say word for word?"

Tom's the first one who has taken a real interest in my unusual knowledge. Most everyone else is so absorbed in their own first-day-of-school stuff that they don't notice my odd quirks and comments. I haven't thought through how I would explain all of this if someone called me out, so I tell him what's really happening.

"No big deal," I say. "I'm just caught in some sort of bizarre time loop."

He squints at me as we walk down the hallway side by side. "You mean like you're actually an adult or something, sent back in time like the movie *Seventeen Again*?"

"No," I say.

"A little kid sent forward in age? Like *Big* or *Thirteen Going on Thirty*, except you're only sixteen?"

"More like the movie *Groundhog Day*, where I'm repeating the same exact day over and over."

He laughs. "Nice one, Andie. Welcome to Punxsutawney. Hope you get unstuck sooner than Bill Murray did."

"According to the director, his character was stuck in that loop for over thirty years," I say.

"Well, if he could've won his true love a little sooner, he would've been set free, right?" Tom says. "Of course, that wouldn't have been nearly as much fun."

"Right." I turn and face him in the middle of the hallway. "Fun. Let me tell you, it is so much *fun* to start every day in a place where nobody really knows you, and they can never really get to know you because you are perpetually meeting everyone for the first time. Because, hey, isolation is *fun*." Tom's eyes widen as I continue. "And speaking of isolation, it is almost *too much fun* to stand by watching people who can't see past stereotypes, and who make snap judgements about others they've never even spoken to based solely on labels and cliques and clothing."

People in the hallway have stopped to watch our exchange, and Tom bites his lip in amusement. He thinks I'm putting on an act. But this is no act.

I raise my voice and feel my face go pink. "You all need to stop treating high school like it's some giant tournament of rock, paper, scissors, where each social group thinks it's better than the others and nobody ever wins!"

My heart is beating fast, and Tom tries to start a slow clap, but everyone in the hallway just reanimates and goes back to their day.

Tom grins at me. "You're *fun*."

I cover my face with both my hands and laugh as my breathing returns to normal.

When I look back up at Tom, it feels like he finally really sees me. After blinking a few times, he says, "But I still really want to know how you pulled off that trick with Demers."

I smack the heel of my hand against my head and give a growl of frustration.

"Wait . . ." Tom says, but I just wave as I make the turn into the girls' bathroom. It felt good to be sharing the truth for a change, but I shouldn't be surprised Tom doesn't believe me. After all, the Andie he got to know all summer long was a bit rude and totally doe-eyed over Colton. I can't go back in time far enough to undo my drool, and now I doubt Tom will ever be interested in getting to know the real me.

I'm surprised to realize how much that upsets me. I wish I'd paid more attention to him from the start, because the more I've gotten to know Tom, the more I like him. Sort of the opposite of what happened with Colton.

Talking about *Groundhog Day* with Tom inspires me to visit the actual groundhog, Punxsutawney Phil, after school. I don't really imagine the Bill Murray movie was a documentary or any-thing, but the town could be cursed. If so, that giant rodent could be holding all the answers.

One look tells me Punxsutawney Phil is *not* holding all the answers.

He's cute and furry and happily napping on his fat little back inside a warm terrarium attached to the town's library. A mural of a field is painted on the back wall, with fake rocks and trees springing up inside the glass enclosure. Phil is half-buried in woodchips, and sleeping so deeply I wonder if he's even alive.

Ignoring the sign that says, "Do not tap on glass," I give a quick knuckle rap.

Unimpressed, he opens one eye, scans me, and closes it again.

"Not quite what you'd call an energetic fellow, is he?" a deep voice says from behind me.

I whip around. "Sorry, I was just trying to . . ." *What?* I have no idea what I'm doing here.

The man standing behind me gives a chuckle. "You could bang all day. Anytime he's not busy eating, that groundhog is fast asleep."

I turn back to look at Phil's upturned belly. I wish I could tickle it. "That's really all he does?" I try to keep the disappointment out of my voice.

The man leans in toward the glass. "Well, every now and then, he does manage to escape."

I grab the man by his wide shoulders and force him to look at me. "He escapes?" I practically screech. "How? Where does he go?"

"Easy there." The man takes a step backward away from me. "He's been known to climb through the ceiling tiles and escape into the library."

I press my whole face against the glass and look up at what appears to be a newly painted ceiling inside the terrarium.

"Actually," the man says, "I do recall they replaced the tiles a while back. No more escaping for Phil."

My eyes swing back down to Phil, who opens his one eye at me again. We stare at each other for a long time, and I imagine the fun he was having back when he could wander free inside the library. Probably surprising patrons by popping out his fat-cheeked face between the books on the bottom shelves. Maybe even getting a pet from a child, or acting naughty by leaving poop pellets in drawers and making the librarians scream.

I can feel how trapped he is now.

"You get it," I whisper to him through the glass, and he knowingly closes his eye.

● ● ●

I continue cycling through variations on my day, getting bolder and bolder with my choices, and teaching myself skills of questionable integrity such as picking locks and hotwiring cars. Finally, taking inspiration from the movie *Ferris Bueller's Day Off*, I borrow my neighbor's red Ferrari one morning and drive it all the way into Pittsburgh.

As I cross over the Liberty Bridge into the city, I smile over how lucky I am to live just a few hours from such an incredible city with so many bridges for me to explore. I peer through the guardrail at the Monongahela River far below and get a thrill of freedom that makes my fingers tingle.

Once I'm in the city itself, I head downtown and park the car illegally right in front of the big stone building of the Andy Warhol museum. Inside, I study mannequins covered in dots and stand in a room filled with silver Mylar pillows with my arms spread wide. And of course I consider rows and rows and rows of perfectly painted Campbell's soup labels. For some reason, the blandness of the logo soothes me. They are familiar and common, yet endless and eternal, and each one is exactly the same in an organized way that makes me feel in control.

After the museum, I drive over to the Southside to ride the Duquesne Incline, which is basically a cool old trolley car that runs up and down Mt. Washington at a steep angle. As it climbs,

I look out the antique wooden car's windows, and the skyline rises into view.

I've always loved the way the city is surrounded by three rivers that make a Y where the Monongahela and the Allegheny become the Ohio River, forcing the city into a point. Once we reach the top, I stand on the observation deck and stare down at the Point State Park fountain nestled right in the crook, marking where the two rivers flow into one. The enormous stone fountain isn't always running, but I'm happy to see it's shooting a torrent of water high into the air today. My day.

I've visited Pittsburgh every summer of my life, and I feel a wave of affection for this city. I calculate how long it will take for me to explore every out-of-the-way nook and cranny, and fleetingly wish I could share my adventures with someone. Anyone. My mind wings to Tom, and I picture us sitting in the Regent Square Theater down on Braddock Avenue waiting for a film to start. Probably a classic like *Casablanca* or *Charade*. It's one of the spots my family has always made a special point to visit. Of course, it's usually Mom's idea.

I feel a pang over how panicked my parents must be feeling by now. I didn't leave a note, since I figured there was a chance I wouldn't even be missed as a new student at school. My hope was they wouldn't know anything was out of the ordinary until later.

I turned the ringer off my phone for the day, but when I check my call history around one o'clock, it's clear the school put things together and called Mom and Dad a couple hours ago. They've been calling almost constantly since then, and I need to push down the burning guilt I feel with the knowledge they won't remember any of this tomorrow.

My guilt dissolves into hunger, and my stomach growls as I walk along the row of restaurants that overlook the cityscape. The Vue 412 smells delicious but looks expensive, and while it would be easy enough to borrow a credit card off a table or to simply dine 'n' dash since I'm living a zero-consequences existence, I'm trying to keep my stealing down to a minimum.

I mean, aside from the neighbor's red Ferrari, of course.

Instead, I grab a burger at the Coal Hill Steak House and then climb onto one of the amphibious vehicles to take a "Just Ducky" tour around the city. The view from the bus/boat shaped like a giant rubber ducky is amazing, but I wish it wasn't so overcast today. I feel like the families and couples taking the tour together are all judging me as I sit alone, so I decide to listen to the library of messages my parents have left on my voice mail.

Which is a mistake. I can hear the suffering in their voices as they move from anger to concern to fear over my disappearance and nonresponse. This behavior is so very unlike me that I can trace the growing panic in their voices. Finally, I can't take it anymore and delete the rest of their messages.

My plan shifts to staying in the city all night to avoid any consequences at home. I remind myself that all debts will be wiped free in the morning, and devise a plan to sneak my way into a motel room once it gets late. That is, if I can find a hotel willing to rent a room to a teenager.

I may be sleeping in the Ferrari, since after my tour and an exciting Steeler football game, I have a hard time just getting myself into one of the nightclubs with my underage ID. I manage to slip into one dark place down along the Strip while the oversized security guard is busy holding up a pair of handcuffs and threatening a small, bald man who is obviously intoxicated.

"If you handcuff me, you'll be hearing from my lawyer," he shouts to the bouncer who's three times his size. "Wait, I *am* a lawyer!" The bald man's tirade of outrage is interrupted as he stops to puke on his own shoes.

The bouncer looks disappointed that he didn't get to use his handcuffs as he puts them away and instead pulls out a hankie to hand to the guy. I slip inside unnoticed.

My thrill at gaining entrance to the coveted indoor portion of the club is quickly squelched by the sight of the dreary interior. There are clusters of people gathered around small waist-level tables, and the bar seems noisy and lively, but the middle-aged woman up on stage singing a Billy Joel song is messing up the lyrics and slurring all the words she does get right.

Her obvious drunkenness is so unappealing, I make a quick note to self: if I ever do make it to middle age, no drinking while singing karaoke.

Deciding to make the best of things, I put my name on the list to sing. I figure I'll have plenty of time to decide which song to pick, and maybe work up enough courage to actually get onstage. Instead, it's a matter of moments before the drunk lady stumbles and has to catch herself by hanging onto the microphone stand.

The thin silver pole promptly collapses under her weight, sending her sprawling onto the floor. She sits up, looking dazed. "And for my next trick," she calls out, "I'll disappear." And with that, she crawls gracelessly down off the stage and is gone.

The next thing I know, I'm standing center stage, in the

middle of the most awkward karaoke moment of all time. In honor of Ferris, I've made the split-second decision to sing "Shake It Up, Baby." Except I'm bringing zero percent of the fun and charisma Matthew Broderick showed off on the parade float in the movie. My voice is flat and I'm basically reading the words off the screen as if reciting everyone a bedtime story.

Suddenly, out of the depressingly dark and musty room, I hear someone practically scream, "Andie!"

I'd be relieved at having my performance cut short, if it wasn't for the desperate tone of the voice. A voice that I instantly recognize.

Shading my eyes from the spotlight, I can see Mom and Dad barreling in between tables as they head toward the stage. Dad turns on a guy in a tight white tank top, who stands up and tries to slow their approach. I watch as my mild-mannered author-therapist-always-use-your-words father punches Tank Top Guy dead in the face.

The guy falls so hard and fast, I'm pretty sure Dad's knocked him out cold. My first thought is that I never knew my father was capable of such violence, and my second thought is that it's my fault he's expressing so much anger in such a nonconstructive way.

It turns out that Mom and Dad have been tracking me down using the GPS in my phone, and Mom sobs uncontrollably as she hugs me in a death grip. The security guard grabs my dad and joyfully pulls out his handcuffs.

"You can just sit tight and cool off," the guard tells Dad as he clicks the handcuffs on him. I'm pretty sure it's the first time he's gotten to cuff someone, because he takes a quick selfie with my father looking miserable.

Once Tank Top Guy regains consciousness and my father starts apologizing profusely to everyone, the security guard grudgingly sets my dad free. The guard looks disappointed that Dad and the guy didn't attack each other as he puts his shiny cuffs away again.

Tank Top Guy accepts Dad's apology for knocking him out, but I catch the short, bald, drunken lawyer slip a business card into the guy's hand while whispering into his ear. The guy's eyebrows go up as he listens, and he puts the card in his pocket.

The rest of the night is basically a blur of me trying to get my mom to stop crying so I can explain to everyone that I'm fine and won't ever do anything like this again.

The panic and hurt on both of my parents' faces is so devastating, I know I'll never bring myself to take another big day off in Pittsburgh. They may both forget about my going off-script when they wake up in the morning, but I'll never get Mom's traumatized expression out of my head. Or the sight of my dad's sweet pancake-making hands locked in handcuffs.

chapter 16

There are many things one can master when one has access to the Internet and lots and lots of free time. Once I've finished watching endless hours of otters holding hands while sleeping, puppies running in slow motion, and panda bears falling down, I start working my way through a long list of impractical skills, mastering one thing at a time.

I learn to create pancake art using a technique of layering batter to make dark and light shades. The learning curve is very steep since I start off not even knowing how to make regular old single-shade circle pancakes, but with time and practice, I get pretty good.

Finally, I surprise my dad one morning with a pancake shaped like a portrait of Sigmund Freud that looks too nice to even eat. He's so happy, I'm almost able to forgive myself for nearly getting him arrested on my big day off.

Next, I teach myself how to decorate elaborate cakes with modeling icing, and present a series of movie-themed ones to my mother. There's *Ferris Bueller's Day Off*, featuring a red Ferrari-shaped cake driving past a water tower that reads SAVE FERRIS.

Then I painfully construct a black-and-white-and-pink *Pretty in Pink* confection with the movie poster image stenciled on top.

Finally, I make a *Sixteen Candles* masterpiece with two handmade Claymation-looking characters sculpted with fondant icing, who sit cross-legged on a table as they lean over a cake to kiss. As a small ironic detail, I've added tiny kissing characters on top of the cake they're leaning over, and then I use tweezers to create an even smaller version on top of that cake. I envision the characters repeating until they're nearly microscopic, but don't want to add to my issues by getting sucked into a cake-decorating vortex forever.

Mom is so impressed and delighted by my *Sixteen Candles* cake and its Droste effect that my burning remorse at taking off and making her freak out is finally extinguished.

I watch every movie I can get my hands on, and even break into Mom's glass case to watch the DVD special features from her classic film collection. Obviously, I leave *Pretty in Pink* alone, but there are lots of interesting interviews and commentaries on the others.

I find myself deliberately manipulating my days so that I'm able to discuss the movies I watch with Tom. He's like a walking collection of cinema tidbits and trivia and behind-the-scenes stories. Whether it's before school, outside the choir room, during lunch, or in the hallway beside Tom's locker, I don't feel like I've totally processed a movie until I've taken the time to discuss it with him.

I learn his movie favorites and storyline pet peeves, along with the exact way he twists his lips and squints when he's thinking.

Because I can only do so much with the day I'm given, it feels like my friendship with Tom is somewhat one-sided. I'm careful not to reference our past conversations, but it grows increasingly more difficult.

"I thought you had an issue with Johnny's attitude toward women in *Dirty Dancing*," I say during a movie discussion we're having one afternoon at the mall.

"When did I say that?" His lips give that twist, and he leans forward on the bench we're sharing.

I think fast. "Maybe you never actually *said* that . . ."

He is watching me, which distracts me from coming up with a good explanation of how I somehow know his opinions.

Finally, I mumble, "I guess I just assumed?"

Thankfully, he says, "Well, *obviously* there's an inherent predatory vibe when a guy with his kind of experience hits on a girl who is so much younger than him."

I breathe a sigh of relief as he goes on about the innocence of Jennifer Grey's character. He has many thoughts on this particular topic, and I love how protective he is of her.

These conversations are great, but I'm constantly reminded that there's no way I'll ever undo a whole summer of pursuing another guy right in front of him.

It hits me every time we laugh too loud over something one of us has shared, or when I show agreement by shoving him in the chest just a little bit too hard, or when our gaze catches and holds for a wide-stretching moment too long.

Again and again, I watch him pull a mask down over whatever feelings might be stirring in him. It's as if I can almost hear his thoughts turn to the way I've brazenly flirted with Colton over and over by the light of the popcorn maker. That's the point when Tom will either clear his throat, or cross his arms, or adjust his fedora if it happens to occur during lunch. The sting of him pulling back from me is always punctuated by the sharp knowledge that I fully deserve it.

I can accept the fact I've screwed up, but it doesn't mean I don't need a way to release my frustration. Loud music seems to help drown out the regret that rings in my ears, and once I teach myself how to truly play the bass guitar, I work on learning the song the Mad D Batteries girls like to play. Finally, I'm able to shred the bass so expertly, *in a good way*, that nobody will dare question me again.

Once I'm ready, I loop through with Petra, hanging out at the mall, taking pictures and laughing together after school. I'm hit by the fact that Petra would make a truly great best friend, if only I could figure out how to become best friends with someone who always just met me.

This time when we show up at Katy's basement with our sacks of Spudz World spudz and sporks, I head directly for the bass leaning against the amp.

Picking up the axe, I play the song the girls are about to practice so perfectly that when the final note dramatically rings out, Petra runs over to give me a tackle hug. The rest of the band freaks out, and even Anna can't help but show me her pure approval.

"That was incredible," Petra says, beaming. "We are going to kill it at Battle of the Bands this year."

My smile goes plastic, because unless Battle of the Bands is later tonight, I'm pretty sure I'm never getting the chance to do it. Petra starts handing out spudz and sporks and the girls all gather around, settling into the same comfortable small talk they've recited before.

My ears are still ringing from my guitar playing as I sit, eating my spudz and trying not to zone out over the repetitive chatter. But the spudz tastes extra dry this loop around.

Anna pulls out her camera to share the photos she scored of the perspiring cheerleaders, and shows us the shot of Tammy with sweat streaming off her squinched face as she kicks one leg high in the air.

"Wow," Anna says. "I can practically smell her body odor from here."

"I hope they grabbed showers right away," Katy adds. "That level of perspiration can turn toxic fast."

"The cheerleaders are actually at a house party tonight," I say, trying to humanize them. "Some girl named Maya. Do you guys know her?"

"Wait, what?" Anna looks irritated. "How do you know where they are?"

"Oh, I just overheard that girl Tammy talking about heading to Maya's house tonight."

"Maya?" Petra starts typing into her phone. After a moment she says, "According to the yearbook database, nobody from our school is named Maya."

"Oh, I'd just assumed she went to Punx High. Maybe the girl goes to a private school or something." I shrug.

Anna says, "Wait, are you talking about *Maya's House*?"

"Yeah, that's what I said; Maya's house. They're joining a dance party there or something."

"I doubt it." Anna laughs. "Maya's House is the town's *retirement* home."

"Retirement home?" I say. "Why would there be a dance party

in a retirement home?" I picture the cheerleaders table-dancing at some old persons' place and laugh. "Guess I had that worked out all wrong."

"Maybe they're performing there," Petra says. "Like, as some sort of public service to make up for getting caught breaking the law. Or for brownie points on their college applications."

"So, wait," Katy says. "You think the cheerleaders are going to Maya's House as some sort of charity?"

"That doesn't sound like them," Anna says.

"Maybe they're just going to visit someone's grandma," Katy says.

Petra says, "Half the town is related to somebody who lives in that home. And the other half at least knows someone there."

I say, "It sounds sweet if they're going to cheer up all those old people with their dancing."

"Too bad we didn't know about this earlier," says Anna. "We could've tried to get a few shots of the cheerleaders making spectacles of themselves."

But I can barely hear her, since I'm already heading up the stairs to go home and hit the restart button again.

I'd love to see what happens when cheerleaders and brainiac girls go head to head at a retirement home. And now I know exactly how to make such a thing happen.

● ● ●

The next day, when Anna, Petra, and I walk through the front doors and into the lobby of Maya's House, Punxsutawney's retirement home, the cheerleaders aren't anywhere in sight.

Looking around at the spacious entrance hall, I lean over to ask Petra, "Was this an old hospital or something?"

She shrugs. "It's just always been here. The place where everyone from town ends up if they aren't living with family."

Anna makes a wide berth for a nurse pushing a wheelchair that carries an elderly woman hunched underneath a knitted shawl.

We make our way over to the main desk, where we're greeted by a strikingly attractive woman wearing nurse scrubs. She introduces herself as Dawn and asks if she can help us.

Anna holds up her camera. "We're from the Punxsutawney High yearbook committee, and we were hoping to get some shots of the cheerleaders performing for your, er, clients."

Dawn says, "You mean the girls who come in here to dance with the residents once a week?"

Petra looks at me, and Anna says, "I guess that must be them. Are they high school students?"

"Oh, yes. And they're so patient with the residents, we all love them here." Dawn gestures toward the hallway across from the main entrance doors. "Everyone's already in the recreation room with the music playing, just waiting for the girls to arrive."

She takes our school ID cards and directs us to follow the yellow-carpeted corridor. "Follow the yellow brick road, and don't get lost on your way to Oz," she jokes. Petra and I give her a smile and turn to make our way in the direction she's pointing.

Hanging on the walls on both sides of the hall are vintage photos of movie stars from the mid nineteen hundreds. Back when the residents were young. The images make me indescribably sad.

We pass a swinging door that's propped open, and inside I can see theater-style built-in seating with a big white screen across the front wall. Surprised, I say, "They show movies here?"

Petra points to the classic poster of the movie *Casablanca* hanging on the wall outside the theater. "Yeah, but it looks like they only play old stuff."

The poster is in a light-up frame that proclaims the film is "Now Showing." Beside that poster is one of *Breakfast at Tiffany's* that's labeled "Coming Soon."

I look up at the image of an ultra-glamorous Audrey Hepburn covered in diamonds and holding an extra-long cigarette holder.

"*Breakfast at Tiffany's* is pretty good," I say. "I'd love to see it on an actual movie screen."

"Maybe you should come back here and watch it with the old folks." Anna continues down the hallway.

"Maybe I will." I pause a moment before following behind her and the rest of the group. *If only "Coming Soon" didn't mean "Coming Never" for me.* But I can come and watch *Casablanca* any night I want.

Finally, we reach big, heavy double doors with a silver plaque on one side that reads "Recreation Room." When Petra and I open the doors and walk through, we're greeted by a sea of bald and cottony heads turning to watch us enter.

One man wearing suspenders in a non-ironic manner grumbles, "You're not cheerleaders."

"See that?" Anna says. "They're not even going to show up. Those girls are terrible."

I point to an oversized clock on the wall. "It's not even six o'clock."

Just then I hear synchronized clapping coming from the hallway haunted by old movie stars behind us. The sound builds as it draws closer.

I turn just in time to see Tammy fling the door wide open. She marches into the room with her hands in the air and calls out, "Who's ready to get this party started?"

The whole room springs to life. Wrinkled faces draw up into smiles and bald and fluffy white heads begin to nod more deliberately. The old man in suspenders who waved us off raises his arms partway above his head and gives a loud, "Woo!"

Anna says, "I can't believe this is happening."

"*Is* this really happening?" Petra asks.

"This is happening." I smile. "And they all look so happy."

The cheerleaders have already moved out onto the floor, and I picture the first few moves of their routine as the whole room waits for them to start.

I had no idea this was where they headed after our long, grueling practice each day. I'm curious what motivates them to take time out to perform here.

I suppose this room is indeed bigger than the cafeteria crowded with folded tables, so maybe this is just so they can test their routines in a space as big as the gym. Plus, they get the added benefit of seeming like good people for spending time with the elderly.

Everyone loves a teen doing charity work, and these girls are earning some high-quality good-job gold stars right now.

Except that when I think about it, back when I was friends with them, they never mentioned Maya's House to anyone outside their group. And according to what Dawn said, and the old folks' reactions, they've been at this for a while, but not even Anna and Petra knew it was happening. And they seem to be aware of *all* student body happenings.

Anna and Petra stand beside me, wide-eyed, as the music starts. The cheerleaders give a surprised look when they notice us, but Tammy just gives an acknowledging nod.

They assume their positions on the dance floor like they're ready to perform, and I catch Anna rolling her eyes at Petra. But the Maya's House residents seem to be confused. They're taking hesitant strides, shuffling their orthopedic shoes along the smooth wooden floor like a group of elderly fans rushing their favorite band. In slow motion.

I'm expecting the cheerleaders to guide them back to their seats, and Anna must anticipate the same thing, because she says, "Here we go," and holds up the camera like she's getting ready to take a shot of the Punxsutawney cheerleaders bullying the elderly.

Instead, the only thing she sees through her camera lens is the group of girls smiling while they greet the slowly approaching old people with outstretched arms. Anna peers over the top of the camera she's still holding in front of her face.

The music shifts to an upbeat tune straight from the dance party scene in *Grease*, and Tammy and her crew each start doing a modified swing dance with the residents.

And when I say "modified," what I really mean is super embarrassing. It's a bit like watching a movie mashup between a zombie flick and *Grease*. But when I see the faces of the residents, I recognize such deep joy, it turns their clumsy dancing beautiful.

I can't help but grin. Anna drops the camera to her waist, and she and Petra look at each other with their eyebrows raised and their mouths slack.

"This is amazing," I whisper, and ease the camera out of Anna's hand.

Petra points to Jacynda holding hands with an elderly gentleman as the two of them hop and kick together. "Get that shot," she tells me. "Look how happy he looks."

A few of the men are coupled with the cheerleaders, but it's the ladies who dominate the dance floor. All shapes and sizes, they're laughing as they twist and skip about with varying degrees of spryness. One woman even climbs on the front pedals of her friend's mobility scooter, waving her arms in the air. I look to Dawn to see if she's going to put a stop to the shenanigans, but she's busy clapping along with the music.

I look at the smiling faces and realize that this dance party is about the least-selfish act of charity I've ever seen a cheerleader perform. And to think I'd assumed they were all heading to some party.

Anna says, "Someone's going to break a hip."

"Well, they'll have fun doing it." I look at her. "You know, I'm sure these people have suffered plenty of pain over their lives, but look at them now," I say. "Moving forward. Chasing joy."

One of the residents lets out a whoop, and Anna swings her attention to the wild scene on the dance floor. The music shifts to a more modern song that's been all over lately, and Petra grabs Anna's arm.

"Come on," she says, "this is your jam."

Anna shakes her head no and tries to pull away. Petra hangs

on to her with both hands, trying to force her onto the floor, but Anna wants no part of what she is witnessing.

Once the song's chorus hits, Petra can't resist bursting into song. With her arms held wide, she twirls onto the dance floor and the cheerleaders make room, giving a shout of approval. Petra looks so happy as she joins hands with a tiny woman who's clapping with even worse rhythm than I used to have.

Jacynda leads a rowdy conga line past us, and I can't help but jump onboard. As the line curls back around itself, I pass a laughing Petra, and she calls out to me, "Everyone is so happy! This is unbelievable!"

I smile back, but don't think she can hear me when I say, "Yeah, this was a really good day."

Reaching back to grasp the textured hands on my waist, I guide them so they're holding the gentleman's hips in front of me. Once the gap is closed, I step out of the conga line and smile as I watch it move past. I'm ready to head home.

As I pass Anna, she uncrosses her arms. "I can't believe I had those girls all wrong," she says, half to herself.

"Yeah," I say. "I did too at first."

"Maybe they didn't prank me at Gobbler's Knob after all," she says. "This changes everything."

I beam at her, but of course for me, it doesn't change anything—tomorrow morning I'll be waking up on my living room couch and nothing will be different at all.

I look at Petra now doing a hand jive with a woman sporting a thick white pompadour. "I'm really tired, but Petra's having too much fun right now," I tell Anna. "Can you let her know I'll get a ride home from my mom?"

"You sure you don't mind getting your mom to pick you up?" Anna seems distracted as she watches the spectacle playing out on the dance floor.

"Of course not," I say. "Do you want my mom to drive you home now too?"

She doesn't answer right away, and I think she's suffering from some form of pretentious social shock over all of this.

Then without warning, the beat drops and Anna takes a hop step into the center of the dance floor and starts doing an unselfconscious robot impression, one that seems completely out of character. A group of residents form a circle around her and goad her on with offbeat clapping.

It's a really beautiful moment.

Everyone is having such a great time, it's almost okay that nobody will remember this in the morning. Almost.

I text my mom for a ride, and she texts me back that she's nearly finished watching the end of *Pretty in Pink* from last night, and do I mind hanging tight for a little while. Even though last night is now many months ago, that movie is still finding new and creative ways of interrupting my life.

As I wait for Mom to come and pick me up, I wander down the opposite hallway, checking out the movie star pictures on those walls. I recognize most of the actors even though I don't know all their movies. The ladies look so glamorous and the men are overly groomed, with their hair slicked back and their mustaches trimmed. Eternally young.

I wonder for a moment which stars will be framed on the wall when I'm old. And will they use posed portraits like this, or will they just frame the most scandalous tabloid shots for each celebrity? I'm stung by a slap of sadness. I don't know if I'll ever get old and find out.

Outside of a picture frame, eternally young is no way to really live.

chapter 17

ello, Andie. Are you lost?"

I'm standing in the lobby of Maya's House, waiting for my mom to pick me up, and I startle at hearing my name. Turning, I see Tom haltingly walk down the yellow carpet toward me. On his arm is an old woman with her hair in two long braids. She's fairly tall despite her evident age.

I try to remember if I've spoken to him yet in today's loop, and snap my fingers when I remember: "The mall." He looks surprised, and I add, "Er, how was it?"

"Pretty much the same as every other mall across America, thanks for asking." He laughs. "How was the mall for you?"

"Great." I need to dial back my enthusiasm. He doesn't know how close the two of us have gotten. I ask, "So, who's this?"

Tom smiles as he holds the woman's delicate hand toward me. "This is my grandma. You can call her Meemaw. Everyone does."

We shake hands, and she surprises me with a firm grip. "You two are missing quite the show over in the rec room," I say. "The cheerleaders are teaching the other residents how to dance."

"I'm good," Meemaw says. "Ready for my *Rampage*!" She aggressively claws at the air.

I give Tom a confused look and whisper, "Is she okay?"

"Nope." He laughs. "Not one bit. Follow us."

Tom's grandmother holds out her free arm, I take it, and the three of us shuffle forward together.

At the end of the hallway we walk through two doors similar to the ones that led to the rec room. I'm greeted by a row of video arcade games standing side by side, all lit up and waiting to be played.

The colorful marques above the screens advertise each game: *Ms. Pac-Man*, *Donkey Kong*, *Space Invaders*, *Centipede*, *Asteroids*. Tom says, "All of the old classics are here."

Meemaw has broken free from us, and she's making her way along the row of games. At the end, she stops at a game unit that has a screen filled with skyscrapers. The lit-up name across the top reads RAMPAGE, with a bodybuilder wolf and a strong ape each punching a lizard man's face from either side.

I reach into my bag and ask, "Do you need some quarters?" I carry extras around now since there's a soda machine at the mall, and I do love a refreshing beverage from time to time.

"No worries, the games are all free." Tom turns the key that's sticking out of the front panel and opens the small door. Reaching inside, he jimmies the coin switch wire repeatedly, and his meemaw claps her hands as the machine beeps to indicate a plethora of player credits adding up.

Finally, she can't hold in her excitement anymore and shoves her grandson out of the way. "Let me at it," she says, grabbing the set of game controls on the right-hand side of the console. She gestures to the center controls. "You can be the wolf."

He moves into position and tells me, "It's three players, if you want to get in on this."

I laugh, but cut off when Meemaw gives me a sharp glare. "You can be the lizard, but stay out of my ape's way."

The profile images of our three characters come up, and I must say, the graphics are rather archaic. My lizard's name is Lizzie, and every one of the monster's pixels is clearly defined. It's hard to believe this was ever cutting-edge technology.

But once the game starts, the primitiveness is forgotten as we all jump and climb up the skyscrapers, punching out windows and eating the screaming people that appear. I accidentally punch Tom's wolf, and the wolf reacts by covering his eyes with his hand.

"Sorry," I say. "He doesn't have much of a defense, does he?"

"Nope." Tom's wolf punches me back and my lizard man covers his eyes.

"Hey," I say. "That wasn't very nice."

We both laugh, and Meemaw snaps, "You two stop messing around and help me take down this building."

Tom dips his head toward me. "Be careful not to hit her ape. Meemaw has been known to retaliate by punching back in person."

I laugh, and he looks at me.

"She's freakishly strong," he says. "One time I kept messing around, and my arm was completely numb by the time we were done playing."

"I'll steer clear of the ape." Tom looks at me, and I call across to Meemaw, "I mean ape in the game. I wasn't calling you an ape."

Meemaw mumbles under her breath, "Wouldn't be the first time."

Tom laughs, and he and I focus on punching buildings and eating cars.

When I look over, Meemaw has her tongue sticking out one side of her mouth as she smacks her punch button with her open palm. Tom's tongue is sticking out the same way, and the look of focus as the two of them call out instructions to each other is adorable. Meanwhile, my lizard man forgets to jump off one of the buildings before it collapses and I lose a life.

"So, what did you think of *Pretty in Pink*?" Tom asks as we both tap our buttons like mad. It takes me a minute to remember I'd mentioned going home to watch it when I was at the movie theater, just before the whole world went wonky on me.

"It was . . . okay," I say while my lizard reaches into an apartment window and eats another guy. The man must go down the wrong pipe, because my lizard closes his eyes and breathes out fire as if he's choking.

"You didn't love it? I thought with your name and red hair, that movie was supposed to be some sort of next-level, life-changing experience."

"I guess you could say it made an impact." *Enormous understatement.* I groan as my character reaches into a broken wall and gets electrocuted. "Wrecking buildings is a lot of work."

Meemaw says, "Less talking, more smashing."

Tom laughs and bumps his hip against mine. "Tell me. Did you think Duckie should've gotten the girl?"

I let go of my lever, stop punching my buttons, and look at Tom. "Absolutely. How did you know?"

He doesn't take his eyes off the screen. "Well, it's pretty *obvious* that was the original intent of the movie. Didn't you watch the special features?"

"I . . . didn't have time." I almost laugh out loud at my lie. I have more time than I have anything else. *Why didn't I think to watch the* Pretty in Pink *special features?*

As Meemaw yells out instructions for destroying the buildings, Tom explains that John Hughes' original screenplay had Andie and Duckie ending up at the prom together. Then test audiences all wanted to see her get Blane, the handsome rich guy, and apparently test audience reactions are majorly important to film studios.

"Didn't you notice how horrible Andrew McCarthy's hair looks at the prom in the end?"

"Focus up!" Meemaw says, "You two can discuss the prom some other time."

Tom and I laugh and keep playing, and by the time I get the text from my mom saying that she's out front, we've helped Meemaw take down at least a dozen buildings.

"I'm just going to walk Andie out," Tom tells her. "Keep the rampage rolling, Meemaw."

"Fine, Tommy, but you owe me another life when you get back."

He leans over and kisses her forehead. Tom lowers his voice, but I can hear him say, "I owe you all my lives, Meemaw."

She playfully swats him away, and he pretends to hold his arm in pain. I tell her good-bye and it was nice meeting her, and she just nods without taking her eyes off her ape rampaging alone onscreen.

As Tom walks me down the hallway toward the entrance, I say, "Your meemaw seems like a trip."

"Yeah, she used to live with us, but her care needs were getting to be too much once my mom went back to work. She can get a little sassy when she eats too much sugar."

"It's so nice you come and visit her," I say.

"I usually try to stop by and play a few rounds with her before my shift at the theater. I'm working tonight." He looks at his watch. "In fact, I'd better get back there to finish destroying the city before I have to take Meemaw back to her room."

We move within earshot of the music flowing from the rec room. "It's nice they have so much cool stuff for the seniors to do."

"Yeah, it's pretty nice here." Tom looks back toward the arcade room. "Sad though too. The residents are often lonely, and each time Meemaw makes a new friend, they seem to die on her."

"That is sad."

"Yeah, outliving everyone can be an isolating thing. The folks here really love it when their families come to visit, but, you know, most people have busy lives."

"I imagine your visits really mean a lot."

"Yeah. And the cheerleaders help a lot too. Being around young people is like a shot of vitality to the residents. It gives them hope."

We stand looking at each other for a moment. I long to give him a hug, but know that clinging to these feelings will just make it hurt even more when today is erased. There's no way for me to rewrite this thing between us.

"Well, I'm going home to catch those *Pretty in Pink* special features," I say. "Thanks for the tip."

Tom looks almost wistful, then checks his watch again. "You got it. I'm off to finish rampaging the city." He brushes a hand against my arm as he turns and strides back in the direction we came.

I will him to look back the whole time and am rewarded when he finally gets to the doors. As he shoves the door open, he glances back over his shoulder, almost by accident, and smiles when I give him a final wave good-bye.

It's the closest I've come to making progress in our relationship, and tomorrow it will all be undone again. And that especially sucks tonight, because I'm pretty sure that seeing Tom playing video games with his meemaw just made me fall the rest of the way in love with him.

chapter 18

When Mom and I get home, the television is turned off, but the *Pretty in Pink* DVD case is still sitting out on top of the player.

I point to it and casually ask her, "Do you mind if I check out some of the extra features?"

"I had no idea you liked the movie so much," she says. "You looked like you were ready to fall asleep watching it last night."

I think back to that night so long ago, when I had the luxury of blowing off any deeper meaning that *Pretty in Pink* might have. "I guess you could say the ending got my attention."

Trying to hide her excitement, she asks, "Do you want me to watch the special features with you?"

"Would you?" I smile. "Pretty please?"

Mom says, "That's pretty *in pink* please. I'll pop some popcorn." She grins. "You get your PJs on and get ready for a thorough discussion of this movie. I have many thoughts."

"You know what, Mom?" She looks at me with anticipation, and I say, "This has been a good day."

Once we're all settled in on the big pink couch with our snacks, Mom loads the DVD into the player. As soon as the rolling clips from the film begin to play and those first familiar notes of the main menu tune reach my ears, I flinch. Grabbing the remote from Mom, I click on *Special Features*.

She gives me a strange look, and I say, "Sorry, just excited to get to it."

"We should maybe start by watching the interviews with other filmmakers," Mom says. "They each talk about John Hughes' influence, and how they all felt the first time they saw his movies . . ."

But I can barely hear her because I'm scanning the list of special features with names like *Zoids and Richies* and *Prom Queen: All About Molly.*

Finally, on the second page of extras, my heart starts beating faster as my eyes fall to the menu item labeled *The Lost Dance: The Original Ending.*

I'm hopeful that the answer to what's happening to me lies in wait beyond this click. It feels like I'm about to unlock all the mysteries of my universe.

But if this is supposed to be some sort of hint toward what's happening, it would seem my universe imploded back in 1986 during a dance at a John Hughes prom.

As we watch the cast interviews and deleted scenes, we learn that in the original ending, Andie shows up to the prom, and Duckie is there and they see Blane, but she chooses to dance the moonlight dance with Duckie.

According to the actors, the first sign of trouble was Molly Ringwald feeling sick the day they originally filmed the prom. Grown-up real-life Duckie says the movie almost ended as *Pretty in Projectile Vomit.*

On top of this, Molly claims there was never any romantic

chemistry between her and Duckie. Like, zero attraction. She describes the original ending as feeling like she was hooking up with her brother. So not ideal.

Then, at the test screening, the audience loved the movie but booed at the ending. *Actually* booed.

Onscreen, Andie and Duckie dance sweetly together at their awesome mid-80s prom, and I am filled with rage.

Stupid, handsome Blane was never meant to get the magical kiss at the end. It was supposed to be Duckie all along. Which makes perfect sense now. He's the one who deserves Andie. He sings for her and rides his bike past her house and epically dances his heinie off in the record store. He even tries to beat up Blane's awful jerk friend, Steff.

Duckie is the one who truly knows and loves her.

Everyone involved in making the movie believed Andie should end up with Duckie. But ultimately, they had to give in.

They reshot the prom scene with Blane wearing some awful wig, since the actor had shaved his head by then. And once they edited everything together, the people loved it. *Because people are idiots.* And Andie ends up with the *wrong guy* forever.

Just like with me. Instead of spending my summer days appreciating Duckie's charms, I wasted them chasing after stupid, handsome Colton. One day after another. As if days didn't even matter.

"Of course she should get the cute guy she wants in the end," one of the actors says onscreen. "The story is a fairy tale."

Mom says, "See, Andie. Even the people who were initially against the happy ending came around."

"This was *not* a happy ending," I say. "Duckie and Andie

together would've been a happy ending. This was just . . . pandering to the lowest common denominator."

"No, Andie. The movie showed that coming from different social cliques doesn't mean a couple can't work things out."

I think about that for a moment. It's true I've seen that social cliques are overly ironclad in high school. I picture the scene where Andie and Blane hang out in the courtyard together and the whole school loses its collective mind.

I try to envision Tammy and Czyre, or even Petra and Chuck, walking down the hallway together, and can't help but think my mom may have a point.

"I hear you on the good clique-crossing message," I say. "But Blane doesn't even confront his rich friends until the prom, when school is over and none of it matters anymore."

"He comes around late, but he does come around," Mom says.

"He *comes around* because Andie couldn't ignore Blane's blue eyes long enough to appreciate Duckie waiting on the sidelines, just loving her." I don't add, *Just like I was so dazzled by Colton I barely even noticed Tom.*

Because I don't need anyone to tell me that Tom is my Duckie. And now the indifference I showed him will always be too recent for me to ever fix it. I can't go far enough back to win him over, and I can't just plop on some prom wig and edit together new footage to make things okay.

Mom says, "Well, I think it's nice that they broke through the social walls that were keeping them apart, and I like to believe they ended up happily ever after."

I pull my lips into an artificial smile. "Well, they did say the movie was a fairy tale."

• • •

I go through several more loops trying to win Tom over in my single-day allotment, but it's pointless. Despite getting very good at playing *Rampage* with him and his meemaw, I can't seem to break through the cinderblock walls he's built around his heart.

The only two things that can even make punch marks in those walls are Tom's two favorite topics: movies and his meemaw.

He loves to engage her in our conversation by asking questions about her years acting as an extra on television shows in New York City.

"Go ahead, Meemaw," he'll say. "Tell the story."

"I've always loved being a background actor." She turns away from *Rampage* and looks at me, her eyes shining. "There's nothing quite like the longevity of a film career that flies way, way under the radar."

Tom says, "Meemaw was always more about having fun than she was about gaining exposure."

"Lots of actors turn their noses up at corpse duty," she says. "But I loved it, and I was one of the best." She tells me she wouldn't move or flinch, even between takes. "I was always in character, and if that character was dead, well, I was lying there, staying dead."

She licks her lips before telling me the story of the time her breathing was so shallow and her eyes so glazed over that the director actually called cut and asked if she was okay. To her delight, he approached Meemaw as she lay there, and she stayed completely still until the man put his fingers against her throat to check her pulse. As soon as he touched her neck, she sprung up and pretended to try and bite him.

"He was so shocked, he screamed like a girl." She grins proudly. "The camera was rolling and the whole thing is online somewhere."

Tom has been scrolling on his phone and holds it up to show me the video Meemaw just described. Sure enough, the big, beefy director looks genuinely afraid as he approaches an old woman lying dead on the ground. I can barely recognize Meemaw in her bloated corpse makeup, but when she makes the director startle in fright, there is no mistaking that familiar grin.

I laugh. "That's the best thing I've ever seen."

"Yeah," Tom says. "Meemaw's always been a practical joker."

She tells me about an ongoing prank she had going with one of the other residents until the Maya's House staff finally started locking up the plastic wrap.

"The people here have so much playfulness and life left in them," Tom says. "The children and grandchildren who don't make time to come here are really missing out."

Finally, I ask why he seems so upset about people not visiting. Apparently, he was here a few weeks ago (by his calendar) and there was a grandpa who was so excited because five of his grandchildren were supposed to be coming to see him.

Meemaw had whispered to Tom that they usually didn't show up, so he spent an hour playing chess with the old man while he waited. Tom says it was heartbreaking to witness the man's slow realization that his stupid grandkids weren't coming.

"Thankfully, the theater was playing *Ocean's Eleven*, so I was able to convince Meemaw to go watch it with him."

"I thought they only showed really old films here," I say. "I mean, not that the original is all that new. It was released in, what? Two thousand?"

Tom laughs. "The remake was done in two thousand and one."

I narrow my eyes at him. "Remake? You mean *Ocean's Twelve*?"

"The original *Ocean's Eleven* was released in nineteen sixty and starred Sinatra and Sammy Davis, Jr."

I slap my forehead. "Now I remember. The Rat Pack, right?"

"Yup." Tom grins. "Meemaw loves them. She and the guy with the rotten grandkids went together and had a really nice time."

"Another movie saves the day," I say, and Tom gives me a wide smile.

He says, "Movies make everything better."

After a beat, I sense his guard go up, and the spark goes out of the moment as he launches into a benign discussion about movie remakes. He points out how different two films can be, despite having the same original plot. And I laugh so hard I tell him I have to go.

Every day of my life is a remake now, and I'm getting a little sick of the recurring plot point where I lose Tom's interest.

• • •

Tom's movie knowledge goes even deeper than mine, and as I continue looping through I spend many nights staying up late to watch his vintage film suggestions.

I'm not all that surprised to discover he's a big fan of John Hughes. Besides supporting my obsession with Duckie and

Andie belonging together, he loves my theory that *The Breakfast Club* could never happen today.

Leaning against the Ms. Pac-Man game he's playing, I say, "The whole group would just sit around looking at their cell phone screens the entire time."

Tom laughs and turns toward me, abandoning his game mid-*wonka*. "I can see the updates now," he says. "Hashtag 'this sucks' with a selfie from on top of that giant metal sculpture in the middle of the library." He gives me that shy, crooked grin that I've come to know so well.

Filled with boldness, I dip my head toward his, hold up my camera phone, and call out, "Multi-person selfie."

He barely smiles for the picture, then says, "I'm not really into that whole 'let's document every second of our lives' mentality. I like living in the moment."

"Well, I wasn't going to post it anywhere or anything . . ." but he's already turned away to stand beside his meemaw and help her destroy a particularly tall and sturdy row of skyscrapers. I'm torn between feeling sad that I've lost Tom's interest for the night and excited that I finally have a photo of the two of us together.

When I look at it I realize that *of course* my eyes are closed in the picture.

And, as usual, it's been deleted from my phone the next morning.

Using my trial and error system, I'm able to determine that not even staying at Maya's House until later does any good. Meemaw eventually destroys as many buildings as she can in one night, and then lets us know she's ready to go to bed.

Once we've tucked her away back in her room, Tom turns to me and says, "Welp, time for me to head over to the theater." And it's as if by mentioning the theater, he's reminded that I've been flirting with Colton there all summer long. Every single time.

No matter how far or friendly we've gotten on any particular day, we never get beyond that point without his expression going blank. Even when I say, "I was thinking of stopping by to catch a movie," his only response is to shrug and tell me that he thinks Colton's on the schedule before turning to walk away.

And he never looks back at me from the doors again.

I even try looping through as a cheerleader, staying for practice and agreeing to go to Maya's House with the girls this time.

When I arrive at the retirement home with the other cheerleaders, I look around the lobby for Anna and Petra. It takes me a moment to remember they only show up when I tell them about the cheerleaders coming here.

Dawn smiles at our group from behind her desk and gestures toward the rec room. "You know the way," she says. "I'll be down in a minute."

Tammy thanks Dawn and then calls the rest of us to come on over and huddle up. We obediently move to the center of the lobby and make a circle.

Leaning our heads together with our arms around each other, we wait for Tammy's instructions as we breathe in the air freshener that's not quite able to cover up the underlying scent of rubbing alcohol. Tammy focuses on each face and stops at mine.

"First, I want to welcome Andie again." Everyone smiles at me and the circle hugs in a tiny bit tighter. It's not the first time I'm hit with a wave of affection toward these girls. I was a bit rusty while working on the routine after school, but they stepped in to help me along. Particularly Tammy.

"This is the most important thing any of us will do all week," she says now. "Your goal is to spread as many happy memories as you can."

"Yeah," Jacynda says under her breath. "Whether those memories last or not."

Tammy shifts to give her a small shove.

"Just saying." Jacynda shrugs. "My favorite dance partner in there has introduced herself to me at least a half-dozen times."

"Hey, all we have is right now," I say. "That's true for every single one of us."

"Yes! Let's make it count." Tammy grins at me and nods. "Ready?"

We all call out, "Okay!" as we rise from the huddle.

Tammy starts a slow clap and leads us as we make our way down the hall toward the rec room.

Jacynda whispers to me, "If any of the residents gets overly excited or out of breath, Dawn is the nurse you want to deal with. She considers her patients' experiences more important than following protocol, so she usually won't report minor incidents."

Our synchronized clapping picks up speed as we get to the end of the hallway and, finally, we burst through the double doors into the rec room together. The smiles that greet us are positively glowing.

The music kicks up a notch, and I move toward the man wearing his non-ironic suspenders. There's pure happiness in his grin, and I find odd comfort knowing I'm not the only one here who's just living for the moment. Building permanent memories isn't always the point.

Sometimes, we're simply enjoying whatever day we happen to be in.

chapter 19

'm surprisingly filled with hope the next morning when I peel my face off the pink leather arm of the couch, dressed in my scratchy polka-dot dress.

Tom wasn't overly impressed by my cheer outfit when I broke from the group partying in the rec room to "accidentally" run into him and his meemaw in the arcade last night. It wasn't until he saw how awesome I am at playing *Rampage* that I managed to catch his attention.

But revisiting my old cheerleading skirt reminded me of something else. Tom is literally the only person in the whole school who doesn't change how he treats me based on how I'm dressed. Sure, he especially loved the pink dress and my own individual pajama day, but he's been nice to me from heels to veils and everything in between.

To everyone else, belonging to different cliques means I'm a completely different person.

And yet, if I've learned anything from my time at this school, it's that the students at Punxsutawney High are more similar than they are different.

Just like Anna finally seeing that the cheerleaders aren't as bad as she thought, all everyone needs is a chance to see each other more clearly and learn each other's stories. They only need someone to draw them all together.

And now, I think I have an idea of just how I can do it.

Last night, Tom told me again how much getting visitors means to the residents of Maya's House. And it was like his words formed the missing puzzle piece that clicked all the others into place.

This isn't only about breaking myself out of the cycle anymore. It's about using all my experience and knowledge and especially my wide range of *contacts* to create one day that will enlighten as many people as possible. It's about making the time I've spent spinning around in my hamster ball finally count for something.

After a quick shower, I pull on dark jeans and a black shirt. While I consider my reflection, my mind rolls over my still-forming plan. Dressing in a way that strikes the perfect balance is crucial to step one.

Since I'm the point person, I'll need to be able to cross back and forth over social barriers. I must create a look that the goths will relate to, without alienating all the other groups who populate my school.

And *yes*, I do realize that categorizing and manipulating people based on labels and looks and cliques is hurtful and isolating and seriously *not cool*, but at this point I need to gain every advantage I possibly can.

All the makeup tutorials I watched online are about to majorly pay off, because my look needs to be just right. Expertly, I create a slightly smoky eye paired with dark lips I can mute to a lighter shade once I've secured the goths' support.

My first mission is to convince Czyre to draw a cool cartoon for the flyers promoting the giant gathering I hope to arrange.

If this event is even half as successful as I envision it being, this school is never going to be the same.

• • •

I accept my morning ride with Colton when he arrives, but make it clear I think of us as just buddies now. Our tour of the school seems more relaxed than ever, despite the loud whirring inside my head as I try to fill in the remaining pieces of my plan.

When he and I reach the cheerleaders, I impress them with a few moves despite my more restrictive clothing.

Once I've won them over, I grab Tammy by the hand, saying, "I wish I could learn how to tweeze my eyebrows into an arch like yours."

Which I know sounds like a bizarre comment, but I happen to know Tammy carries tweezers in her purse and is famous for pulling them out to expertly shape the eyebrows of anyone brave enough to ask.

The two of us head to the bathroom together, where she gives me what I must confess are the most awesome-looking eyebrows to ever grace my face. She even uses cold water compresses to help reduce the redness.

I'm careful to time things perfectly, so as we leave the girls' room she runs directly into Czyre in the middle of the hallway. Right in the same spot he and I always used to collide.

Except Tammy walks with more purpose than I do, and so the two of them knock into each other much too hard. Tammy staggers back, and I can see an angry bump already forming where his chin hit her forehead.

I feel terrible, but I catch Tammy before she falls and think fast in hopes of finding a way to redeem this. Czyre is bent over, picking up his Sharpie, and I ask, "Didn't I see you drawing a cartoon on the side of one of the bleachers?"

Tammy reacts as I hoped, dropping her hand from the growing red lump on her forehead and staring at Czyre.

He stops testing if his jaw is broken, and his eyes go wide as he stares at me.

Thankfully, Tammy grabs Czyre by the arm and steals his attention. "Did you really draw that cartoon?" she asks. "The one with the stressed-out toddlers? Wait? Are you the vandal artist who's been doing *all* the drawings?"

Czyre looks back and forth between Tammy and me as he opens and closes his mouth. He has always protected his identity so carefully that I've completely blindsided him. "Who *are* you?" he asks me.

Tammy practically shrieks, "Those drawings are *amazing*!"

Looking around, Czyre holds a finger to his lips before he breaks into a slow smirk. "They're also *illegally* posted," he whispers. The two of them look at each other for four full beats before he finally asks, "You want to see my latest one?"

As Czyre leads Tammy toward the dark open mouth of the stairwell, she gets a sudden look of fear in her eyes.

Catching up to them, I hook my elbow around hers. "Lead the way," I say.

Czyre glares at me like I'm third-wheeling it hard, but I can see that he needs my help. Tammy must've watched too many horror movies or is maybe a bit weirded out by guys who wear eyeliner. Either way, she needs my presence because she's about to bail.

When we reach the point where we have to duck our heads beneath the undersides of the steps, Tammy says, "I've never really been *inside* here." Her voice sounds timid and makes it clear that it isn't the movie tropes or the eyeliner that are bothering Tammy. It's the goths.

"This is a first," Bridget says. "Welcome to our lair."

From the back corner, I can hear a quietly mocking, "Ready? Okay!"

"Funny," Tammy says without laughing.

I want to scold the whole group. Can't they see that she's being very brave right now and that Czyre and Tammy are meant to be together forever and that everyone here is ruining things for them?

"Come on, guys," Bridget says. "Be nice." *There's my girl.*

Tammy must've just spotted the drawing Czyre did of her, because she moves slowly toward that wall.

When she reaches it, she raises two fingertips to touch the sneakered feet of the cheerleader calling out, "Care!" Tammy's head turns toward the crowd calling back, "We can't," and she moves her fingertips from the wall to her lips.

She stares at the cartoon.

"Tammy," Czyre says, "I hope you don't—"

"This is . . . *me*." Tammy turns toward Czyre, and the two of them stand, looking at each other. "You've captured my struggle. Caring is hard enough. Sometimes it feels like nothing matters. And then trying to get *others* to care is . . ." Her voice breaks and her eyes well up in the dim light.

"I know," Czyre says, and finally the rest of the gang under the stairwell can see what I already knew.

That these two were clearly meant to be together. Tammy hooks her hair behind one ear and looks up at Czyre in a way that says the Goth vs. Cheerleader wall has just crumbled down a bit in one spot. She's seeing him.

"Well, I'm going to get a little air," I announce, and it's as if I've just stuck a pin into the balloon of awkward that's been expanding inside the small space. The rest of us move from underneath the stairs in one big *whoosh*.

Of course, Czyre and Tammy stay behind, which was kind of the point.

Czyre now owes me. I smile as I glide a more neutral rose shade over my lips. I'm happy that they finally connected, but it's time to move on to phase two of my plan.

When I find Anna and Petra standing in front of their lockers, I falter a moment. It's not as if I can just waltz up to them and start talking. And how do I even bring up the topic of their rock band when I should have no way of knowing about it?

Before a solution fully forms in my brain, Anna closes the locker they're standing in front of and I need to act.

Snapping my cell phone up to my ear, I open my mouth in mock surprise. "Oh no!" I say loud enough that the girls can obviously hear me. "What are we going to do?"

Anna looks annoyed. Maybe because I've nearly bumped into her in my attempt to make sure I have her attention. She says, "There's this thing? It's called *personal space* . . ."

"I'm *so* sorry," I say, gesturing to my phone as I put it away.

"Did you just hang up on someone?" Petra asks.

"They'll understand." I wave my hand awkwardly and make a mental note to become better at acting. "I'm just really in a jam. I don't suppose either of you knows of a band that might be free to play a gig tonight?"

Petra looks excited, but bites down on both her lips as if forcing herself to keep quiet, while Anna crosses her arms. Clearly, they don't trust me.

"I need everything but a bass player," I say. "I'm really good on bass." I mime a few riffs as I will the two of them to go for the bait. It takes me naming a few songs that I know they play for Anna to finally uncross her arms and ask for more details.

As soon as she hears there will be jealous hordes of classmates present, she's in. I lean forward to give them the details, marveling at how well things are going already.

Which is when I see Tammy striding past with her nose in the air. Alone. I quickly pretend to gather the contact information that I already have from Anna and Petra, and run after Tammy.

"What happened?" I ask when I catch up to her. "I thought you and Czyre were really hitting it off."

She turns to face me. "I'm sorry, but what did you say your name was again?"

"Andie?" I say softly. "It's my first day."

"Hi, Andie. I'm not really sure how you knew Czyre was the cartoon artist, or what else you think you know about me, but really, you need to back off."

"What happened? Did he try to kiss you or something?" I'm still traumatized by my own kiss/kick experience with Colton, but I can't imagine Czyre acting inappropriate.

"No," Tammy says, confused. "Things went fine. I just barely know him."

"But he drew your cartoon," I say lamely.

"Okaaay . . ." The way Tammy draws out the word, I know I've totally lost her. "See you around, Andie."

Without getting Czyre to draw up the flyers for me, I'm cooked, and Tammy was a big part of that plan. Looking around the hallway, I suddenly get an idea.

"Girls? Can we talk about flyers?" I wave my hands toward Anna and Petra.

If Czyre and Tammy won't help me, I need new recruits.

"That's final bell," Petra says as the two of them turn away from their lockers. "Do you need help finding your homeroom? Andie, was it?"

"Yeah," Anna adds, "good luck with that."

"My homeroom is right next to yours," I tell Anna loudly as they begin striding down the hallway. "Hey, let's walk together."

To be honest, our homerooms are in opposite directions, but I've gotten much better at making up fake last names.

"Beuford?" the teacher calls out when I arrive just steps behind Anna. Petra broke off three rooms ago with a friendly pat on my arm, but Anna is the one I need to convince if I hope to get anyplace.

Once I'm settled in beside her with my fake last name, I lean in and start my pitch. It sucks to be redirecting my plan so soon, but I always knew that flexibility would be key to making this happen.

This unending day will not bend or stretch for me, but it's all I've got to work with, so I'll just need to be the one to adjust.

• • •

At lunch, I sit with Tom and his friends and casually bring up the subject of Maya's House. "Did you know that they have a movie theater inside?" I ask. "It seats about fifty people or so."

Tom nods his head. "Yeah, they show all these cool vintage classics."

"Have you ever watched a movie there?" I ask.

He laughs. "Yeah, and I think they like to stick with the classics, since otherwise the films get overrun with the residents calling out, 'What did he just say?'"

I smile. Tom and I have had this conversation before about how frustrating it can be to watch a film with someone who expects you to miss portions of it in order to explain the parts they just missed. "I was thinking of going over there tonight," I say. "Who's in?"

"I'm there all the time with my meemaw," Tom says. "But she's not much of a movie buff. She prefers the games in the arcade."

I say, "Well, I looked it up, and tonight they're playing *Casablanca*, so . . ."

"Oh my goodness." Chuck hooks both thumbs around the straps of his yellow suspenders. "I am genetically required to watch that movie at every given opportunity."

I already knew this, but I act surprised. I smile and give him the showtime, explaining just how easy it is to gain free access to a classic movie playing on a big screen. As long as one doesn't mind a few shouted interruptions of, "*What?*"

As Tom and his friends pledge to come tonight, I think things are starting to get back on track.

<h1 style="text-align:center">chapter 20</h1>

The entrance hall to Maya's House is eerily quiet when I arrive about five hours later, and I feel a tremor in my resolve. Actually, the tremor is more like an earthquake with a magnitude of 9.6 on the Richter scale. *This is crazy.*

I don't know if I have the strength to make it this far again if this time doesn't work, and there is still so much that can go wrong. Way too many moving parts, but at least things are moving.

Instead of focusing on myself and what I'm going through, I'm determined to help as many others as possible today. No matter how long it lasts.

The flyers were thoroughly distributed around the school and through social media and various message boards with the event's address and time. Spreading word ended up becoming a group effort, and the flyers looked something like this:

#PrettyinPunx

Hello, Punxsutawney High students, and welcome to another year of higher education!

The first day of school is off like a dirty shirt

and we've got the best way to celebrate. Put together your most volcanic ensembles and come one, come all, to an epic start-of-year social gathering. Don't waste good lip gloss or miss out on the chance to say *you were there.* Come, be admired. Talk. Connect. Be #prettyinpunx

We are about to throw the biggest high school inter-clique party this retirement home has ever seen.

I start unloading the supplies I've picked up and head in to tell Nurse Dawn the parts of my plan she needs to know. It's a good thing she's more interested in happy experiences for the residents than she is in following protocol, because we're about to break a whole lotta Maya's House house rules.

• • •

"Hey there, Andie, where've you been all day?"

It's Colton, and his arrival with his friends means this event is officially *on* in a big way. His invitation was the longest shot. I'd sent him an anonymous text that the cops had been tipped off to the traditional *epic* party at his buddy's house. I also gave him details about this event and let him know there'd be free video games and drinks.

Naturally, my text didn't mention that the games are arcade classics from the 1980s and the drinks are primarily a selection of juices to encourage good digestion. All nonalcoholic.

"Wait a second," Colton's friend Motko says as he moves in beside him. "This is the place where my grandpa lives."

"Welcome to Maya's House," I practically gush.

Kaia sidles up close to Colton and gives me a suspicious look. I grin, and her penetrating glare morphs to mild confusion. I desperately want to take her perfectly airbrushed face in my hands and look her in the eyes and tell her that she doesn't need to make herself sick anymore. That she deserves so much better, and that we are not enemies. Being a girl is not a competition.

But she flinches when I lean toward her, and so I just say, "Hi, I'm Andie."

As if she can sense my original crush on Colton, she hooks an arm possessively around his bicep. "I thought you said there were drinks and video games," she says. "This is just an old people's home."

Just then, my Mad D Batteries bandmates walk in dragging armloads of equipment. "Where do we set up?" Anna asks me. I can see she's truly a little excited to see the others here.

Kaia laughs mockingly. "This, I need to see."

"Come on then," I say. "The rec room is this way."

Instinctively chivalrous, Colton grabs an amp and Motko picks up one end of the electric drum set Katy is dragging. The two of them share a smile that fills my matchmaking heart with happiness.

As we haltingly make our way down the hallway toward the rec room, I'm starting to wonder if I can pull this off when I hear the giggling chatter of more classmates arriving.

Timing seems to be working out perfectly, and Tom should be showing up for the movie with his colorful friends any minute. I'm excited for them to meet the residents, since a number of them have similar taste in clothes.

I even made sure the goths will come by inviting their tattoo-ist buddy, Rodney, here to give temporary tattoos to everybody who wants one. He's happy for the practice, and is busy setting up a chair in a corner of the arcade. Residents are already lined up, waiting to get faux-inked.

Nurse Dawn was a little skeptical of Rodney, particularly when one of the elderly ladies ran up to ask if she can have her new boyfriend's name permanently tattooed onto her chest. But Rodney was kind yet firm with the woman, convincing her that a long-lasting temporary tattoo was the better choice.

"You have a lot of life and love left in you, I can tell," Rodney said. "There's no point in limiting your options."

Dawn gave Rodney a wink and told the woman, "See, Rosa. I've been telling you, *he's* the lucky one."

I'm hoping that once Czyre gets here, he and Tammy don't ignore the spark that was ignited between them this morning. And it would be so nice if Petra and Chuck finally got to spend a little time together—not to mention Katy and Motko, who are talking to each other right now as they carry in the rest of the band equipment. I've even noticed that Bridget has a lot in common with another close friend of Colton's, who doesn't drink due to his dedication to football.

This event is jam-packed with romantic potential.

I may not have a shot with Tom, but that can't stop me from trying to match up as many other couples as possible. I feel like I'm channeling the ultimate courtship ambassador: Cher Horowitz from *Clueless*.

Above all, my goal today is to spread joy and happiness and love, so I especially more-than-anything hope we aren't all about to get arrested over the teeny-tiny, minor fact that we're completely overrunning, invading, and hitting the maximum occupancy level for this whole retirement community right now.

• • •

It turns out, I needn't have worried. Various residents jump up to greet many of my classmates, and it takes me a moment to realize that Petra wasn't kidding when she said half the town has relatives who live here.

It isn't long before the cheerleaders are clapping their way down the hallway as the usual classic playlist blasts from the speakers. Anna earnestly breaks into her robot onstage and the crowd goes wild, including Tammy, who makes a beeline for Czyre right away. It's the biggest and most diverse and energetic dance party this place has ever seen.

The. Old. People. Love. It.

When Chuck arrives, the old man wearing non-ironic suspenders is dancing with Petra to a crooner tune by Elvis. The two guys in suspenders admire each other's accessory choices, and Petra smoothly switches partners to dance with Chuck.

Everyone around me is so happy, I can't help but to imagine this might be it. The final cycle to break me out of my curse.

The night has everything: People breaking down social walls like in *The Breakfast Club*. There's a wacky Ferris-Bueller-dancing-on-the-German-float feel to the retirement home surroundings, and there's even a bit of *Some Kind of Wonderful* sprinkled in as we jump up onstage to start our Mad D Batteries set and Petra starts wailing on the drums as hard as Mary Stuart Masterson ever did.

If only we could full-on *Pretty in Pink* this party with the original ending; the strong and proud and resilient redhead getting her moonlight dance with Duckie. From where I'm standing onstage I look across the crowd for Tom.

I notice one of the orderlies is also searching through the crowd. He runs up to Nurse Dawn and starts waving his hands dramatically. I'm too far away to figure out what he's telling her, but Dawn's eyes land on me. As soon as she's calmed the orderly down, she makes her way over to the foot of the stage where I am.

"We may need to shut this down," Nurse Dawn calls up to me over the music.

"Oh no, what is it?" I stop playing my bass, instantly filled with regret for my recklessness. "Did someone break a lamp or a bone or somebody's heart or something?"

"No, it seems there's a problem over in the arcade," she says.

"Is Rodney giving real tattoos?" I practically screech.

"No, he's doing fine," Dawn says. "In fact, he gave me this." She shows me a delicate hummingbird inked onto her inner wrist.

She stops to smile at it a moment, and Anna hisses my name from center stage.

I gesture for the band to keep playing without me and leap off the stage, landing neatly beside Dawn. "What's the problem?"

"There's a rowdy group of boys hogging one of the arcade games, and we have a resident who's pretty worked up. The nurses are dealing with her, but we can't have our people getting upset."

"Please give me a chance to make this right," I say. "Which game is it?" I already suspect the answer as I drop my bass and move toward the rec room doors.

"*Rampage*," Dawn calls. I'm sprinting toward the arcade when she adds, "But be careful, that elderly woman is freakishly strong!"

On my way to the arcade, I see that Bogart and Bergman are embracing onscreen, and realize that Chuck was still in the rec room instead of coming in here to catch *Casablanca*, despite the fact Dawn had previously announced the movie was starting. This happens to be a Very Big Deal. I mean, he named his cat Humphrey after Bogart, for goodness' sake. But there Chuck was when I left, standing and nodding as he watched Petra play the drums.

When I get to the arcade, the place is packed with the same group that was at the house party with Colton the night I flex-kicked him. I spot Colton playing *Rampage* with Meemaw and Motko. The three of them are banging the buttons so hard, the whole machine is rocking.

Colton yells at the screen, and Meemaw hits him in the arm. "Less crying. More punching."

Colton rubs the spot where she connected with his arm. "Ouch, you hit hard."

Motko laughs. "We're not supposed to be actually punching each other, Meemaw."

Apparently, somebody else already intervened. I look around for Tom and finally find him playing *Ms. Pac-Man*. He doesn't look up when I approach.

"I heard your meemaw was giving the football team a hard time," I say.

"Yeah, they were hogging her game for a while."

"Glad you got them to let her play."

Tom looks up from his maze of dots and glances over to where Meemaw and Motko are high-fiving each other. "That was all her," he says. "Nobody was gonna keep her away from *Rampage*. It's her favorite game."

I laugh. "I know."

He gives me a strange look and goes back to playing *Ms. Pac-Man*. I belatedly realize I'm not supposed to know anything about *Rampage* or his meemaw, but I can certainly show him a thing or two about *Ms. Pac-Man*. I hit the two-player button.

"You know you can't just join in on these games, right?" he says. "They're from the early eighties."

"Oh, yeah." I laugh. "Practically need to wind them up with a crank."

"Kind of like that." I can tell from his voice that something is bothering him, but in this version of today I don't know him well enough to call him on it. Then again . . .

"Are you mad at me or something?" I ask.

"What makes you think that?" he says without looking up.

"Because you're acting like you're mad at me."

"I'm not acting like anything, Andie. It's not like the two of us are friends. What're you getting at?"

I sigh. "Nothing, I guess." It appears the *Pretty in Pink* part of today is simply never going to happen. My Duckie is so close and yet still so far away.

I can't be sure, but I think Tom lets his Ms. Pac-Man die on purpose. When the game finishes running through the credits, he asks if I want to go first.

I step up to the single controller. "Sorry, I forgot we can't play at the same time either."

"No worries." Tom watches me play and is increasingly impressed by my skills. As I clear board after board, he begins to cheer me on.

"Guess I should've let you go first," I say.

"Oh, I'm not playing after this," he says. "It would be too shaming. I'm just watching now to see how far you go."

We're quiet for a few minutes while I gobble dots and cherries and blue ghosts like it's my job. Finally, I ask again, "Did I do something different today? Something that upset you?"

Tom leans his back against the machine. "I don't know what you mean by *different*, Andie, but right now I'm wondering why you're not over there playing a game with Colton."

"Why would I be playing with Colton?" I ask as I quickly slam the joystick back and forth, counting in my head before the ghosts change back from blue.

"Well, I mean—" Tom runs a hand through his hair. "You seemed pretty into him this summer at the theater. And then you invited him to come here to the retirement home. I'm just wondering what your angle is, playing *Ms. Pac-Man* with me right now. Or should I say, schooling me at *Ms. Pac-Man*?"

That's what I did different; I invited Colton to Maya's House. "But I invited everyone here tonight," I say. "I'm the one who came up with the fliers and helped make them and hang them around the school. I'm the one who sent text messages and posts and invited everyone I ever talked to."

Tom looks over toward the rocking game of *Rampage*. "It's just that I deal with his arrogant nonsense enough at the theater, now he's with my favorite girl."

"You like Kaia?" I ask. This is new.

"What are you talking about?" Tom gestures to the end of the row. "He's Rampaging over there with my meemaw."

I laugh. "Of course your meemaw is your favorite girl."

"You've obviously had a huge crush on Colton all summer," Tom says as my Ms. Pac-Man chomps a strawberry. "Are you picturing those dots as tiny Kaia heads?"

"Colton was all wrong for me." I shift away from my game so I can look Tom in the eye.

This is it. Even if he never remembers this moment, I have to try.

Over the sound of Ms. Pac-Man rolling over to die, I tell him, "Tom, I like *you*."

He laughs, but I don't go back to playing my game and I don't break eye contact. Finally, he says, "Well, you didn't have to martyr poor Ms. Pac-Man just to make a point."

"I want you to believe me." I look at him imploringly. "I really like you."

"I . . ." Tom's expression fills me with hope. "Andie," he says, "forgive me if I need a few days to process this."

"No!" I say, and he startles. "I need you to get this *right now*."

He looks at me for a moment, and I know him well enough to read his expression. He wants to believe me. But based on how I was treating him up until my epic time travel loop, he's just not going to be convinced. A single day cannot undo a whole summer, but I'm so very close. *One more day*, I think. *That's all I need.*

I lean in closer, and the two of us just sort of hover there a moment, before he seems to wake up. "I'm working the closing shift at the theater tonight," he says. "I should really get going."

And just like that, he turns to leave. "Tom?"

He turns back, and I think of all the things I want to say to him right now. All the inside jokes we've shared that he's forgotten. All the conversations. But it's not fair to expect him to believe what he is to me. He has a right to ask for more time. "I'll see you tomorrow," I say.

"Yes." He smiles. "I'll see you tomorrow."

The lilt in his voice makes it clear that this is a "To be continued . . ." conversation. I just wish it wasn't actually a "The End" that will morph directly into tomorrow's "Once upon a time . . ."

But as I watch him walk over to kiss his meemaw goodnight, and see Colton and Motko give him friendly slaps on the back, I wonder. I didn't quite manage to win my Duckie, but the party has been a roaring success, with so many of the walls dividing the different cliques coming down. People who never spoke before are busy exchanging numbers and screen names. Not to mention all the new romances already starting.

Everyone around me looks so happy and connected, I can't help but think this could be it. I may have just fulfilled my calling.

And a thin beam of hope says I might wake up free.

chapter 21

nd it's that sort of optimistic thinking that finally breaks me. I go to bed that night truly believing the anticipation building inside me means something. Like I've finally broken the curse. I envision myself waking up in my bed, wearing my pajamas. I *will* my vision to come true.

When I wake up the next morning, I'm so blind with excitement that it takes me a few moments to connect the dots and figure out where I am.

On the couch. With my face stuck to the pink leather. In the poufy, polka-dot, scratchy dress. With the *Pretty in Pink* DVD menu playing on the television.

I stand up and just stare at the screen, vaguely aware my hands are rolling in and out of fists. I twist my neck from side to side until it cracks, and then I weave my fingers together and stretch my palms out in front of me until my elbows lock and all my knuckles pop.

Then . . . I completely lose it.

Flinging my fist out, I punch over the table lamp. It bounces instead of smashing, which I find even more infuriating.

The music coming from the television feels like it's eating a hole in my brain, so I hit eject on the player and snap the disc in two. Then four. Next, I wrestle with it for a few minutes before finally flinging the pieces so I don't end up slicing my hands open on the broken disk's sharp edges.

Reaching down, I pick up my blanket and try to rip it in half. My face turns hot as I pull and twist, but evidently the fuzzy material is much stronger than it appears. After marveling for a split second at how sturdy something so lightweight can be, I'm reduced to screaming in frustration.

Both of my parents come running into the room.

I pound the back of the pink couch with both of my fists. "Czyre and Tammy have never met and fallen in love," I wail at them. "And Petra doesn't realize that she and Chuck truly belong together."

Dad leans over to Mom and whispers, "What movie were you two watching last night?"

I go on. "There's a stupid picture of Kaia stuffing her face that's absolutely devastating, and Anna will never know how nice the cheerleaders are and that they *didn't* prank her."

"We were watching *Pretty in Pink*," Mom says to Dad. "I don't know what movie she's talking about." She tilts her head at me like a dog listening to a high-pitched noise.

"*Everybody* has problems." I raise my voice. "They're all just drowning in the same stupid stuff, and I can't fix *anything*."

Mom tries putting an arm over my shoulder, but I shrug it off. Looking back and forth between my parents, I yell at them, "I am *never* going to graduate high school!"

Dad starts laughing at this. "Okay, sweetie, you're clearly having some sort of episode due to the stress of changing schools.

You've always gotten good grades. I'm pretty sure graduating isn't going to be a problem."

"I'm not going to school today," I say. "No way. Everything will be undone. It'll be like nobody ever danced together at the retirement home." I try to climb back underneath the blanket, but Mom pulls it off me.

"I need to stop pushing the stupid boulder up the hill!" I say. "There's *no point* in any of it."

I drop onto the couch and cover my face with both hands, but I can feel the two of them having a nonverbal conversation. And it's probably some version of "*I'm* not talking to her, *you* talk to her."

Dad must lose the argument, because he's the one who finally sits down beside me on the couch.

"I know starting over at a new school is difficult, Andie," he says. "But trust me, you've got this. We wouldn't have moved you here if we weren't positive you can handle it."

"It's all in the attitude," Mom says brightly as she sits down on the other side of me. "Today can be a good day or an awful day. It's all up to you."

I nod as if I'm agreeing with her. Then announce, "Yeah. It's going to be *awful*."

• • •

When Colton arrives, I'm still wearing the pink polka-dotted number, and my parents are watching me nervously as I argue with myself while pacing back and forth.

Mom lets him in and gestures in my direction. "Andie's all set to go . . . I think."

"You know something, Colton?" I snap, and he looks at me expectantly. Like I'm about to say something flirty. "You can be a real jerk."

He flinches like I've slapped him, and Mom moves into the room. "I'm sorry," she says. "My daughter isn't feeling all that well this morning."

"I'm fine, Mom, really." I poke Colton in the chest. "But *this* guy here. He's only concerned with everybody liking him."

Colton looks vaguely afraid of me. "Um, we'd better get going," he says. "Unless you'd rather wait for the bus?"

"Oh, you'd like that, wouldn't you?" I snap at him. "No crazy redhead in a wild pink polka-dot dress interfering with your flirting game. Leading girls on to feed your own ego."

"Um, okay then . . ." He gives my mom a look that is a clear cry for help.

"Let's just go," I snap, and head for the door.

Mom calls out a good-bye, but this time she doesn't try to take our photograph together.

• • •

Colton tries to ditch me just inside the front door to the school, and I call after him, "You don't even deserve that cool job at the movie theater!" The crowded hallway of students turns to see who the yelling redhead in polka dots could be.

"Get a good look, everyone," I call out in my crazy-person voice. "I'm the new girl, *Andie*! And I'm going to be here *forever*."

As I walk down the hallway, my dress rustles with laughter as my ballet flats whisper the truth over and over. *Nothing matters. Nothing matters. Nothing matters.*

I run into Czyre and pull the Sharpie from his hand. "Hey there, *George*." He gives me a startled look and I call out, "Does everyone here know *George*?"

He asks, "Have we met?"

I snap the lid from the Sharpie and grab his face, trying to draw a mustache on him. He fights me off, so I drop the Sharpie and announce, "George here is the one who's been drawing those powerful cartoons and posting them anonymously around the school."

I walk away before I can witness the fallout, but catch someone excitedly saying, "Czyre! I had no idea!"

I open the door to the gym and call out to the cheerleaders, "You know, you should really be proud of the charity work you do." They're all frozen, staring at me in their cheerleading skirts. I add, "You don't need to hide what nice people you are after hours."

I'm going through the motions of my day as if in a fog. Yesterday was all about spreading as much happiness as possible. And now today's about throwing truth bombs.

I tell Motko, "Go and visit your grandfather. You don't know how much longer he'll be around!" *Kapow* . . . truth bomb.

I tell the guy in my science class, "You're so afraid of rejection, you reject everyone before they get the chance to reject you." *Kapow* . . . truth bomb.

"Suzie talks about you behind your back. And you talk about her behind hers. How about you two talk *to* each other instead of *about* each other?" *Kapow* . . . truth bomb.

"You need to stop thinking only of yourself. Your best friend is having a hard time right now and you haven't even noticed." *Kapow* . . . truth bomb.

"Everyone can tell that you're high. Everyone. And you might want to consider keeping what brain cells you have left." *Kapow* . . . truth bomb.

"Stop obsessing over whether he likes you. Do *you* like *you* is the more important question." *Kapow* . . . truth bomb.

By the time I reach Mr. Demers' English class I'm getting lots of dirty looks, and I suddenly get the feeling I should be watching out for villagers with pitchforks.

When the topic of Sisyphus comes up, I calmly raise my hand and answer the question about repetitive situations before Mr. Demers finishes asking it.

When Tom repeats his classic comment that Sisyphus should just stop doing that, I'm ready for him.

Which basically means I explode. Jumping onto my chair, I scream at him, "Maybe Sisyphus just *can't* stop." I hop from my chair to my desk, and the legs squeak in protest. I say, "Maybe the rock won't stop rolling down the hill no matter what Sisyphus does, and maybe, just *maybe*, he has no choice but to keep pushing the stupid thing back up."

I look down at the blanket of shocked faces staring up at me.

"Maybe we're all simply doing the best that we can with situations that don't make any sense to us." I step down from my desk to my chair, then to the floor. "Our boulders might be all different shapes and sizes, but I think we all know the effort of pushing something heavy. And the pain of risking hope that *this* time, maybe, when we reach the top"—I feel tears forming in my eyes—"things just might be *finally* different. Better, even."

As I slide back into my seat, my puffy pink polka-dot skirt claws at my legs, reminding me how ridiculous I just looked.

"Wow," Mr. Demers says, and starts a long, slow clap. He doesn't seem upset when nobody else joins in. "That passion was fantastic . . . Andie, is it?"

I nod, and then lay my head down on the desk I was just standing on.

Mr. Demers continues with his lesson, and eventually I sit up and slouch back in my seat. Tom leans over and whispers, "I'd heard you were making quite the impression around here today."

I turn and look at him with rapidly blinking eyes. "I think I've been falling in love with you." *Kapow . . .* truth bomb.

● ● ●

At lunch, I continue my tirade, reaching new levels of anger and honesty.

"Take your blinders off," I tell Anna and Katy while pounding the lunch table. "You're not the outcasts you think you are—you are the *pulse* of this school. You have the power to connect everyone. Don't divide the yearbook into sections by groups. Focus on the similarities between us all."

I move my face close to Anna's. "Forget about Colton—you can do *so* much better. And delete that stupid picture of Kaia enjoying food. A girl deserves to eat in *peace*."

Petra is watching me, and I shift in front of her. "You need to stop operating in Anna's shadow and think for yourself for a change. Petra, you're a good person. You should be free to date whoever you want. And, by the way, you and I could've been best friends in a different life."

Taking a step back, I look around. "Just . . . try to do better."

I make my way over to Tom's table. He hasn't said anything to me since the big confession I dropped on him in English class.

"Well, if it isn't our newest dramatic actress," Chuck says. Tom must've told the rest of them about my outburst.

"My psychologist father would call it more of a *histrionic episode*." I shrug. "Thankfully, he doesn't believe in diagnosis during adolescence."

Tom scratches the back of his head and asks, "Is that what made you say that thing about liking me?"

"What I *said* was that I'm falling in *love* with you." I move in close to his face. "I just wish I'd realized it this summer, before it was too late."

"What's too late?" he asks, and I check the clock on the wall. Glancing over, I see that Kaia and Colton have already left their table.

"Looks like *I'm* late." I head for the cafeteria doors without looking back.

I walk into the bathroom with such swiftness, the girls preening at the mirror stop and turn to look at me.

With all the authority I can muster, I ask, "Do you mind clearing the room?"

One of the girls leans over, and I hear her whisper to her friend, "That's her. The one I was telling you about."

I say, "If you've heard about me, you know I'm not playing around today. Please leave."

The girl's friend puts her hands on her hips. "Do you really need the whole bathroom to yourself?"

"I just want to talk to Kaia privately." I glance over and see her kitten heels underneath the usual stall door. I sigh and tell the girls, "You all look great. Now it's time to please make your way to the exit in an orderly fashion."

Everyone stands in place until I'm forced to yell, "Go! Live your lives!" My voice must sound desperate, because the girls finally start scampering past me into the hallway.

The stalls open one by one and girls quickly rinse their hands on their way out of the bathroom. Finally, Kaia's stall door is the only one left closed.

I take a deep breath, trying to figure out how I'm going to deliver this particular truth bomb. It scares me more than any of the others, even telling Tom I'm falling for him—because I can't just *kapow* Kaia. Dropping truth on someone whose thinking is distorted can be unpredictable, and explosive, and may cause even more damage. But I have to do something to help her.

Walking down the row, I'm trying to remember all the stuff my dad has talked about and the things I've learned about eating disorders. I give a soft knock. "Kaia?"

Holding my breath a moment, I wonder if she'll just ignore me. The only sound is the faucet's steady drip. Finally, the toes of her kitten heels move into view, and with a metallic click she unlocks the door, opening it partway.

She peers at me through the opening. "How do you know my name?"

I move back to give her space, and she opens her stall door wider.

"I know more than your name," I say. "I know what you were about to do in there. And I know that bulimia can be extremely dangerous."

She moves back, pulling the stall door halfway closed.

"Wait." I put up my hand. "I'm not going to say anything about this to anyone. I just . . . I really want you to know that you deserve so much better. You only get one body, and it should be treated with kindness and nourishment and love."

"You don't know anything," she says, but opens the metal door a tiny bit wider.

"I know that you probably have a distorted body image, so telling you how amazing you look won't really help anything. Although I'll still go ahead and say you look amazing."

She strides past me and up to one of the sinks, where she starts washing her hands.

"And one more thing I know. The shame surrounding an eating disorder often keeps sufferers from seeking help."

Kaia closes her eyes a moment, and when they open they meet mine in the mirror.

"Listen," I say. "If there's a name for something, it means someone else has already done it. You are not the first girl to ever have *bulimia*." Kaia winces at the word. I go on. "But you don't need to be defined by this. Getting help is scary, and it may be embarrassing, but from what I've seen, you have the strength to kick this thing."

In the mirror, Kaia's gaze slides from me to herself. She stands, looking into her own eyes until they begin tearing up. "Who are you?" she asks her reflection.

I whisper, "You are Kaia, and you are going to break free from this oppression, and you are going to be okay."

She turns to me. "No, I mean who are *you*?"

"I'm your new friend, Andie. And I'm rooting for you." She

gives me a small, if confused, smile, and I turn and walk out of the bathroom.

When I pass Colton, I say, "Be there for her."

My truth bombs continue getting less explosive until they're barely truth grenades, which gradually in turn become truth suggestions.

I tell a sullen teacher monitoring the hallway, "Appreciate your blessings."

One girl, I just walk up to and hug. "You are worthy of big love. Believe in you." She immediately begins to cry.

The whispering murmurs behind my back make me glad that nobody will remember me tomorrow. But there's one person who doesn't seem to mind all my blatant honesty.

When I go to my locker at the end of the day, Tom's standing there waiting for me.

"I heard you told Colton off about not deserving to work at the theater," he says.

"Yeah," I say. "It's the truth. That must be the coolest job on earth, and the guy doesn't even know what a meet-cute is."

"Tell me about it." Tom traces a finger along the edge of my locker door. "So then why did you spend half the summer there doing his work for him?"

"I thought I liked him." I shrug. "But I finally realized I don't."

"So, you won't be coming by the theater anymore?" Tom asks.

"You just try keeping me away." I don't specify if I'm talking about him or the theater, but I mean both.

He smiles. "Well then, I was wondering if maybe you'd like to pick up a shift or two of your own."

My mouth drops open. "You're actually offering me a job at the movie theater?"

"You've proven you can be a hard worker," he says. "I think you'd be great. We may have to do a background check since you eerily seem to know something about everyone in this school, but it'll probably be okay."

I smile. The first one since I woke up this morning. Apparently, I was wrong about today being an awful day, because this is a *very* nice surprise indeed.

chapter 22

I tell Tom I'm free to lend a hand at the theater tonight, and he says he'll meet me there to show me the ropes later. After he visits a "very special girl."

I think he's trying to either throw me off or make me jealous, but I just smile and say, "She must be a lucky girl too."

Before the school bus even reaches my house, someone has already posted my cell phone number to my classmates. I'm immediately inundated with text messages asking how I know the things I know. And who do I think I am. And a couple of other blistering endearments.

Mom is impressed by how much my phone keeps buzzing and assumes I've had an amazing first day. I decide to let her have that one, particularly since I'm borrowing her car to go to the theater tonight with the warning I'll be home late.

I think Dad is forcing her to watch some sort of documentary with him about an outrageous thing that's happening in the medical . . . *snore* . . . whatever . . . never mind.

When I walk through the theater doors, Tom greets me with a grin, and I ask how his *very special girl* is doing.

He blushes. "She's my meemaw. I went to play a video game with her."

My smile is genuine as I picture them together. "So then, I was right," I say. "She is lucky."

It's already late, so the two of us get busy tidying up around the counter. Since I was here all summer, I pretty much know how things run. As we work, I keep glancing over at him, then looking away at the exact moment he tries to catch me watching. We're both acting pretty smiley.

Next, I follow Tom as he gives me the official tour, explaining the equipment and sharing little anecdotes about his experiences at the theater. Apparently, he's been working here since he started ripping tickets at fifteen.

"Welcome to the heart of this whole operation," he says as he ushers me into one of the small projection booths. An enormous machine taking up the center of the space whirs with a trivia reel that's being mostly ignored by the audience in the theater below us.

"This is beyond cool," I say as my gaze tries to take in every detail of the booth. "Like magic." I feel my eyes glowing like a cat's as I look out the little window, following the beam of light to the giant screen.

When I turn back, Tom is watching me. "I knew you'd love this."

"I do," I say simply.

Tom smiles. "The retirement home where my meemaw lives has a little theater inside."

I keep my expression neutral. "You don't say."

He points to a stack of smaller reels in one corner of the shelves. "I help out by running the movies there when I have time, and in return they loan us some of their classic reels every now and then. They run on the old projector, not the digital one, but they're pretty cool."

"I'd love to watch a few of those."

He smiles. "I'm predicting we'll get the chance at some point in the future."

I wish, I think. But at least we have right now.

The two of us stand there grinning at each other. Tom's eyes wander over my face, and my heart starts to flip-flop.

So naturally, that's right when Tom's cell phone rings. The tune sounds hauntingly familiar, but I can't quite place it.

He answers the phone. "Oh, hey, Colton." His brow furrows a moment, and after a longer pause, he says, "Okay, got it." *Pause.* "No, really, it's fine." Tom looks at me. "Yeah, we've got you covered. Good luck."

When he hangs up, Tom explains that Colton can't come in tonight.

I think of Colt hanging out at the rowdy house party and realize he's been blowing off the late shift at work this entire time.

"He was on the schedule to close," Tom says. "But he said something about his girlfriend, Kaia, needing him. Apparently, she's going through some stuff."

I'm hopeful this means our talk today inspired her to ask for help. And that Colton is being supportive.

"I don't mind pitching in," I say.

Tom smiles. "Thanks, Andie. It really sounds like you'll be helping him and Kaia out."

"Glad to do it," I say, and mean it.

I'm glad it's a slow night, because it gives Tom and me a

chance to talk while we work. As he guides me in setting up the projector for the last show of the night, he tells me how much he loves this theater.

"We're doing well," he says, "but independently owned places like this are really suffering financially."

"So that's why you nearly forced me to eat a whole carton of malted milk balls when we first met," I say.

"I couldn't lose that snack bar sale." He laughs.

"That was humiliating."

"Come on, the chocolate drool was adorable."

Our smiles both fade at the same time, and I imagine Tom must be remembering Colton wiping my drool with a napkin, just like I am. I can't believe that gesture made me swoon so hard and for so long, it kept me from even noticing Tom.

The projection booth suddenly feels too stuffy, and Tom says we should go downstairs to get ready for our final wave of moviegoers.

And just like that, another magic moment has passed me by.

● ● ●

While cleaning up the final theater after the last movie ends, the two of us discuss the differences between watching a movie at the cinema versus at home. We both agree it isn't just about the size of the screen.

"The movie theater is all about the shared experience," he says.

"Exactly!" I hold up my broom in triumph. "I've noticed the same film can have a different feel at different showings, depending on the audience."

Tom smiles. "There's one woman who comes in here who has the biggest, most infectious laugh."

"I know the woman you mean," I say. "I love when she comes. I swear people who experience comedies with her in the audience are so lucky. She enhances the show for everyone."

Tom nods in agreement. "And then it's so cool when people come out of a movie talking a mile a minute about the film."

"It's like riding an hours-long roller coaster together," I say. "By the end, you know each other's screams and hopefully laughter, and even if the movie isn't what you expected, or if you happen to forget it the next day, you've shared something with a roomful of strangers."

"I love that," he says, and the two of us stand there smiling at each other some more. Finally, he says, "I'd better go make sure everyone's gone and lock up."

After he's been gone a few moments, the screen of the theater I'm in whirs to life with a black-and-white film. It must be one from the retirement home.

When Tom comes back, I'm sweeping a small mound of spilled popcorn that was left on the theater floor. "Nice touch," I say, pointing to the screen.

The movie makes the shadows and light dance over the empty theater seats in an eerie way. I feel lightheaded as I slowly sweep the popcorn into a long-handled dustpan.

From across the aisle, Tom says, "Sometimes the movie itself isn't as important as who you're watching it with."

He's studying me in the flickering light. I stand up straight and get another small wave of dizziness.

He points. "The garbage is just outside the door."

I look down at my pan filled with popcorn and say, "Oh. Thanks."

As I walk up the aisle toward the exit doors, I wonder if we've just hit that point in the night when Tom remembers how I've acted all summer. I sigh as I push open the door, thinking, *Well, it was nice while it las—* "Aaaaahhhh!!"

A man is standing directly in my way, and I blindly swing my dustpan at his head.

It isn't until I hear Tom's laughter from behind me that I realize I've just assaulted Victory Man. Or rather, the cardboard cutout version of Victory Man. I spin around, tingling with adrenaline.

Tom is laughing so hard he can't catch his breath. "I'm . . . sorry. I couldn't . . . resist."

Dropping my weapon, I pick up the limp cardboard cutout of the masked superhero and begin hitting Tom with it. Which only makes him laugh harder.

"Are you kidding me?" The release as my adrenaline drains makes me feel more disoriented than ever.

The two of us stop a moment, breathing hard and looking at each other. The mirth that sparkles in Tom's eyes reminds me of his meemaw, and I have to twist my mouth to hold in a smile.

"Really, Andie. I didn't think you'd react that strongly." He lets out a small laugh and tries to look serious. "Pranks are really big around the theater, and I just thought . . ."

Finally, the endorphins that were set loose after my big scare take over. I feel my face break into a wide smile.

"You're . . . okay?" Tom starts laughing again, and this time I join him. We laugh long and hard as he throws the cardboard cutout on the ground and starts beating it up.

"Defending my honor now?" I tease.

"I'm really sorry." Tom says. "But that was so worth keeping Victory Man around."

Between laughs I ask, "Did you learn that prank from your meemaw?"

He stands up to look at me. "How did you know she's a big practical joker?"

Whoops. I stammer, "Oh, well, you know. You just went to visit her and all . . ."

He steps closer. "Andie, you are a surprising girl."

"You know what?" I look down at Victory Man's remains and think back to when Tom was only "boss-man" to me. "You surprise me too," I say. "And that's really saying something."

He smiles. "Wait till you see the pranks my meemaw taught me using plastic wrap."

"Well, you just wait for the payback," I say. "Prank war starts now."

Our laughter pops back up in small bursts as the two of us clean the popcorn I've respilled and make our way back into the theater. We sit down side by side to watch the black-and-white movie still playing onscreen. It's one of those old, grainy slapstick comedies. This is definitely one of those cases where who I'm watching it with is the part that really matters.

"Hey, Andie," Tom says quietly. "Open your hand."

I do, and he pours a stream of perfectly round balls of chocolate into my palm.

"Are these what I think they are?" I ask, excitedly popping one into my mouth.

"We still don't carry Whoppers, but I thought I could make

an exception on outside food for one night." He holds up the tan box and makes it rattle. "A reasonably sized portion, of course."

With a grin, I toss one of the malted milk balls into his open mouth, and the two of us turn our attention to the movie screen.

On it is a classic scene that has a guy comically dangling from a giant clock face high up on the side of a tall building. The huge iron minute hand he's hanging on keeps moving around the clock as he kicks his legs helplessly far above the ground.

Tom and I laugh and lean closer together. Without thinking, I lay my head on Tom's shoulder. He doesn't seem to mind.

We comfortably share the rest of the box of Whoppers, with me eating most of them. Once they're gone, we keep watching the movie together in silence, and my eyes gradually grow heavier and heavier.

Tom turns to tell me something, and I can't make my brain focus enough to understand what he's saying. Intently, I look into his face, with the screen's light dancing off of it, and feel as if I'm being hypnotized.

As much as I don't want this time with Tom to end, I'm losing the fight to stay awake.

"Some roller-coaster ride, huh?" Tom says, and I wonder how many times he had to repeat this before I heard him.

"Yeah," I say, my throat dry and hoarse. "Some ride."

I softly smile as I close my eyes and finally, unwillingly, submit to sleep.

• • •

When I wake up, the theater is still dark and Tom is lightly shaking me. "Andie? Wake up. Sorry, I fell asleep too."

I stretch and smile. "No problem. How long was I out? An hour?"

"Oh, Andie." In the dim glow of the aisle's safety lights, I can see Tom's eyes are wide and worried. "You're going to be in so much trouble with your parents."

"Trust me. They get over things *really* fast." I yawn. "They probably won't even remember me coming in late by tomorrow."

"But, Andie," Tom says, "it *is* tomorrow. The sun's already rising."

I stare at him with my mouth opening and closing. I try to ask what time it is, but no words will form. *Is it possible?*

I stand up and rush to the theater doors. Flinging them open, I'm blinded by the pink light of early dawn bursting through the opening. I can practically hear a garage band of angels drowning out the choir as they joyfully rock out.

It's morning. And I'm not on the pink leather couch.

I run back to Tom. "It's tomorrow!"

Without stopping to think, I grab him by both sides of his face and kiss him directly on the lips. When I pull back, he looks utterly startled.

"Oh." I blush. "I'm so sorry, I just—"

Tom cuts me off mid-apology by kissing me right back.

My first kiss—my first *real and welcome* kiss—is not exactly what I'd call movie-perfect. In fact, it's a tiny bit awkward, and it's kind of obvious this is Tom's first kiss too. Plus, we both still taste a little like malted milk balls. But Tom's lips are soft, and I can't stop my fingertips from trailing up and down his face. Making sure he is here and this is real.

But I know deep down it *is* real. And the best part is, it is happening in my tomorrow. "We're finally here," I whisper.

Tom pulls back and looks into my face.

Grinning, he reminds me I've already agreed to work at the theater again tonight. "That is," he says, "if you're not grounded."

"Oh, I'm grounded, all right," I say. "But my mom is going to think me working here is the coolest thing ever, so I'm pretty sure I'll swing it."

"Well, I'll keep the shifts flexible to start, but just know that since I handle the scheduling, you and I will be working together . . . a lot."

I smile. "That's one Sisyphean situation I'm happy to get stuck with."

It's finally happened. The curse is over, and it was never about some miracle kiss breaking it. It was about me discovering where I really belong.

Or maybe it was about learning to not care about fitting in. Or perhaps about making as many people hate me as possible, because now that I think about it, all those truth bombs basically blew up my chances of ever being well-liked at Punxsutawney High. I mean, it's not like I expected to become prom queen or anything, but this is not exactly the ideal version of reality for me to be left with. Talk about *kapow*.

I look at Tom. Then again . . . *kapow*.

Everything that happened yesterday brought me to this moment. Kissing Tom.

Who cares about the fallout back at school? My mind rolls through the outrage that is probably already storming its way across the Internet, and I make a mental note to check in with Mom about any chance of being homeschooled for the rest of high school.

Thinking of Mom reminds me … "I seriously need to get going."

After a second kiss (and a third), I tell Tom good-bye and rush out the doors. I'm going to be in *so* much trouble when I get home.

But it's okay, because I'll finally get to see my parents as one day older than they've been, and there is hope for the future, and anything is possible because this is a *brand-new day.*

The sky is no longer overcast. For the first time in months, I can see the sun.

Also, I may keep the dress, but there's a giant pink couch in the living room that is totally getting dragged straight to the curb.

Acknowledgments

To Ammi-Joan Paquette, thank you for connecting this book to the perfect editor, and thank you, Jillian Manning, for being that perfect editor. Special thanks go to the rest of the incredible teams at Blink and EMLA: Jacque Alberta, Ron Huizinga, Sara Merritt, Jennifer Hoff, Erin Murphy, the GANGO, and everyone working to share their love of books with book lovers everywhere.

Thank you to my warrior sisters who know how to move mountains with mustard seed faith: Dorene Pirro, Jamie LeGrand, Katie Melanson, Cathy Bates, Gina Lopez, Katy Moore, Sue Harlin, Vicki Barlin, Sarah Northwood, Mary Pearson, Christine Coscia, Mary Phillips, and so many others. You are true rock stars. To Mom, Gerry, Pops, and the Boyles, Giels, Pirros, Cromptons, Spadolas, and Courtneys: I am abundantly blessed to call you all family.

To the loves of my life: Brett, Trinity, and Aidan. If I could choose one day to live over and over, it would definitely be one spent with the three of you (but probably not on Rodeo Drive—ha! Too soon?). Thank you for loving me despite my Deadline Mommy days. This book should have all our names on the cover.

BLINK®